TAKE MY BREATH AWAY

TAKE MY BREATH AWAY

MARTIN EDWARDS

FIVE STAR
A part of Gale, Cengage Learning

GALE
CENGAGE Learning™

Detroit • New York • San Francisco • New Haven, Conn • Waterville, Maine • London

GALE
CENGAGE Learning˙

First Edition in the United States.
Previously published in the U.K. in 2002.
First Printing June, 2011.
Set in 11 pt. Plantin.

LIBRARY OF CONGRESS CATALOGING-IN-PUBLICATION DATA

Edwards, Martin, 1955–
    Take my breath away / Martin Edwards. — 1st ed.
        p. cm.
    ISBN-13: 978-1-4328-2531-7 (hardcover)
    ISBN-10: 1-4328-2531-3 (hardcover)
    1. Serial murders—England—London—Fiction. 2. Law firms—England—London—Fiction. I. Title.
    PR6055.D894T35 2011
    823'.914—dc22   2011007746

First Edition. First Printing: June 2011.
Published in 2011 in conjunction with Tekno Books and Ed Gorman.

Printed in the United States of America
1 2 3 4 5 6 7 15 14 13 12 11

Suppose, finally, we succeed in explaining our entire instinctive life as the development and ramification of *one* basic form of the will—namely, of the will to power . . . the world viewed from inside . . . it would be "will to power" and nothing else.

—Friedrich Wilhelm Nietzsche,
from *Beyond Good and Evil,* sec. 36, Walter Kaufmann transl.

CHAPTER ONE

The dead woman smiled. *So far, so good.*

As she walked into the room, the party was in full swing. Glitzy laughter and listen-to-me voices. No one gave her a second glance, except for Nic Gabriel.

"It can't be Ella," he told himself. "This isn't happening."

He whipped off his Ray-Bans, but she was still there. Skirting the crowd of young lawyers, taking care not to brush against them. Perhaps she feared they might sue if she nudged their elbows and made them spill their champagne. Nic was standing on the terrace at Westminster, watching through open French windows. A breeze from the Thames chilled his neck. The moment she'd appeared in the doorway, he'd recognized her.

Ella Vinton. But a stone in a Sussex graveyard bore her name. She'd been left to rest in peace.

A waiter bearing an ornate salver offered him another glass. He should have said no; he'd already drunk too much on an empty stomach, but he took it anyway. He barely noticed the flinty taste as his eyes followed the woman. Threads of hair flapped over her face as she glanced this way and that, like any nervous latecomer, on the lookout for a familiar face. A thought jumped into his mind.

I know the man you're searching for. The man who invited me here, the man you killed yourself for five years ago.

His skin was tingling. He was witness to something he couldn't understand. A mystery, a pleasant torture. How could a suicide be recalled to life? Five minutes earlier, he'd been yawning, sedated by booze and gossip about golden hellos and gourmet food. Wishing he had never let Dylan Rees tempt him into coming here with a weird tale about addiction to murder. Now he'd seen a wraith with a split skirt and purple fingernails. Talk about drop-dead gorgeous.

Ella? Surreal. He knew it was time to sober up and start thinking straight, but a function room in their Lordships' House was no place for getting to grips with reality. People said things had changed, that the dust of tradition had been vacuumed away. Since being ushered through the gate into Black Rod's garden, he hadn't caught a glimpse of ermine. The corridor leading here stank of new paint. Even inside the air wasn't fresh. The reek of Chanel and silver polish was suffocating.

In one corner, a Steinway tinkled: a floppy-haired Hugh Grant clone picking out "The Tender Trap." The young advocates talked louder with each gulp of Bollinger. Nic gazed through the glass at the flushed faces. Destinies mapped out, the kids were doomed to succeed. They would flatter judges, woo juries, and worsen the statistics for professional alcoholism. Obituaries would extol their observational powers and attention to detail, but none of them noticed the revenant gate crashing their party.

Ella Vinton. But it was impossible. Ella had bought a chain and padlock from a hardware shop in Wembley and tied her left wrist to the outer rail of the main line to Euston. She'd tossed the bag containing the key out of reach to preclude second thoughts and waited for the West Coast express. For once the train had not been late. The driver had seen her kneeling on the line, waving him on with her free hand, as if impatient to be done with everything. He'd braked at once but had no chance of stopping in time. Her head and limbs were sliced from her body, bits of her flesh and bone tossed along track and verge like a scattering of pulped grapes.

Ella had been an acquaintance rather than a friend. Nic remembered her by that habitual half-smile, half-frown, which seemed to anticipate betrayal. Not that Dylan blamed himself for her death. When he spoke of it, he implied a million-to-one accident. A twist of fate, an act of God.

She edged through the crowd, a pale skinny woman with scarlet lips and a tangle of russet hair crying out for a comb, toting a cavernous leather bag on her shoulder. She kept looking around, but even if Nic caught her eye, it would make no difference. Dylan was the one she wanted.

Nic squeezed the stem of the empty glass into his palm. His throat was dry. Was he drunk or simply daydreaming? He'd always had too much imagination to make it as a lawyer.

A hoax, it had to be, a sick joke. A spooky Ellagram dreamed up by someone wanting to give Dylan a fright. Nic glanced over his shoulder. Dylan stood farther along the terrace, outside Ella's range of vision. Leaning against a tub of red begonias, thumbs hooked in the pockets of a spotless white jacket. His violet bow-tie distracted the eye from his splayed nose, smashed years ago by a mistress's husband and badly reset. He was holding forth to a handful of the youngsters. The piano had fallen silent, and his voice drowned the shouts from the protesters blocking traffic on Westminster Bridge. He was doing what he did best: telling his audience things they wanted to hear.

"You're the chosen few," he insisted. His lilt became pronounced when he talked to strangers. He thought of it as a marketing tool. Now he was declaiming in the manner of a primitive preacher, reminding the elect of their superiority over the damned. "The country's most promising young trial lawyers. So it's time for me to let you into a secret. Litigation is better than sex." A sly smile crept across his battered features. "You'll find out once you lose your courtroom virginity. Believe me, you'll always remember your first case."

A couple of the girls giggled; one young fogey had an absentminded expression on his squashed features. Nic guessed he was thinking wishfully, dreaming that there might be truth even in Dylan's rhetoric. Perhaps lawyers really did make marvelous lovers.

Down the terrace, another cocktail party for the great and the good was in full swing. Fragments of Vivaldi, performed by an unseen string quartet, drifted through the air. Nic saw a handful of new aristocrats—Pimm's-drinking thirtysomethings with ponytails and neck tattoos, heard their chortling as they talked about parties at Number Ten and private finance initiatives. People with no time for pomp and circumstance, for doffing caps or hierarchy. The rich man in his castle, the poor man at his gate, all that didn't wash anymore. These people were meritocrats, modern, streetwise, and brilliant at networking. The old coteries were dead; long live the new.

On the bridge, police were loud-hailing orders to the demonstrators, but no one paid attention. Back inside the Cholmondeley Room, the peer hosting the party wore a Mustique tan and Calvin Klein loafers. He was bragging to a girl in a backless gown about how he had claimed a ten-day fact-finding tour of Caribbean beach life on expenses.

Nic glanced back indoors. The room was slightly out of kilter. If only he hadn't gulped down that last drink. Ella had drawn nearer. A strange light of triumph shone in her eyes, and he guessed she had caught sight of Dylan. Her gait had become as unsteady as a marionette's. Nic had seen the black skirt before. The outfit was a favorite, and she'd worn it the last time they had met for dinner, in that organic food place off Marylebone High Street. Probably the last time Dylan, a red-meat man, had ever touched anything remotely akin to green cuisine.

According to Dylan, there had been little enough left of Ella to identify after the train had done its worst. Nic peered at the white unmarked flesh of the woman's neck and cheeks. She was studying Dylan with the concentration Nic remembered. He'd always been struck by the single-minded way she focused on her lover. As if trying to hypnotize him into belonging to her alone.

"I'm a partner in an agency called Valentines." Dylan winked at a blond girl who had been lapping up his rodomontade. "Apposite, in a way. Because there's a touch of romance in what I do. Even though Saint Valentine was decapitated. Didn't you know that was the poor devil's fate? You learn something every day. People call me a headhunter, but it's not a tag I care for. No, I'll take you into my confidence. I'm a matchmaker. I marry up people like you to the job of your dreams. So that you consummate the perfect union."

Nic saw Ella flinch at the words. Dylan still hadn't seen her. He always got carried away when talking about sex. Ella closed her eyes. It *must* be her. Yet it could not be.

This was all Dylan's fault. Dylan, who had seduced him with all that talk about dead lawyers. Dylan the yarn-spinner, the myth-maker, the Celtic bard in an Armani suit. Of course he'd known that Nic could never resist a story about strange and sudden deaths.

The rich man who burned in Paradise. The giant who chopped himself in half.

There was a connection, Dylan had insisted on the phone, and not just because the dead men were lawyers in the same firm. Forget about suicide or accident. Think murder for pleasure.

"As for the boy who died of shock," Dylan said dreamily, "the real culprit wasn't the guilty creature who killed him. Trust me."

"Now you're definitely asking too much," Nic muttered into

his cell phone. "What are you on?"

"Hey, you're the man who made his name with a tall story. You love to prove the truth's the opposite of what everyone else believes. Who else ever said that Crippen was innocent? Come on, you stubborn bastard. Suppose you show up, what's the worst that can happen? You get raw material for that second book. It's about time."

Nic couldn't help laughing. Dylan always played games, even when he wasn't as high as a kite. He loved to tantalize; he always knew just which buttons to press.

Nic shook his head, trying in vain to banish the fuzziness from the champagne. His brain was out of gear. Ella had opened her eyes again and reached the door that opened to the terrace. A few yards away, Dylan paced up and down as he talked. He was restless, forever itching for action. He kept glancing down at the freckled cleavage of the girl who had taken his fancy. Behind him were screens displaying the Valentines name and heart-shaped logo, together with the agency's slogan. *We'd love to help you change your life.*

"Let's pursue the analogy a little further," Dylan said. He'd lowered his voice in a pastiche of an intimate whisper. He might have been confiding a trade secret, or swearing eternal devotion. "The candidates the top firms need are those who are prepared—to go all the way. The ones who aren't interested in giving up, opting for the quiet life. No pleasure in fudging a deal, settling your case at the door of the court. Think coitus interruptus, eh? Such an anticlimax. No, the litigators who command the big money in the marketplace have one thing in common. They finish what they started. And they never, ever let go."

His listeners sniggered. They were too smart to fall for a headhunter's bullshit. All the same, they realized there was a grain of truth in what he said. They were stars in the firmament of trainee lawyers. They had slaved to reach this stage in their careers, putting in long hours of overtime trawling through calfskin-bound law reports and dusty statute books while their friends screwed around. They were ready to prove themselves as warriors. Hardened in battle, trusted by their paymasters, feared by all who crossed their path.

Ella was standing in the doorway, on the threshold of the terrace, tension stretching the flesh tight over her cheekbones. Nic tried to focus on her, wanting to read her mind. She must be an actress, a look-alike hired from an agency by someone who wanted to give Dylan a shock. Her hand was deep in the shoulder bag. She had moved to within touching distance of Dylan. Absorbed in his peroration, he was still unaware of her scrutiny.

"They never let go," Dylan savored the phrase. "They never . . ."

The words hung in the air as at last his gaze strayed to Ella. His eyes widened, his body seemed at once to become rigid and old. It was as if a single glimpse of her pallid cheeks had snapped his spinal cord and he'd been paralyzed by his unrighteous past.

"Remember me, Dylan?" she asked. Her voice was clear, melodious, less scratchy than Nic recalled.

In that instant Nic realized what she meant to do, guessed the truth even as she withdrew her hand from the bag. She was clasping the black haft of a butcher's knife.

"*No!*" he shouted.

He had to save Dylan. Had to. His legs felt as if shackled in irons, but he forced his way through the crowd, bundling a girl to the floor. An angry boyfriend jabbed him in the ribs, but he kept on going. Someone yelled, a roar of incoherent horror.

The blade shone in a ray of light as the sun emerged from behind a cloud. Dylan was motionless, his face creased in bewilderment. As if he realized something, but could not fathom the explanation for it. He spoke in a hoarse whisper.

Nic could hardly make out the words. They sounded like:

Why not jazz?

Ella frowned and said, "I've been waiting for this for so long."

She brought the knife down even as she spoke. Even as Nic sprang, arms flailing as he tried to catch hold of her. He found himself clutching air as she evaded his grasp. Tears stung his eyes as his head crashed against the ground. He had a dazed idea that he was drowning, surrounded by a blur of bodies swimming wildly for the shore. Girls screamed, young men yelped in disbelief. Nic's ears filled with Dylan's cry of pain as the serrated steel ripped through his throat.

She looked at Nic, and he wondered if he was about to die. There wasn't a hint of recognition on her face. He felt consciousness floating away. She frowned, as though puzzling over a mathematical conundrum. Solution found, she gripped the knife in both hands and plunged it into her heart.

Chapter Two

Roxanne Wake danced through the revolving doors and out on to the Strand. Traffic was shuffling to a standstill, but for once she didn't care about breathing in the fumes. She shimmied between the cars and trucks; limbs loose, energy boundless as a child's. A motorbike courier almost struck her as she crossed the far traffic lane, but she skipped out of reach of his pounding wheels, and her heart didn't even miss a beat. Nothing could go wrong, not today of all days. The day she had begun a new life.

People in the pavement throng jostled past, didn't give her a second glance. It was wonderful not to be noticed. Finally she could say that she'd escaped from the past. She was free.

The last seven years might never have happened. Her first morning in the new job was over, and she had survived. No, forget it; that was lawyers' understatement. Truth was, it had gone like a dream. The law meant so much to her, but she had never worked for a firm of lawyers before today. Let alone an outfit like Creed.

Yet as the human resources manager took her on a whistle-stop tour of the office to meet her new colleagues, she was made to feel as if among friends. She couldn't remember all the names, let alone match them to the blur of faces. Creed boasted a welfare counselor, a client-care czar, and a team of knowledge-dissemination executives. There was an office reading group, led by a Brixton poet celebrated for being tough on rhyme, tough on the causes of rhyme. She'd seen the staff gym, the Jacuzzi, and the whole-food restaurant, she'd shaken hands with the in-house masseuse and the part-time sculptor-in-residence, she'd been invited to dress down every Friday. No one asked a single awkward question. She'd not picked up the slightest hint that anyone doubted who she was.

She could hug herself. Everything was going to plan. Her secret was safe.

Okay, so there had been one moment of alarm. It had come during her meeting with Fergus McHugh, the firm's director of public relations. Cool yet charming, he'd asked for a few crisp words for a news release about her appointment. Conjuring up a quote proved easy enough. She'd discovered an unsuspected flair for the superlative-laden sound bite.

" 'I'm thrilled to have joined Creed. Everyone recognizes this is the country's leading human rights law firm. I've always admired senior partner Will Janus and his passionate commitment to civil liberties.' Will that do?"

"Perfect." Fergus McHugh's smile dazzled like the streaks of blond in his hair. "Couldn't have scripted it better myself. All we need now is a head and shoulders snap to send out in the press pack."

Shit. She should have foreseen this. She swallowed hard. Absurdly, she had the sense that Fergus could read her thoughts, found in them a source of cruel amusement. But that was just paranoia. Luck was on her side—it had to be, on this day. The photographer was delayed by gridlock caused by a demonstration heading for Whitehall, and in the end Fergus ran out of time. He confessed that he and Will Janus were overdue for lunch with the home secretary.

Roxanne uttered a silent prayer of thanks. Her new name meant nothing to anyone, but there was just a chance, a remote chance, that a photograph might stir memories that she needed to stay buried. Seven years was a long time. She looked so different now. Interviewing witnesses at the advice center in Hengist Street had taught her that most people could be relied upon to forget what they'd seen last week, let alone a picture in the papers from long ago. But there was still a risk. *Never mind,* she told herself. *You've got away with it.*

On her way into work that morning she had bought herself something to eat in the middle of the day, but she was in the mood for something special. Creed's restaurant was said to be excellent, Egon Ronay was a fan, but she wasn't ready to share lunchtimes with her new colleagues. She needed to get out for half an hour. At last she had something to celebrate, if only with herself. It wasn't every day that you started afresh. She hurried up Southampton Street to Covent Garden. Thorntons had a shop there, and she treated herself to a thick bar of fudge.

She had this love-hate thing with chocolate. During her darkest days, she could never keep it down. Things were so different now. Food wasn't a problem anymore. She inhaled the sweet perfume of the shop, hardly bearing to postpone the moment when she unwrapped her prize. Her skin was in goose bumps just anticipating the taste. Since she'd started working at Hengist Street, she had put on half a stone, but these days she was relaxed about that. It was good to sin, every now and then.

Creed's offices filled the seven stories of Avalon Buildings, a skinny block squeezed in between Savoy Court and Carting House. Reception was a large and airy space, fringed by a jungle of potted plants. Interior designers had eschewed minimalism in favor of comfort and touches of luxury. The armchairs for visiting clients were soft and deep, and the aroma of Kenyan coffee wafted from a filter machine in the corner. A feng shui expert had positioned the fountain to perfection. It gushed soothingly as Roxanne walked in from the street. *GQ* and *Granta* were laid out on a wrought-iron coffee table; the table's mosaic-tiled top

17

spelled out the firm's logo. Glossy brochures describing the firm's specialities were scattered around, each boasting a foreword by a celebrity client. Large abstract paintings hung on the wall, random doodles of blue, brown, and green. Celine Dion crooned from concealed speakers, promising that her heart would go on. Visiting a lawyer had become a lifestyle experience.

Not, Roxanne told herself, that this was a lawyers' firm like any other. Creed prided themselves on that. All the literature, the advertising, had this common theme. *Lawyers who are different.* The firm had earned a reputation as a scourge of both private and public sector employers who treated staff unethically. The partners didn't handle divorce, property work, or criminal law. Their specialty was civil rights in the workplace, and clients included trade unions, whistleblowers, and a lobby full of equal opportunities campaigners. Advocates from Creed had acted in landmark cases transforming the balance of power at work.

"Creed has three priorities," Will Janus had once famously said. "Litigation, litigation, and litigation."

It was a jest, a snippet of self-parody, a reminder of what a self-deprecating, regular guy he was. Professional traditions had passed their sell-by date. Will often evangelized about the need to fight the forces of legalism. He wanted to make justice available for the many, not the few. Creed didn't so much employ staff as have profit-sharing executive stakeholders. Will preached solving disputes by e-mediation and spreading the gospel via Creedlaw.com. His firm led the way in providing joined-up legal services. Yet everyone knew that, if there had to be an old-fashioned bare-knuckle fight in the courts, there was no better advocate to have on your side than Will Janus. He'd been a winner all his life.

The catwalk blondes behind the reception desk had scarily

perfect smiles. Roxanne did not miss the charm-laden efficiency with which they greeted her by name, even though she'd forgotten to clip her identity tag back on to her lapel. One more thing she would have to learn. So much to do, so many habits that had to become second nature. Even if she had not changed her appearance and name, even if the short résumé she had sent to Ben Yarrow had not economized so savagely on the truth, she would have been an impostor. At least she had a chance to become a new woman. Remembering her badge was only the start. She must *be* Roxanne Wake, every single second that she was here.

She'd been given a room of her own, even though she was an unqualified lawyer with no track record to speak of, and she'd half expected to be herded into a noisy open-plan office along with a clutch of colleagues. Lucky. These days she liked being alone. The room was crammed with gleaming computer equipment, installed that morning by geeks bearing gifts from the information technology department. Potted plants with shiny green leaves warded off bad chi, otherwise the decor was limited to a virgin year-planner on one wall, an internal telephone list tacked to another. When she'd settled in, she would give her surroundings a little more personality. Better be careful, though, about the personality she chose. No family photographs, no loveable drawings of stick people crayoned by infant relatives. Think Roxanne Wake, she instructed herself. Think Roxanne Wake.

She closed her eyes and experimented in her mind with color and knickknacks. Better play safe and put up a couple of theater posters and a Monet print. Nothing distinctive, nothing that invited comment or gave chatterboxes with time on their hands an opportunity to ask tricky questions. It was so easy to let something slip. At Hengist Street she had succeeded in keeping herself to herself. Everyone was so busy that few opportunities arose for friendships to build. Roxanne needed it to be the same at Creed.

"Everything all right?"

Even before he spoke, she knew that Ben Yarrow, head of the Ethical Employment Department, had opened the door. His aftershave was unmistakable. "Eurotrash" by Wal-Mart, or some such. It smelled as if he soaked in it. He wore a wedding ring, and she wondered why his wife hadn't urged him to douse himself less liberally or at least with better taste. As for his dress sense . . . but perhaps Ben wasn't accustomed to taking advice. He spent too much of his life giving it.

She opened her eyes and switched on a smile. Not simply because Ben was one of Creed's senior partners, and her ultimate boss. What mattered was that he was the man who had picked her out, given her the chance to change her life. She owed him.

"People have been very kind," she said.

He fiddled with the ends of his blood-red tie. "I have something for you. Joel Anthony is working on a new discrimination case, writing up the statements. You can help him interview the witnesses."

"What sort of discrimination?"

"Specifically, sexual harassment. *Alleged* sexual harassment."

His puckish face creased into a grin. He was a small man, balding, with a ginger beard. In her mind she reinvented him as a troll, lurking under a bridge and plotting mayhem. She bit her lip, not wanting to give a hint of what was passing through her mind. She doubted whether his talents encompassed a capacity to laugh at himself.

"Who are we representing?"

Ben chuckled. "We're on the side of the angels, Roxanne. That's the first thing you need to learn here. Our clients are always the victims of circumstance. Even blue chip companies bleed. It will make a change for you, not having the chance to embark on a crusade on behalf of a wronged applicant. Oh, one more thing I have to tell you. As it happens, the allegations concern a director colleague of Ali Khan. Remember him?"

How could she forget? A few weeks earlier, Ben and Roxanne had fought against each other at a tribunal hearing in Woburn Place. Roxanne's client, Tara Glass, had worked in the finance department of Thrust Media. Thrust was owned by the legendary entrepreneur Ali Khan. After ten days Tara was sacked, the stated reason her bad attitude. She kept coming in late and spending half her time on the phone to her boyfriend. Tara said the truth was that she'd threatened to blow the whistle on Ali Khan for bribing people of influence and putting his personal bills through the company's accounts. The company offered big bucks to settle, but she wanted her day in court. What's the claim worth? she had asked. Unlimited compensation, Roxanne told her, if the case was proved.

At first Ben's cross-examination was gentle, almost sympathetic. Maybe he wasn't so fearsome after all, Roxanne thought, or perhaps he was simply smart enough to recognize when he was on a loser. Then suddenly, the questions started coming like machine-gun fire. Why hadn't Tara walked out the moment her conscience was troubled by the frauds? Why wait until she was sacked before speaking out?

"Or perhaps the brown envelopes you talk about never existed," he suggested, casting a sly glance at the tribunal members.

"I saw them," Tara insisted. "I had to wrestle with my conscience every day I was in that office."

"Your conscience, yes." Ben shook his head. "So, Ms. Glass, you believe in always telling the truth, do you?"

"Of course I do." She leaned forward in the witness box,

meeting his gaze. "Passionately. I wouldn't be here otherwise, would I?"

"Sure about that?" He paused. "Would you care to turn to page fifteen in the bundle, Ms. Glass?"

Sitting in silence in the stuffy tribunal room, Roxanne felt her heart begin to pound. *Where is this going?*

All at once, as she leafed through the pack of documents in front of her, Tara's hands began to shake. As if she could see an abyss opening up, but could not help plunging toward it.

She whispered something inaudible.

"Speak up," the tribunal chairman insisted.

"I have the page," Tara said with difficulty.

Ben smirked. "It's your job application form, isn't it? See the box where you said you had no previous convictions? Were you telling the truth when you filled that in?"

Tara's cheeks were ashen. "All that stuff was a long time ago."

Ben's eyebrows shot up. "A little less than five years?"

"I was a student then."

"Who earned part-time cash selling her body to businessmen in a hotel near Russell Square?"

"I was broke! Up to my eyeballs in debt. You have no idea."

"And the incident eighteen months ago, when you were caught smoking heroin in your boyfriend's flat? Too relaxed to recall that when you signed the drugs-free declaration?"

"You bastard!" Tara choked back a sob. "This has nothing to do with my case!"

"Ms. Glass," the chairman said in a warning tone. "Mr. Yarrow is merely doing his job."

Roxanne felt an emptiness in her stomach. The case was hemorrhaging in front of her eyes. She'd been so fired up with the injustice of what they had done to Tara, so determined to make the company pay. Meanwhile Ben Yarrow had been doing what Ali Khan paid him handsomely to do. Digging deep.

"Easy, isn't it," Ben said coldly, "making loadsamoney out of rich businessmen? But you graduated in more ways than one, didn't you? You moved from working for those sad punters in Bloomsbury to taking a post with Ali Khan's company. A colorful figure, isn't he? Ideal for your purposes, I suggest."

"I had no purposes!"

Ben's face darkened. Roxanne thought he looked like something small and nasty out of *Peer Gynt*. "You had the prospect of a quick buck if you claimed your boss couldn't keep his fingers out of the till, smeared him as corrupt and dishonest. Very useful for someone with an expensive habit to feed."

"He did those things! It's true. Everything I said is true."

Ben shook his head. "We've already established your difficulties with the truth, Ms. Glass."

Tara Glass ran out of the courtroom in tears. All her fight was gone. Roxanne caught up with her in the corridor. She didn't have the heart to ask why Tara had never mentioned the heroin. Tara said she was withdrawing her claim. She wished she'd never been born, she sobbed, as she fled from the building.

Roxanne's instinct was to hate Ben Yarrow for the ease with which he'd destroyed the woman. She still felt sure that Tara had been telling the truth about the brown envelopes. Yet a still, small voice of calm told her he was only doing his job. On the way out, she had to share the lift with him. To her surprise, he didn't gloat the way most company lawyers did after a crushing victory. When he asked if she'd ever contemplated working in private practice, she found herself feeling oddly flattered. Disappointed, too, that having raised the subject, he said goodbye without making any attempt to take it further.

A month later, he'd called out of the blue and asked if she was interested in joining Creed. At first she'd played for time, said she needed to think it over. She didn't regard herself as streetwise, but she knew enough about career moves to realize it was a mistake to sound too eager. Inside, she'd always known that she would say yes. Creed was a firm that had its heart in the right place, and Ben Yarrow was offering her the opportunity to make the new start of which she'd dreamed. The biggest gamble of her life, but a risk she had to take.

The department needed an extra pair of hands at a busy time. The firm had more work than it could handle, and employment lawyers with advocacy experience were in short supply. She'd won most of the cases she'd handled at Hengist Street. A two-in-three success rate was worth shouting about, given the number of no-hopers with which she'd been lumbered. He interviewed her along with his junior partner, Joel Anthony. An old-fashioned question-and-answer session. No psychometric tests, thank God. She didn't want anyone exploring the secrets of her personality. When they offered her the job, Roxanne's only qualm was that perhaps she should have come out up front and told them everything. She was so much more of a phony than poor Tara Glass. But did it matter? She'd earned the offer on merit, on the strength of her own performance before Tara's case fell apart. She might be a novice joining the ranks of a renowned human rights practice, but that proved that the firm's commitment to its equal opportunities recruitment policy was more than skin deep. Besides, it was too late to tell them who she really was.

"You needn't worry," she said. "I went on a crusade for Tara Glass, but that doesn't mean I won't fight to win for Ali Khan's companies. That's what lawyers ought to do, isn't it? Put their personal feelings to one side and do their best for their clients?"

"You're an idealist," Ben said with a smile. He lifted a hand as Roxanne started to say something. "No, no, it's a compliment. Really. This firm was built on ideals. Don't forget, Ali

Khan wasn't always the celebrity he is today. Will Janus's greatest success as a young immigration lawyer was when he acted for Ali, the first time he wanted a visa to stay on in the U.K."

"I remember the passport application case. It was a *cause célèbre.*"

"You know, Roxanne, that's the trouble with this country." Ben sat down on the edge of her desk. Invading her space, ever so slightly. "So many people hate success. Then there's the racism. Ali is a powerful man these days—and he was born in Karachi. No wonder he's unpopular in some quarters, especially with the jingoistic press. With our help, he won each battle and finally the war. He got his British citizenship. But he didn't always have money. He had to claw his way up. He's suffered discrimination all his life. And I tell you this. If there's any truth in these sexual harassment allegations, you can help Joel make sure the culprit is hung out to dry."

"I'm touched by your faith in me."

"Don't be. I picked you out, remember? It may seem like a gamble, but I've never been averse to the occasional punt at long odds. I'm not afraid of backing my own judgment."

It struck her that he and Joel Anthony had taken an extraordinary risk in recruiting her. Nine out of ten of the other lawyers she'd met in Avalon Buildings were seasoned attorneys. Yet Ben had offered her a twelve-month contract and a fat paycheck after watching her lose a case for a client who had expected to win. She'd heard about the recruitment crisis in her field of law, but hadn't guessed it might make her such a sought-after commodity. It was a fresh experience to be so wanted. A single reference from Ibrahim, her boss at the agency, had sufficed; Ben hadn't even asked for copies of her exam certificates. She supposed he often advised his clients on the importance of adhering to punctilious recruitment procedures. Handwriting analysis, competency tests, questions about her attendance record. Yet the laxity wasn't surprising. Lawyers never acted themselves in the way they advised others to behave.

"What's this?" The voice belonged to a woman who was peeping around the door. Roxanne had an immediate impression of red hair in a bob, pale powdered cheeks, and vivid scarlet lipstick. "Dumping a sure-fire loser on the new kid on the block, Ben?"

Far from appearing to be offended, Ben chortled. "Practicing the noble art of delegation, as it happens. Management in action. Roxanne, have you met my ill-mannered personal assistant? This is Chloe Beck."

Chloe Beck trotted into the room, high heels going *click-clack, click-clack.* She was tall and skinny, and her black skirt barely existed. Roxanne saw Ben's eyes feasting on Chloe's legs, but the girl took no notice. As if she expected nothing less.

She studied Roxanne through Calvin Klein eyeglasses before putting out a ringless hand with long, cool fingers. "Hello, Roxanne. I missed you on your whistle-stop tour of the office. I work for Ben and Joel Anthony."

"And from now on, for you as well, Roxanne," Ben Yarrow said. "I'm sure you'll make good use of our voice recognition system when you start dictating letters and stuff. The technology is cutting edge. But we all need secretarial support from time to time, and Chloe will be glad to help."

Chloe gave Ben a sidelong glance. "The computer wizards haven't managed to phase me out altogether yet. You've come from an advice center, then, Roxanne? I gather you were at Hengist Street."

Unaccountably, Roxanne felt a chill of unease. Or perhaps it wasn't so unaccountable. "You're very well informed."

"The grapevine here is marvelous," Chloe said. She was sizing Roxanne up, as if trying to decipher a code.

"Chloe *is* the grapevine," Ben said. He was smiling at his PA with every appearance of amiability, yet Roxanne sensed a tension between the two of them.

"Don't listen to him, Roxanne. Everyone says I'm nosey, but I'm simply interested in people. Joel Anthony keeps encouraging me to qualify. He says I'd make a good lawyer, simply because I'm so fascinated by other human beings. Never mind all the technology we have here. A litigation department's business is all about people and the way they behave. Finding out what goes on in their minds." Chloe gave a teasing giggle. "Uncovering their darkest secrets."

Roxanne lived in Leytonstone. Not exactly Hampstead, but the station was on the Central Line and on arriving in London, she'd at least managed to find a flat within her price range. Now she was on Creed's payroll, she could pick and choose. But really, she thought, as her train slowed down and she picked up her briefcase ready to get off, Leytonstone was good enough for her. If the past seven years had taught her nothing else, she had learned that, over time, it was possible to become accustomed to anything.

She lived on the first floor of a converted shop. Once upon a time it had been a butcher's, but that was okay as long as she didn't try to picture the carcasses hanging from hooks in the cold storage area below the ground floor. The woman who lived downstairs was a veggie, but she didn't seem bothered by the building's history. She was undertaking happiness research at the London School of Economics. Roxanne wondered what had prompted her to live in Leytonstone. Presumably trying to get away from the day job.

Roxanne put on a leotard and slipped a yoga tape into the video recorder. She needed to make amends for that shameful lunch of fudge, but she hadn't wanted to brave the aerobics classes that took place each evening in Creed's gym. Time for a little calm surrender in the privacy of her own home. The zest she'd felt in her lunch break was a distant memory. Her head had begun to throb and her limbs were aching, but she couldn't lay all the blame on the crush of commuters on the Tube. She had left Avalon Buildings on the stroke of eight: hardly a late finish by the standards of ambitious city attorneys. Yet she felt exhausted, and not just because Ben Yarrow was a hard taskmaster. At Hengist Street, she'd dipped a toe in the waters of legal practice, but she could have given it up at any time. By joining Creed, she'd made a commitment to becoming a top-flight lawyer.

"Change your shape and you can change your life," cooed the woman on the tape. She was a blonde in her forties, sickeningly supple.

Roxanne hadn't underestimated the demands of the work. There were no restrictive practices in the employment tribunal: a wet-behind-the-ears paralegal might find herself doing battle with eminent barristers and streetwise solicitor advocates. That didn't frighten her; she'd always nourished the belief that, with experience, she might be a match for even the wiliest opponent. But her new colleagues might become curious about the stranger in their midst. She must find a way of preserving her privacy without raising eyebrows.

"Inhale. Lift those arms. Stretch up and keep your eyes on the ceiling, still with a full lung. Exhale . . ."

Was Chloe a threat? As Roxanne kept her eyes on the ceiling, she told herself not to imagine dangers where none existed: Chloe simply liked to talk.

"Shall we try the warrior posture?" Anyone would think this was a litigator's training film, compulsory continuing professional education. "Bend your front leg and aim your thigh flat. Keep that back leg straight! Can't you feel the gorgeous, gorgeous movement? Inhale now, and up you come."

Roxanne stretched, feeling her joints creak.

"You did really well," the woman said.

"Patronizing bitch," Roxanne hissed as she breathed out.

Already the exercises were working. She was starting to relax, the anxieties of the day fading from her mind.

Everything was going to be fine.

CHAPTER THREE

"He's sleeping, Sergeant," the doctor said softly.

It wasn't true. Nic seldom slept, anyway. He had closed his eyes because seeing wasn't believing, and he needed to get his brain into gear if he was ever to make sense of Ella's resurrection.

The policeman grunted. "You said he was fit to be questioned."

Nic strained to catch bits of the murmured reply. *Head injury . . . not severe . . . badly shocked . . . keeping him in for observation . . . you never know.*

"This won't take long."

Nic heard the doctor sigh and then his footsteps, departing. The policeman bent over him; he smelt of curry. When his shoulder was jogged, Nic grunted, turned on his side, allowed his lids to ease apart. The overhead light was harsh, made him blink. The policeman resembled a slab-faced scion of the Kray family. Nic guessed he would be more at home kicking the shit out of football hooligans or anarchist agitators than conducting a murder inquiry. Assuming it was a murder enquiry.

"Mr. Gabriel, we have to ask you about what happened."

Nic's head was swimming. He was afraid of what he was about to be told, but he had to know. He muttered, "Dylan. He's dead, isn't he?"

The sergeant nodded. "Yeah, Mr. Rees died at the scene."

Nic wanted to throw up, but he felt too weak to manage it.

He buried his face in the pillow, uttered a silent scream. How could he not blame himself for what had happened?

"Sorry," the policeman said unapologetically, "but I have to press you. Can you take me through what happened at this cocktail party?"

Eventually Nic forced himself to say, "What happened to Ella?"

The sergeant leaned closer. Nic felt as though about to be suffocated by the fumes from a stale takeaway meal. "Ella?"

"She cut his throat."

The sergeant breathed out, a fearsome tandoori gust. "So you know the woman who did this?"

"Ella Vinton, yes. She's dead."

"No, Mr. Gabriel, she's still alive." The sergeant scratched the stubble on his chin. "But only just. She's in intensive care."

"You don't understand. She died five years ago."

The policeman took his statement but made it plain he didn't like what he was hearing. When Nic said he'd been getting loaded at the party, the interrogation became perfunctory. Even before he confessed to being a writer by profession, his credibility was already in tatters. Somehow he felt it wouldn't help if he said he hadn't published anything for ages. Lazy as well as unreliable; scarcely the ideal witness.

Later, a nurse came to check him over. Middle-aged, spookily cheerful, like someone out of a propaganda broadcast. He half-expected her to reel off the cuts in hospital waiting times, to tell him that recruitment of nurses was at an all-time high.

"You'll be right as rain in no time."

Wasn't this the hospital where bodies had been piled high on a mortuary floor because of staff shortages? Where a gynecologist had molested a hundred patients before being fired? Where one in five patients contracted a fresh ailment while under the hospital's roof? He wasn't reassured.

He tried raising himself up on the pillow. Every muscle in his body seemed to protest at the same time. He had a blinding headache, but he didn't want to mention it in case they told him he had to stay here.

"I'm fine. When can I leave?"

She ignored him with the ease of long practice. "There. You've overexcited yourself. What you need now is a jolly good rest."

Phil's face, looming over his. On her heart-shaped face, a characteristic mixture of irritation and excitement.

"It's me, Phil."

He wanted to say *Of course it bloody is, we've been sleeping together for months. I haven't lost possession of all my faculties.*

He managed a hoarse, "Hi."

"It's incredible. Dylan dead. At the hand of a mystery assassin. Wow, who would believe it?" He could almost see her mind working, wondering how it would play in the media. "You were almost a hero."

"You're so good for my ego."

"Don't be like that. You know what I mean. Anyway, frankly he's no great loss."

But he was my friend.

He muttered, "I couldn't save him."

That was what tormented him, so much more than the knock that had caused him to finish up here. He'd kept his eyes on the dead woman since she'd walked into the room, but he'd been too concerned with trying to fathom how she had risen from the grave. He should have stopped her from carrying out her revenge.

"Of course you couldn't." Her tone suggested that someone else might have. Someone with more focus, the sort of man she'd once thought he was. But it didn't matter, since she'd never liked Dylan. She frowned. "I wonder who the woman was."

He didn't want to tell her about Ella and when he feigned sleep, she didn't hang around. His brain was fuddled, but one clear thought formed as the door closed behind her. It was never going to work with the two of them. He'd realized a long time ago that they didn't actually have much in common, but he'd fought against the knowledge, wanting to make the thing work without being sure why.

Phil was a public relations manager who specialized in advising companies in crisis on how to limit the damage to their reputation occasioned by fraud, scandal, and other calamities. He supposed she was what they used to call gamine. No breasts or bum, but she was beautiful. They had met at a publishers' party, and she'd told him the story of a law firm she acted for. The senior partner had sent an inflated bill to a woman client who ran a small business. The morning it arrived she drank three tumblers of whiskey and pulled a plastic bag over her head. According to Phil, her clients were neither greedy nor callous, just ordinary decent folk who wanted to make an honest living and made a mistake once in a blue moon.

When he suggested that the senior partner's gravestone ought to be licensed for dancing, she said, "I suppose the pressmen of the day thought the same about Hawley Harvey Crippen."

"Touché."

"I adored your book. Not that I believed a word of it. I'm sure he was as guilty as hell. But I love a good whitewash."

"Should I be flattered?"

"Don't laugh! The way you reinvented the little shit is brilliant. It's spooky, meeting someone who can not only think himself into the mind of a murderer but even make out that he's been sadly misunderstood. You give the old stuff a new spin. Take an all-time loser and rebrand him as a captive of the heart. I love it. Perhaps you and I ought to go into business together."

Instead they finished up in bed together. The sex was great. She was an inexhaustible lover who liked to do fun things with strawberries and cream, handcuffs and leather, silk scarves and whips. For a while he believed the relationship might work. He understood his mistake the first time she complained about his unwillingness to repeat the formula that had made his book a word-of-mouth phenomenon. When he told her there wasn't a formula, she'd stared as if he'd spoken in Swahili.

"There's a formula for everything."

"Not for this. I just wrote the book the way it had to be written."

"Fine." She shrugged: it was so simple. "Do it again."

He didn't want to keep thinking about her. Dylan was *dead*. He would never cringe again at Dylan's lousy jokes. They would never speak again about anything. And it was his fault.

In his mind he played back that call to his cell phone. Dylan's voice booming in his ear. The king of bullshit at the top of his form.

"You'll love it, I swear."

"A reception for learner litigators? If I wanted to commune with lost souls, I'd sign up for a pagan mass."

Dylan guffawed, a deafening blast of noise. "Why are you always so cynical? Look, those kids' souls aren't lost. They're about to be sold, and they won't be cheap. Come on. Think of this as a trip down memory lane. You were a hungry young advocate once. Give tomorrow's gladiators an idea what it's like out there in the real world. Private practice."

"What if I tell them to quit the law and get a life?"

"Frankly, what else would they do?" A conspirator's chuckle. "You can spell out what a good deal I can swing for those kids. Assuming they sign up with us, that is. Valentines is sponsoring the whole shebang, no expense spared. It's an investment. I swear, after a couple of drinks, you'll start feeling all nostalgic. Reminiscing about victories snatched from the jaws of defeat. Wondering about what might have been."

"Balls."

"You were a loss to the profession. Everyone says so. Can't imagine why you gave it up. This true-crime stuff is all fine and dandy, but when are you going to write another book? You can't live on the royalties from *Crippen* forever. You're wasting your life away, do you realize?" Dylan was on a roll now. "Okay, you wrote a best seller about a famous murder case. You won a couple of prizes, that's great. Surely you've got the bug out of your system by now. That's why you've not written anything but the odd article in ages. You ought to be racking up the chargeable hours, doing stuff that really counts. Judicial reviews, heavyweight corporate lawsuits. I could place you tomorrow, you know that? You can name your price, I guarantee."

"Piss off, mate."

"Look, it isn't every day you get the chance of free booze at the Mother of Parliaments. You can inhale the history. To say nothing of privilege. Hey, did you know a peer of the realm who was condemned to the gallows had the right to be hanged by a silken cord?"

"Is that so?"

"Don't yawn. It'll be fun. Peeking at the priceless wallpaper the Lord Chancellor splashes whenever he has a wee. The president of the Young Advocates' Society featured in the last Honours List. Services to vote-rigging. He's called in a few favors, made sure we got a cut rate for the room. You and I can go out for an Indian afterward, chew the fat, put it down as a business expense. Food always tastes better when you're cheating the Revenue with every mouthful."

"Why don't you tell me what you're really after?"

Dylan sniggered. "No fooling you, is there? Well, it just so happens, I have a story for you. There has to be a book in it. This is something extraordinary. Unique. Trust me."

"Now you're definitely asking too much."

"Two hot-shot lawyers have died." Suddenly Dylan was whispering. "They aren't the first, and they won't be the last."

"So what? Lawyers die. Didn't I read somewhere the mortality rate for lawyers under forty is three times as bad as for other professions?"

"Yeah, some people might quarrel with *bad,* but it makes you think. Seriously, there's a connection here." Rhetorical pause. "Three people dead, and it won't end there. I'm sure of that."

"Give your crystal ball a wipe."

"You can scoff," Dylan said, with pretended dudgeon. "This is all about murder for pleasure. I want to prevent another killing. The woman who put me on to this won't be safe, if something isn't done soon."

"What woman?" Humoring him.

"I had a fling with her one weekend in Oxford. That's how I became involved. It all became too much for her. She was at her wits' end. She needed someone to confide in. At first I thought she was nuts. I didn't believe a word of it."

"What did she tell you?"

"You'll find out tomorrow evening. You're coming, right?"

"Tell me now."

"You must be joking. It will take hours to explain. I've checked her story. Jesus, it's bizarre. No wonder she's spooked. She's up to her neck in it. The first to die was a boy she'd slept with. This was years ago, but she never got over it. A couple of times she's taken an overdose, once she cut her wrists. I've seen the marks." Dylan sighed. He was talking as much to himself as to Nic. "She's so mixed up, she'll never utter a word to anyone else. Twisted kind of loyalty, I guess. She made me swear to forget what she'd told me. I gave a promise, just to keep her quiet."

Dylan made a lot of promises to women just to keep them quiet. Nic said, "What are you on?"

"Nothing, not even the humblest little joint. But we are talking about a craving here. An addiction to murder." Dylan sighed. "I've kept all this to myself for long enough. I'm afraid something may happen to her. It would be so easy."

"Okay, okay, you win."

Dylan teased him with a chuckle. "After the last young advocate has sloped off home, I'll give you the lowdown. Assuming I don't get lucky, in which case you may have to be patient a little while longer. But I'm not wasting your time, promise. This is a story about seizing the power of life and death. Trust me. This is a story that will take your breath away."

And now a dead woman had taken Dylan's breath away, before he had time to spin his yarn. All he'd managed were those odd last words.

Why not jazz?

Nic rubbed his eyes. He knew about bereavement, about the dull ache that lingered long after others expected you to get on with your life. Losing Dylan wasn't the same as losing family, but Phil was wrong: it was a loss, all the same. One more empty place in his life. Funny, he'd never thought of it before, but in a strange kind of way Dylan reminded him of his father. Did that explain why he'd always relished the company of his scallywag friend? For Bryn Gabriel had been a storyteller too.

CHAPTER FOUR

"Let me have a love contract?"

Joel Anthony was teasing her, Roxanne decided. Or maybe not. With Joel, it was hard to tell. His face was straight; surely he wasn't flirting? He was willowy and handsome with elegantly manicured fingernails and a gold stud gleaming from his ear. When she'd first met him, at the interview, she'd assumed he was gay.

"A love contract?" she repeated. She leaned back in her chair, annoyed with herself for being baffled and sounding naive.

He smiled. "Not come across the term before?"

She shook her head. "Sorry."

"Don't be. I should have explained. It's an American idea. Dreamed up by lawyers acting for employers who are sick of being sued for millions of dollars when a relationship at work goes sour. Say two colleagues have an affair, then one of them moves on. If the other can't come to terms with rejection, the next move may be a harassment suit."

"So the company asks the couple to sign an agreement not to litigate if they split?"

He nodded in approval. "You've got it. When the relationship starts, they are supposed to confirm in writing that they've embarked on it voluntarily. Personally, I can't think of a bigger turn-off, but there you are. We act for the London subsidiary of a Boston corporation, and they've discovered the finance director is seeing his secretary. So in-house counsel wants them to

38

confirm in writing that it's consensual nookie."

"It won't work in this country," she said. "You can't sign away your right to bring an employment claim. And if the boss is a bully, why couldn't he bully her into signing just as easily as bully her into having the affair?"

He grinned. "You spotted the flaw. Never mind. If the client's willing to pay and we've disclaimed responsibility, all we have to do is write up the agreement and send in our bill."

The people who consulted her at Hengist Street hadn't wanted advice on love contracts. For them, going to law was a matter of survival. Many worked in the garment industry, earning a pittance in factories down Brick Lane.

"Fine," she said. "Anything in the precedent books?"

"Uh-uh. All the sample documents I've seen are iffy. You're better making it up."

She so nearly said she was good at making things up. Joel was someone with whom it would be easy to loosen your tongue. An uncommon man, she sensed. Gay or straight, who cared? He was good to look at and an expert listener. She liked his company, but she'd have to watch herself with him.

He opened the door of her room to leave, then turned to face her, Columbo fashion. "So—how's it going, Roxanne?"

"I'm loving it." As the words left her lips, she realized that she meant them. She was in her element here. Day two, and so far Creed was everything she'd dreamed it might be.

"Terrific. So you made the right decision?"

Joel's boyish features would not have looked out of place in a high school yearbook photograph. He'd risen fast. He had a first from Balliol, but even so, few people in a top London firm made partner so young. The legal directories rated him as the outstanding advocate of the new generation. A paragon: it was astonishing that she didn't loathe him. In fact, she found him mysteriously easy to talk to. There was no sign that success had gone to his head.

"This is the chance of a lifetime," she said. "Everyone's heard of Will Janus. Any employment lawyer with an ounce of motivation would want to work in his firm."

"You flatter me, Roxanne," a familiar voice said. "May I call you Roxanne? This is a first-name firm."

She turned to see the man who had strolled in to the room. Handsome as a star of a daytime soap, in his mid-forties but looking younger. There was a spring in his step, an eagerness in the way he carried himself, as if seeing her was a long-held ambition. Amazing. Will Janus himself had spared the time to come and look her over.

A couple of months earlier she'd lined up at the Barbican to hear him speak in a debate set up to raise funds for a single parents' charity. The motion was that "lawyers are the guardians of justice in a free society." He'd argued in favor, and his speech was eloquent and witty, charming yet full of conviction. Naturally his advocacy carried the day. Afterward she'd asked him to autograph his manifesto for the legal ethics in the twenty-first century, *Purer Than Pure*. He'd chatted with her and hadn't seemed in the least hurried despite the impatience of his minders from the publishing company.

Quite simply, Will Janus was hot. Whenever a high-profile case was heard, whether at the Royal Courts of Justice or in Brussels or Strasbourg, it was safe to bet that Will Janus would be around. Making a statement outside the door of the court, chairing a press conference, or offering incisive comment to a heavyweight news program. He wrote a weekly column for the *New Statesman* and presented documentaries for Channel Four. He owned a penthouse on the South Bank and a nineteenth-century mock-castle in the Kent countryside, which had been the subject of a photo shoot for *Hello*. He was everywhere. He was so much more than a lawyer with a conscience; he was a celebrity, an icon for his generation.

"Good to meet you." He paused and studied her face, before a faint smile of recognition spread from mouth to eyes. For a moment she was transfixed by fear. Had he somehow fathomed her true identity? "We've met before, haven't we? A seminar at King's College, or that debate at the Barbican, perhaps? You must forgive me. My memory's getting terrible in my old age."

His handshake was firm. There was no doubting either that somehow he'd remembered her or that he was genuinely pleased to see her again. Roxanne stammered something incoherent and he smiled again, a maximum-wattage beam this time, to put her at her ease.

"Joel has been pulling my leg about this tan. Francine and I have just come back from three weeks in the Seychelles, and I'm a bit worried that I may not have been missed. Ben's told me all about you, of course." As Roxanne moistened her lips, he added, "He absolutely raved about your advocacy in that case you fought a while back."

It was true what they said in the papers, Roxanne thought. Will was such an ordinary man. It was a special talent, making success seem like winning the lottery. His life might be yours, or at least what yours might become. He didn't have a posh accent; he hadn't been born with a silver spoon. He worked hard, but he hadn't omitted to get a life as well. His favorite food was cod and chips. He was an ardent football fan. How could anyone so decent possibly make you reach for the sick bag? He was just a nice guy who deserved his fame, his fortune, and his lovely family.

"I lost the case. My client pulled out."

Another grin, frank yet engaging. "Should have taken the settlement when it was on the table, eh? Never mind, we live and learn. I suppose you're finding this different from your last place? Not too many Kandinskys in reception there, I bet. Are you interested in art, Roxanne?"

She cast her mind back to the squiggles and blotches on the wall, wishing she had taken more notice. No doubt he meant to flatter by consulting her opinion, but the pictures meant nothing to her: colorful whizz-bangs with less inner meaning than a bar of Cadbury's Dairy Milk. She thought wildly of saying she didn't know much about art, but she knew what she didn't like, before saying cautiously, "They are very—audacious."

At once she saw that it had been the right reply. Will Janus smiled—no, she thought; he exhibited his teeth—in evident pleasure. "You're so right, actually. They represent some of his most turbulent work. We have a few originals up in the boardroom. Did you know Kandinsky intended to lecture in law?"

Roxanne shook her head. She was out of her league. Best to say as little as possible.

"Yes, he was regarded as an outstanding talent. Yet he gave it all up because he discovered a vocation he believed in even more. A remarkable man."

She felt compelled to say, "I'm not that remarkable, I'm afraid."

"But you are," he insisted. "We don't employ clones, the type of people the big City firms hire by the truckload. You may be a paralegal, but please don't feel intimidated. From what I hear, you're a damned good litigator. A fighter. You gave Ben a run for his money, and that's something not many can say. You hail from Buxton, I gather?"

He bestowed his smile upon her once more, a lord of the manor dispensing largesse to a tiller of earth. He'd taken her by surprise, the mark of a skilled cross-examiner. She wasn't ready with an answer, since she'd never dreamed the senior partner would show an interest in the track record of a newly recruited minion. It shocked her: surely he didn't *know?* She could not have uttered a word even if she had wanted to. She simply stared at his regular features, trying to read what was going through his mind.

"That's right." She found her voice at last, although it was little more than a croak. "I come from Derbyshire."

"Nice part of the world. Bracing."

And that was it. No more probing, no third degree. She was worrying over nothing; perhaps she'd mentioned her home county to Ben and Joel at the interview and then let it slip her mind. Will gave a casual nod, exchanged a little more small talk, and then excused himself because he had to prepare for an interview with the BBC. He was due to be quizzed about the burdens on business imposed by the latest European directive on health and safety. Later it occurred to her that a few years earlier Will would have been campaigning on behalf of workers endangered by dangerous conditions on the shop floor, not speaking up for employers forced to meet the cost of making their factories safe. But it didn't matter. She was just relieved that he hadn't interrogated her about what she had been doing before she'd started work at the agency in Hengist Street.

So much to learn. Not just about the law, but the minutiae of working in private practice, stuff she'd never needed to bother with before. Halfway through the morning she underwent a crash course in the art of time recording. A black art, according to Ibrahim, who had worked in law firms before fleeing to the voluntary sector. Everyone hated it, he said, because there was no way of fiddling the system. If you didn't record your time in full, it looked as though you weren't working hard enough. If you charged for every moment you spent working on a file, you had to convince a skeptical client who asked for a breakdown that you had added value to the transaction. If you wrote off a portion of the time you recorded, to keep the bills low and the clients happy, you had to justify yourself to the managing partner. The only people who liked time recording were the partners whose profit shares depended on it.

"Lawyers sell two products," Ben Yarrow told her. "Time and expertise. Clients take our expertise for granted, so it's all the more important to keep a close check on how many hours and minutes we devoted to working for them. Time is money, yes?"

"Of course it is," she chanted, like an obedient fifties schoolgirl repeating her tables. Perhaps Creed wasn't quite as different from other firms as the partners liked to make out. "Time is money."

"All you need to remember is this. For a lawyer, time is the quintessential legal fiction. Fifteen minutes for us might be thirty seconds for any other mortal being. You see, we divide each hour into four equal units. If you so much as breathe on a file for a couple of moments, you chalk up a unit. And we charge the client for the full quarter-hour. It's not stealth billing, it's all perfectly legitimate and aboveboard. Time-honored practice, you might say."

His lips twitched, and she realized he'd cracked a joke. She managed a smile and gave a sigh of relief when he left her alone in the room to set about acquiring the knack of recording time. Playing by the rules of a strange game which needed to be mastered before she could make headway with the cases she'd been hired to fight. She must concentrate on parcelling up her day into fifteen-minute slices and logging each of them faithfully onto the computer network. Each input included a terse note explaining what she had been up to, the clients she had advised, the colleagues she had consulted. A record of how she spent every fraction of the day. Kafka would have loved it, and Orwell wouldn't have been in the least surprised. The system was intrusive, it was oppressive, and yet she did not find herself itching with resentment. At least she could take it in her stride, after being watched for so long.

Chloe brought the bad news in the afternoon. She put her head inside the door and said, "I took a call while you were having your sandwich. The woman didn't want to leave a message on your voicemail, said she hated talking to machines."

At first, alarm bells didn't ring. Roxanne was scanning a CD-ROM onscreen, checking one last point before submitting her draft love contract to Joel Anthony's gaze. Keeping her eyes on the text, she said, "Uh-huh. You have a number?"

"And a name. Hilary Metcalf. She's a lawyer. She was on her cell phone. Sounded a bit uptight, but she wouldn't give her client's name. She was adamant you were the one she wanted. New case, is it?"

Roxanne stared at her. For a moment she thought she had lost the power of speech.

"You all right?" Chloe asked.

"Fine, yes, I'm fine," Roxanne said. She hated herself for her frailty. She ought to be stronger than this. "Hilary Metcalf, yes. I-I think I know what it must be about. You have her number?"

"Here." Chloe handed her a piece of paper. "Maybe I should have emailed you, but to be honest, I like to have a word with a fellow human being every now and then. Don't tell Ben. He'd have me handcuffed to my desk if he had his way." After a moment she added with lifted eyebrows "If you know what I mean."

"Yes, yes," Roxanne stammered. "Thanks."

Chloe lingered in the doorway. "Settling in okay, then?"

"Fine," Roxanne said quickly, "Yes, absolutely fine."

"Anything you want, just sing out, all right?"

At last she closed the door behind her. Roxanne buried her head in her hands. *Hilary.* She was a problem Roxanne thought she had solved. Of course, that had been too optimistic. She saw it now. One thing about Hilary: she didn't give up easily.

After a minute, Roxanne straightened in her chair. No point in putting off the evil hour. She might as well return Hilary's call. If they had to talk, so be it. She would try and sort it once and for all.

As she punched in the numbers, Roxanne told herself to relax. She had a lot to thank Hilary for, as Hilary had often reminded her. But she didn't want to remain beholden to anyone, least of all Hilary. That part of her life was over. Finished. Gone.

"Is that really you?" Hilary sounded anxious, as if she might be victim of a malicious hoax. Roxanne could picture her twisting the beads of her necklace, the way she always did when something troubled her. "I didn't believe you really would call back."

"Why not? If I didn't, you'd call again, wouldn't you? You wouldn't let me get away with no reply."

"Don't be mean. Let's just say, I'm glad you did call. We need to talk."

"Why? We said all that was needed last time we met."

"Look, Cass . . ."

"Don't!" Roxanne was almost shouting. Then she remembered that Chloe was in the next room. The walls were thin. She ground her teeth, praying the PA was transcribing an audiotape and had her earphones on. In a whisper, she said, "Don't ever, ever call me that again!"

"What's wrong?" The note of triumph was unmistakable. "It's your real name, isn't it?"

"Not now, it isn't. I'm someone else. Roxanne Wake. Do you understand?"

Hilary's sigh echoed on the cell phone. So familiar, that sigh. How many times had she heard it, how many times had her unreasonable behavior—unreasonable in Hilary's eyes, at least—

provoked more-in-sorrow-than-in-anger words of reproach? She almost felt cooled by a breeze of nostalgia.

"Okay, okay, okay. I'll do my best to remember to call you Roxanne, if it makes you happy."

"It's my name," she said through clenched teeth.

"Sure, sure." Hilary was never more infuriating than when she made it obvious that she was humoring you. Some of her clients, the petty thieves and the alcoholic down-and-outs, seemed to relish her condescension—or perhaps they expected nothing else from a lawyer.

"What are you going to do?"

"Like I said, we ought to talk." Hilary had shifted into bedside manner mode. "I'm sure we can work things out between us, you and I. Don't worry, I don't want to upset your apple cart. It's just that I feel we have unfinished business and—"

"No, we don't." Roxanne was spitting out the words. "We were finished a long time ago. If you want to ruin things for me, fine. Of course, you can do it, if you feel the need to take revenge for my ingratitude. But one thing's for sure. It's over between us."

"Roxanne, you don't—"

Enough. Roxanne banged the receiver down on to its stand.

Drafting the love contract helped to drag her thoughts away from Hilary Metcalf. She dictated her amendments and watched the words coming up on the screen in front of her. She'd never used speech recognition software before, and the system was not yet accustomed to her flat Northern vowels, so she had to talk as though to a slow-witted child in order to avoid the contract becoming littered with typing errors. Even so she was fascinated, seeing her words translated into text without needing to put a finger on the keyboard. As she printed off the sheet, she wondered how far the technology might advance. Was

thought recognition the next stop down the line? How dangerous it would be if one day a machine were able to type up what
was in a person's mind.

On leaving the office, she turned in the direction of Charing
Cross and sidestepped a bleary-eyed man who was shifting
blankets and bits of cardboard so as to make himself more
comfortable in the doorway where he'd chosen to spend the
night. Suddenly she became aware of someone behind her,
touching her on the arm. For a moment she thought it must be
another of the homeless, wanting to sell the *Big Issue*. She
already had two copies at home, but she was reaching for her
purse when a familiar voice murmured her name. Or rather, the
name she had been born with, the name she had forsaken on
arriving in London.

"Cass . . . Cassandra. It is you?"

She spun around and found herself facing Hilary Metcalf.
Hilary's expression was one of triumph blended with excitement and apprehension, as if she could not quite believe her
eyes.

Roxanne swallowed. Hilary was dressed in a lilac pantsuit, no
doubt aiming for a look that was casual yet smart and, as usual,
not quite succeeding in the attempt. Hilary scorned makeup,
and her skin was starting to show its age. A week ago she had
reached forty, but Roxanne had not sent a card. She did not
want to offer even a sliver of encouragement, give the faintest
hint that they could still be friends. Yet despite that, Hilary had
turned up here. Of course it had been a mistake to assume that
she was safely tucked away in her first-floor office in Manchester. She must already have arrived in London when she'd called
that afternoon.

"I told you. My name is Roxanne." She was surprised by how
calm she felt. What she wanted was to sound icy and hard, as
though talking to an importunate stranger, but she couldn't

quite manage it. Her voice softened as she said, "I am Roxanne Wake."

Hilary blushed and lowered her eyes. "Sorry. It just slipped out. Honestly, I didn't mean to upset you. I promise to remember in future . . . Roxanne."

She touched Roxanne's arm again in a gesture of conciliation. Roxanne stepped backward, bumping into a passerby. She did not want any contact with Hilary, not one more conversation. Let alone a future.

"You may have changed the way you look," Hilary said, "but I'd recognize you anywhere. You just can't hide those gorgeous cheekbones."

She gave a nervous smile. She was always clumsy when she tried to say something nice. Roxanne felt her stomach contract. The last thing she wanted to hear was that anyone could identify her as Cassandra Lee.

"Why have you followed me down here?"

"You make me sound like a stalker or something."

Roxanne took a deep breath. "Funny you should say that."

"What do you mean?"

"Well, aren't stalkers simply people who obsess about others?"

Hilary said nothing for a few moments. Roxanne gnawed at her lip. She'd meant to wound, but she hadn't enjoyed it. She'd said it many times over the last seven years, and she had to believe that it was true: she hated inflicting pain.

"Look, I'm sorry. I don't want to hurt you."

"Oh, really?" Another thing about Hilary. She could never keep the sarcasm out of her voice for long. "You could have fooled me."

"This isn't helping either of us," Roxanne said.

"It's not easy for you, sure. But think about me. It took courage to call you, believe me, after everything you said the last time we were together. You hurt me then, and you knew it." She paused as a couple of youths jostled past them. "Look, this is no good. We can't have a private conversation in the middle of a busy street. Is there somewhere we can go?"

It was a trap, Roxanne understood at once. Hilary wanted to insinuate herself back into her life. Yet they did have to talk. It was unavoidable. "There are gardens on the Embankment. We can talk there without being overheard."

"Not quite what I had in mind," Hilary said. "I thought— maybe a restaurant? We could have a meal together. My treat. You're still as thin as a rake, you know . . . Roxanne. I'm sure you're not looking after yourself, eating properly. I wouldn't mind betting that your ribs still show through. You ought to—"

"The gardens are just the other side of those buildings," Roxanne interrupted, starting to walk away. "Come on."

"All right, you win," Hilary said, panting as she tried to keep up. "As per usual. You'd better lead me there. I'm just a country girl. I don't know the big city."

Roxanne knew perfectly well that Hilary had been born and brought up within five miles of Manchester Town Hall, but she didn't rise to the bait. She headed for a bench in front of a bed of roses, looking out on to the commuter traffic and the river beyond. When she had settled herself, Hilary said, "You certainly took a lot of finding."

"I didn't want to be found."

"Well, anyway, congratulations. I always knew you were determined, to say nothing of bright. But I never dreamed you would have found a job with the people's lawyers. Creed, no less. Even their telephone holding music is something special. Did I read that Jarvis Cocker composed it as a special favor for his mate Will Janus? Very impressive."

Roxanne breathed in. The perfume of the roses was fighting a losing battle with gasoline smells from the road. "I could say the same for your detective work. Tracking me down here."

"Not easy, I promise you. Or quick. I had to make a lot of calls. You wouldn't guess how many."

Roxanne could imagine. When Hilary set her mind to something, she never gave up. Perhaps that was part of their problem. Each was determined, each regarded the other as ludicrously stubborn. "How did you find out?"

"It's a long story. I asked around. Networked. I may be a provincial lawyer, but I do have a few contacts in the Smoke, you know. Eventually I traced you to Hengist Street. I had a long chat with your old boss, Mr. Ibrahim. He sounds like a nice man. Harassed, of course, overworked, but willing to spare a fellow member of the profession a few minutes on the phone. He told me how proud he was of what you have achieved." Hilary paused. "I take it for granted that he has no idea Roxanne Wake and Cassandra Lee are one and the same person?"

"You're right," Roxanne said. She found herself stifling a yawn; the sheer weight of deception was exhausting. If Hilary had been talking to people, perhaps there was no point in asking her to keep her mouth shut. The truth might already be out. "Before you ask, neither does Will Janus."

"Somehow, that doesn't altogether surprise me, darling." Hilary spoke like a seen-it-all mother in conversation with a teenage daughter confessing she was no longer a virgin. "I mean, I'm sure the great man is broad-minded, but even he might draw the line at recruiting Cassandra Lee. It's taking equal opportunities a bit far. Even you must admit that."

"Are you going to tell him?"

Hilary gazed at her, open-mouthed. "For heaven's sake, Roxanne. What kind of woman do you think I am? After everything you and I went through together. Everything we shared. How can you possibly imagine, for even one second, that I would betray you? Darling, when have I ever let you down?"

51

Roxanne focused on a boat chugging in the direction of Tower Bridge. She felt remorse, tugging at her sleeve. Hilary had rescued her. Without Hilary, she would not have had a life, let alone been here in London, working for a fashionable law firm, starting at last to make her own way in the world.

She gritted her teeth. "That doesn't mean that I want us to be together anymore. I meant what I said last time. I owe you more than I can pay back. What I won't do is work off the debt in bed with you."

Hilary buried her head. "I see."

"Sorry, but you need to understand. My mind's made up."

"All right." Hilary stood up. "I won't waste any more of your time. I'm sorry too, Roxanne. I suppose I needed to hear it from you one more time. Once you'd had a while to reflect. I could never quite believe that you'd come up with the considered opinion that you don't want to share your life with me. Stupid of me, obviously."

Roxanne realized this was a good moment to hold her tongue. She had to expect Hilary to be bitter.

"Tell me one thing," Hilary said, her voice trembling. Any moment now, Roxanne thought, and she would burst into tears. "What on earth possessed you to call yourself by that awful name?"

"Roxanne is Persian for 'dawn.' I read it in a magazine." Roxanne's cheeks were hot. How could she have been so naive? "It seemed to suit a new life somehow. Same with the surname."

"You always were a romantic at heart. An idealist." Hilary's little pointed teeth started to nibble at her upper lip. "I'll say goodbye, then."

Roxanne rose to her feet, and Hilary held out her hand. They shook, an oddly formal, businesslike gesture.

"You do understand?" Hilary asked. "I-I just had to see that you were all right."

"I'm fine."

"I hope so." The serious eyes stared into hers with such intensity that Roxanne winced. And then Hilary turned and walked away without glancing back.

CHAPTER FIVE

Nic still felt dazed, kept reliving the minutes leading up to Dylan's murder, picturing the knife in Ella Vinton's hand. Each time he yearned to rewrite the script, but he never managed to conjure up a happy ending. Dylan always finished up dead, and Nic was left soaked to the skin in blood and guilt.

The police returned. Two different officers this time, but again his account foundered on the rocks of the police department's institutional skepticism. All they told him was that Dylan's killer still had not regained consciousness. One journalist after another showed up; he gave good quote but little else. Until he understood what had happened, he would say nothing to the press about Ella, or the dying man's last question.

Why not jazz?

A puzzle which took on fresh meaning when he listened to the hospital radio. Lots of Chicago, Luther Vandross, and Abba. He hated being cooped up with the Muzak and the disinfectant smells and the squeaking of trolley wheels. Hated it. While the medics deliberated over whether he was all right, he discharged himself. His head throbbed. His brain was messed up, but was it any wonder? After all, he'd seen a friend killed, a friend he'd tried and failed to save. He'd get better quicker in the world outside.

He walked back to Clerkenwell, rather than catching a bus or a cab. Whenever he could, he traveled the city by foot. He didn't drive in London, keeping his old car simply for trips outside the city. As for the Tube, its sweaty stench made him want to retch. Cycling would have saved time, but in the overcrowded streets it was an eco-friendly form of Russian roulette. On a bus he would eavesdrop on the conversations of his fellow passengers, but there were limits even to his curiosity, and when he took a taxi he turned a deaf ear to the cabbie's grumblings about Tottenham Hotspur and the single European currency. So mostly he walked. It was a way of trying to make sense of the place. He wanted to get close to it, to pound the uneven pavements until the city soaked into his being and he felt at last like a native.

Yet however many miles he covered, London remained foreign to him. He'd read all the books, he'd walked far and wide, he knew where Blondin the tightrope maestro was buried and how to find the site of England's first permanent scaffold. But when he was alone and his mind wasn't stretched to the full, a sense of the city's unspoken hostility always crept back up on him. At times he felt like an astronaut stranded on a forbidden planet.

"Spare us a bit of cash."

Someone peering out from under a woolly hat was lying in the doorway of a barber's shop, wrapped up in a pile of old newspapers and a dirty pink blanket smelling of stale tobacco and urine. Nic tossed a pocketful of coins into a grimy hand. The man might have been anything from twenty-five to sixty. London did this to people. It seduced them, and then it let them down.

He'd arrived here on leaving Cambridge and spent twelve months at law school in Lancaster Gate, sharing a house with fellow students, through one of whom he'd met Dylan Rees. He had no career path in mind. The lesson he'd drawn from his fractured childhood was that it was pointless to look ahead. One could spend so long planning the future only to find everything blown away in a moment. He decided to go with the flow and, when the people he knew gave up on fantasies of backpacking around the globe and stayed on to earn serious money, he did the same. At the last minute he found a training contract with a City firm, and when his two years of training were up and he was offered the chance to stick around, he seized it. After all, he had nothing to go back to in Ravenscar. It wasn't because people called it the town that never was. Home simply didn't exist anymore.

He soon made his mark. He could seldom manage more than a couple of hours' sleep a night, and when he was awake he was happy to work. The firm kept hiking his pay and at his performance appraisals, heavy hints were dropped about prospects of partnership. The only problem was, he didn't want to practice law. Rules might be necessary, but it turned out they didn't *solve* anything. For years, he'd daydreamed about writing a book, and the time had come to see if he could hack it. He could have moved anywhere; he only needed a roof over his head and paper and pen. Yet an invisible yoke tied him to London. He couldn't explain it, even to himself. The exhaust fumes made his eyes water, but he couldn't think of anywhere else that he wanted to be.

He bought a houseboat moored near Battersea Bridge. A gesture of defiance. If he could not escape, at least he could pretend that he was out of the city when the midnight racket outside his bedroom window came not from screaming junkies but from geese guarding freshly hatched chicks. He loved the rocking of the boat on summer evenings. He'd started sleeping longer. Even during winter storms, when his books were sent flying from his shelves and an eight-hours-a-night man would have been kept awake, he felt no nostalgia for high-rise living. He'd written *The Innocence of Dr. Crippen* on the boat, and returning to dry land never crossed his mind until after he fell for Phil. The pair of them drank too much one evening and drifted into a conversation about living together. It was out of the question for Phil to share the boat. She became seasick watching *Titanic*. So he'd finished up in Clerkenwell, and the first time he spent the night there his insomnia returned, as bad as ever.

Phil's flat was a stone's throw away from the excavated remains of the House of Detention. Increasingly, he thought of it as an elegant contemporary equivalent of the old jailhouse. He unlocked the front door and paused on the granite curbstone, which formed a step down to the main living area, listening to see if she had come home. The flat was one of half a dozen carved out of a disused Victorian school. Visitors exclaimed at the cleverness with which the architect had converted the shell, keeping the old high ceilings and the sense of airiness within a confined space. Phil liked to say that the place was more than a home; it was a statement. The architect had once been her lover, and she reckoned he would come running back if she so much as whistled. The granite step was supposed to provide the rough, freestanding element that the ex considered necessary to ease the transition from the door to the principal living quarters. There was no getting away from the ex. His pretensions were all around.

Phil was in the kitchen, loading the dishwasher. He caught sight of a single glass on the top rack. She jumped as she heard him come into the room.

"I wasn't expecting them to let you out so soon."

"I'm fine."

She offered her cheek and he kissed it, dutiful as a middle-aged husband. Her skin was cold and her breath smelled. Unlike most of her colleagues at work, she didn't much care for nose candy. She was at least old-fashioned enough for drink to be her vice. In their early days as a couple, they'd often gotten drunk together. They both loved Chablis; it had been a kind of bond.

"Aren't you supposed to be out with that client all evening?"

She pulled away from him, averting her face. She was a little unsteady on her feet. "He canceled at the last minute. The bastard."

Unaccountably, he felt a spurt of sympathy. This particular client was supposed to be trying to keep the lid on an internal fraud, but Nic was sure Phil and he were having a fling. He hadn't checked the fridge to see if they were low on strawberries and cream, but there had been a good many late-night sessions in the past month. If the time spent was justified, the whole of the client's accounts team must have been in on the scam.

He moved to her side again and put his hand on her shoulders. Through the silk top, he could feel the tension in her. "You okay?"

Silly question. Her eyes were puffy and her mascara had run. "Of course I'm okay," she said. "Just tired, that's all."

"Uh-huh." He gave her shoulder a squeeze, wondered how long it would take before she began to pick a fight.

She turned to face him, and he had his answer. "Mel called. Seems the press are taking an interest in you again because you saw Dylan getting his throat cut. *De mortuis* and all that, but maybe every cloud has a silver lining. You could be hot again if you seize your chance right now."

"Meaning?"

"Meaning, when are you going to start work on that the second book?"

"And what should I write about?"

"Hey, you're supposed to be the one with the vivid imagination. You can think of something. It doesn't matter what."

"It matters to me."

"Oh, for Chrissake! It's four years plus since you sold *Crippen*. Three since it came out. No wonder Huckerbys have threatened you with the sack."

He shrugged. She was right. His publishers were losing patience. They'd chafed for a long time. He'd made them enough money to earn kid glove treatment for the first year or two, but lately they'd been muttering about breach of contract. So what? He couldn't write to order.

"Don't tell me you're still waiting for your muse!"

"Fine," he said, aiming to be infuriatingly amiable. "I won't mention it."

Even on the occasions—not so rare now as in the early days—when she looked untidy, there was no hiding her beauty. Rich chestnut hair, cheekbones to die for. Behind her head was a row of spice jars on a fitted shelf; she had been known to hurl them in a drunken temper. He didn't need to ask her why she kept all the jars when she never bothered with anything more exotic than bay leaf and thyme. Apart from their value as projectiles, they were integral to the ambience, another of the ex's nice little touches.

"I'm making a coffee," he said. "Want one?"

Her cheeks were flushed. "Right now, what I want is to get on with my work. One of us has to make a stab at earning a living."

He switched on the coffee machine while she disappeared to her work station. The ex had created a mezzanine level with room for two vast computer desks as well as a spare bedroom. It was reached by the staircase made of aluminium and stainless steel cables, which arced through the air like the shiny skeleton of a prehistoric creature unknown to science. Phil loved it; sometimes he thought she loved the whole place more than she could love any man. The ex had been architect of his own downfall.

59

The phone trilled. His agent had called the hospital only to learn that Nic was no longer a patient. He didn't bother with words of sympathy, cutting to the chase with an offer—"Kid, the money will make your eyes water"—for a two-thousand-word piece for the *Mail on Sunday*. Nic didn't need to think it over before saying no.

Mel was a loud New Yorker who had missed his true vocation as a yellow cab driver. "Fuck me, Nic. You're Johnny on the spot when a legendary headhunter is brutally slain and you don't race straight off to your keyboard? Bad fucking attitude. You'll never make a proper writer."

"Yeah, you're right, but I'm still not doing it. Too much like dancing on his grave."

"Think of it as therapy."

"Even if I did, the piece would never see the light of day."

Mel never wasted time banging his head against brick walls. "Okay, okay, so what about *Son of Crippen*? Plenty of scope for serialization with true crime, that's the way to make a few bucks."

"Don't you start."

"You're afraid, aren't you?" Mel demanded. "Afraid you're just a one-trick pony. Afraid the next book won't be as good as the last. So you'd rather not risk writing it."

Nic said lazily, "When I want to be psychoanalyzed, I'll let you know. It's not fear, Mel. You know that. It's just—I need a story to seduce me. Take over my life. If I'm not obsessed, it won't work."

"Okay, okay. So what's bugging you right now? Apart from the fact that your royalty checks ain't been so handsome for a while?"

"When something comes along, I'll tell you, all right?"

He put the phone down, aware that he hadn't told Mel the whole truth. Something had begun to obsess him. It was more, even more, than the need to understand how Ella had come back from the dead. He wanted to learn about the dead lawyers and find if the answer to Dylan's final question meant anything at all.

Without thinking, he put on a CD. Noel Gallagher, being contemptuous about something.

"For God's sake," Phil called down. "Are you doing this deliberately? You know I need quiet if I'm going to concentrate."

He cut off Noel in mid-sneer. "Sorry. I wasn't thinking."

He sprawled across the red and yellow sofa, an artistically brilliant contrast to the plain birch plywood wall cupboards and as comfortable as a ledge of rock. Thinking about Dylan, not Phil. Later, after she'd finished work, she was in a better humor and came to sit on his knee.

"I had an idea," she said, as he stroked her thighs. "How about writing up what happened to your family all those years ago?"

He stopped stroking. "You can't be serious."

"Sure I am, why not? You could do it." She paused. "Maybe it would help."

"Help who?"

"You."

"So I need help?"

"You became a lawyer so you could discover how to weigh up evidence. You wrote about how a man under suspicion deals with his wife's death so that you could make sense of crimes of passion. Maybe prove that black is white."

"He didn't kill her, Phil."

"You're talking about Crippen?"

"You know I'm not."

She pulled a face. "Everyone else thinks he did it."

"I can't write about it—the whole thing's too close. But there's no way he could have killed her."

"It's the truth. Must be. Why can't you get used to it?"

He bundled her off his knee. "Because I don't believe it. I knew him. He would never do a thing like that, you hear? I'll never accept he was guilty, understand? One day I'll prove it to you."

"Prove what, exactly?"

"That my father was no murderer."

Bryn Gabriel had been a Welshman and a teller of tales. Nic's first memories were of his father recounting legends of King Arthur and his knights of the Round Table. One story that always stuck in his mind was that of King Pellinore's pursuit of the Questing Beast. The Beast was part lion, part serpent, part goat, and made a sound as though thirty couples of hounds were in its belly. It existed for no other reason than to be sought after, and Pellinore hunted after it until he died. As a boy, Nic had asked his father why someone would ever feel impelled to devote his life to an endless and impossible task.

"It happens, Dominic." His father always used his full name, never the shortened version his mother preferred. After her death, Nic never called himself Dominic. "If we want something badly enough, we may have to sacrifice everything else in trying to achieve it, even if in our heart of hearts we know it's hopeless and we're fated not to make it. I don't suppose it's a matter of choice. If something matters so much, it takes over completely and consumes our whole lives. As it did with Pellinore and his pursuit of the Questing Beast."

In those days, he hadn't been able to make sense of what his father said. He loved the magic and mystery of the ancient narratives, but kept hankering after rhyme and reason. His hunger for rational explanations was what had drawn him to the study of law. If so, he'd been disappointed. The logic of the law was only skin deep. He'd come to realize that murder fascinated him more than anything. Was it possible to understand what went on in a killer's mind, as well as in the mind of those presumed guilty, who turned out in truth to be innocent?

At half past two, he went upstairs. Phil groaned as he climbed into bed, but did not open her eyes. He touched the back of her neck with his lips. Her skin was soft, and the whiff of alcohol still clung to her. He stared out across the spiky moonlit skyline. The electronic system which closed the curtains had developed a malfunction so that a gap was always left through which he could survey the city at night. Shadows danced on the ceiling. He dared not close his eyes in case he saw Ella Vinton, her eyes devoid of pity, plunging the knife into Dylan's throat. Phil stirred beside him.

"Still thinking about the headhunter?" she said in a muffled voice. Her eyes had not opened.

She was not a fool. "Yes."

"You can't bring him back."

She might have been talking about his father, as well as Dylan. "I know."

"Well, then," she muttered. "Go to sleep."

She was barely awake, but he felt his chest tightening. It wasn't smart to be hurt by a few drowsy well-meant words, but surely if she loved him, she would have remembered that he was an insomniac.

The noise of the city; there was no escape from it. Beery voices booming out of airless bars, the crashing of builders hauling bricks over scaffolding, the constant bellow of the traffic. The racket of London echoed in his ears. Even as he lay awake in bed in the middle of the night, there was no respite. In the distance a car engine rumbled, a drunk yelled, a group of roaming young people shrieked with laughter.

Lying in the dark, he thought, as so often, about murder.

63

Dylan had known how to touch his nerve, how to seize his attention by talking of an addiction to murder. Nic derided most of the true-crime buffs he'd met, people like the Ripperologists, the puzzle freaks who kept coming up with nuttily improbable suspects for the Whitechapel killings or the sickos who salivated over the details of each evisceration. But on one thing everyone who dabbled in criminology agreed. It was possible for a man to be innocent of a crime when all the evidence pointed to his culpability. The case against Crippen was crushing. Nic had read the notes made by Richard Muir, counsel for the prosecution. Terse jottings so beautifully composed that they'd even made it into a compilation of classic legal literature—as well as playing their part in hanging a man.

A line from Raymond Chandler stuck in his mind. *Nobody ever writes a book about a famous case to prove that the jury brought in the right verdict.* But having an imagination wasn't a must for serving on a jury, and even Chandler had speculated that Crippen might not have meant to murder his wife. While he was at work on his book, Nic had not simply wanted to dream up a way of exonerating Crippen. He'd believed in the doctor's innocence. Believed in it with the same fierce passion that insisted his father was innocent, when all the evidence damned him.

When daybreak came, his heart stopped thudding, and as he stretched out and calmed down, he told himself not to give up, that one day he would feel at ease in London. Self-deception, of course. No matter how long he lived here, even if he stayed until his dying day, in his bones he would never belong.

A few minutes after seven-thirty, the phone rang. Lea Valentine, Dylan's partner.

She didn't bother with preambles or solicitous inquiries after his health. "Heard the news?"

"What news?"

"It was on breakfast television. The woman who killed Dylan.

She's dead. Without regaining consciousness. Guess who she
was?"

Chapter Six

"You've been wonderful," Roxanne said after Chloe Beck book-marked the internet labor law reports on her personal computer the next morning. "I don't think I could have survived even this long without you."

"It's nothing. Anyone would have been glad to show you what's what," Chloe said. "Anyway, I've enjoyed it, showing you the ropes. Making friends."

Roxanne gave a cool smile. Grateful for Chloe's help, but not wanting the other woman to befriend her. It was safer to keep a distance from people at work. She must guard her privacy. Even if Hilary kept her word and did not betray her, it would be so easy to let something slip in casual conversation.

Chloe was a chatterbox, someone who regaled the slightest acquaintance with highlights from her life story. Roxanne had already heard far more of the gory details about Chloe's implants operation than she would have wished. Worse, Ms. Silicone didn't just like talking about herself. She was fascinated by people, endlessly inquisitive. A dangerous companion for a person with something to hide, and avoiding her was easier said than done. Their rooms adjoined each other, and Roxanne had to pass Chloe's in order to reach hers. The only alternative was to hike all the way around the floor in the opposite direction so as to avoid the chance that Chloe might look up from her desk and wave her in for a chat. But that would be both ridiculous and cowardly, and whatever her faults, no one had ever accused her of being stupid or lacking in courage. Usually she just shook her head if Chloe spotted her as she passed, mouthing "sorry" through the glass panel in the door.

Yet it would have been impossible, even if she never asked her for help with an unfamiliar computer system or to do any secretarial work, to escape Chloe's company altogether. Thanks to speech recognition software and the regular absences on business of Ben and Joel, Chloe often seemed to have time on her hands. She liked to pop in for a chat whenever she was at loose ends. Any excuse was good enough. Later that same day, Roxanne even found herself participating, for the first time in her life, in a conversation about lipstick.

"I'd feel naked without it," Chloe confessed. "If my house was burning down, the first thing I'd want to rescue would be my lipstick. You may laugh, but it's true!"

Roxanne had grown up regarding lipstick as something that mattered to people of her mother's age. She thought of it as a generation thing, but Chloe was her own age. At least she guessed so. In super-bitch mood, she might have said that the other woman wore so much makeup, it was hard to tell. But who was she to criticize someone else for wearing a disguise?

"I'm sure you'd look just as good without it," she said.

Chloe feigned self-consciousness. "Oh, do you really think so?"

"Honestly."

They bantered like this for a while. Chloe said, "You know, I'm so glad you've come here. It's fun to talk to you. Makes a change from the girls in the typing pool. And the lawyers. You're—well, it's a funny thing to say, but somehow you're different."

You don't know how right you are. "I suppose I'd better take that as a compliment."

"Of course," Chloe said. And, beaming from ear to ear, she

sauntered back to her room.

Roxanne couldn't help liking her. That was the problem. Chloe was warm and straightforward and possessed a love of life that Roxanne found intensely appealing. Perhaps she was jealous, because Chloe didn't seem to carry any baggage. There was no secret she had to keep forever.

Roxanne was seeing a good deal of Joel Anthony. Somehow she felt safer in his company than when she was with any of the other partners. So far he had neither asked her about her past nor showed any curiosity about her private life. Like Chloe, he was always willing to spare a few minutes to answer her questions, however mundane or naive they might be. Often he spiced his explanations with anecdotes about cases the firm had fought. Triumphs over bureaucracy, officialdom, hallowed legal precedent. Every story cast Will Janus in a flattering light.

"It's like Fergus says. Without Will, this firm would be just another bog-standard law practice. Will's broadened our client base out of all recognition. We don't just serve a narrow interest sector these days. We don't just focus on employers, or on employees. He's found a third way. These days, the great and the good beat a path to our door. Number Ten begged him to talk Ali Khan into sponsoring the Media Zone at the poor old Dome. He was close to Diana in the months before she died. They shared an interest in campaigning against landmines and raising funds for children's hospices. Salman Rushdie's a friend, Bob Geldof, the list goes on. Only yesterday he was asked to call in at Lambeth Palace."

"I suppose I assumed our work would be mostly on behalf of workers and trade unions," she said. As the words left her lips, she wanted to bite her tongue. It sounded like blasphemy, although she hadn't meant to criticize Will Janus or the firm. The trouble with Joel was that he made you feel relaxed, so that you were tempted to drop your guard. She added hastily, "I mean, almost all the stuff I've seen so far consists of files opened for multinationals and favors for the glitterati. It's fascinating, but—"

"We'll represent anyone," Joel said, interrupting her with every appearance of good humor. "As long as they pay our bills. As for the *pro bono* work we do . . ."

Her only reservation about Joel, she thought as he launched into a recapitulation of Fergus McHugh's press release about the firm's free advice clinic for needy residents of the Isle of Dogs, was that he was so on-message. But he was a brilliant lawyer. She was learning so much from working with him on the Thrust Media sexual harassment case.

The victim, Gina Mandel, was a sales rep for Thrust Media's magazine division. She'd complained about her marketing director's conduct at a bonding weekend at a hotel in Brighton. He'd taken the bonding concept too far. She accused him of propositioning her at the bar in the evening and then following her up to her bedroom and pestering her to allow him to come in. When she said no, he'd tried to kiss her, then put his hand up her skirt before she'd managed to slam the door in his face. Roxanne had handled a dozen similar cases at Hengist Street, but this was the first time she'd acted for an employer in such a squalid little story. Howard Haycraft, the director, had given Gina Mandel a poor performance appraisal a week earlier. He claimed she was taking revenge, although she had been off work with stress ever since, and her doctor confirmed that she couldn't face returning to confront the boss who had bullied her. According to Haycraft, she was simply seeking to make easy money and destroy his career in the process.

"Preparation," Joel said, leaning back in his chair with his hands behind his head. "That's the secret of success in advocacy. Never mind the rhetorical flourishes—they're fun, but they're only icing on the cake. You need to know your case inside out. So you can be ready for anything."

"You wrote to the clients about rehearsing the witnesses' evidence."

"I want to put Haycraft under pressure, the sort of pressure he'll be under in the witness box if this case goes all the way. You come, too. See how he reacts to cross-examination."

"You want to play devil's advocate?"

He grinned. "Something like that."

They took a taxi up Tottenham Court Road, heading for Thrust Media's headquarters, a glass building with a cupola that looked like a millennial palace designed by Richard Rogers on an off day. Thrust sold everything from best-selling vegan cookbooks to interactive pornographic software and was a hot tip to win the lottery franchise next time around. Meanwhile Ali Khan climbed closer to the top of the British rich list every year. The bitter litigation over his battle for a British passport was long forgotten. These days, he was a pillar of the establishment. He and Will Janus were very close. Gossip magazines often pictured the pair of them and their pretty wives together, attending opening nights, celebrity weddings, and parties given by pals from the corridors of power.

They stopped at a red light. Newspaper placards on the pavement screamed "Anarchist Protest Fears." Joel shook his head, said that the mayor ought to crack down on the trouble before things got out of hand.

Roxanne wasn't interested in the threatened riots. Politics meant nothing to her. "What do you make of the case?"

Joel drew a slender finger across his throat. "Haycraft will soon be history. The company's dignity-at-work policy is explicit. Harassment is gross misconduct."

"He's admitted nothing."

"We'll see. Ali Khan can't afford to have his reputation

tarnished by managers who indulge in macho posturing. Thrust is determined to root out bullying."

"Perhaps Howard Haycraft should have asked Gina Mandel to sign a love contract."

"Believe me," Joel said, "it would take more than that to save his neck. Listen, Roxanne, once I've finished testing his evidence, you take him for a coffee and a chat. See what shape he's in. Go somewhere in public, so there's no way he'll try anything on with you. Are you okay with that?"

"Don't worry. I can handle a creep like Howard Haycraft."

"I'm sure you can. When you talk to him, he'll be in denial. Doesn't matter. Whatever you do, don't let him forget he's the one in trouble, not Gina Mandel." Joel gazed hard at her before adding with uncharacteristic harshness, "Deep, deep trouble."

They were greeted at the reception desk with the news that Ali Khan wanted a quick word.

"This is quite an honor," Joel said. Roxanne would have sworn that his voice was trembling with excitement. She was reminded of Chang in *Lost Horizon,* breaking the news to Conway that the High Lama of Shangri-La had summoned him for an audience.

In person the great man was tiny, with an oversized head, a warm smile, and a handshake that lingered too long for Roxanne's comfort.

"I'm sure you will both do what is necessary," he said. "For me, reputation is everything. We cannot afford to have the good name of Thrust besmirched by accusations of impropriety."

Something impelled Roxanne to say, "Gina Mandel's evidence is uncorroborated."

Ali Khan considered her. His genial beam did not flicker. "Indeed. But that is no reason to disbelieve what she says. She is a highly intelligent young woman as well as, if it is not indelicate to say so in the circumstances, a very attractive one. I

feel sure she will go far in this organization—once the present
little difficulty has been resolved to everyone's satisfaction."

"Of course," Joel said fervently.

Ali Khan still had his eyes on Roxanne. "You acted for Tara
Glass, did you not? A sad business. Such baseless allegations. I
was distraught. But it is not true what our enemies say, Ms.
Wake, the Khans do not always bear grudges. We sent a floral
tribute to the funeral, made sure her widowed mother had a
little nest egg to keep the wolf from the door."

"The funeral?"

"Ah yes, didn't you know? It was most unfortunate. She took
an overdose of heroin twenty-four hours after the tribunal hearing. As you gathered, she did have something of a drug habit.
And in the end it destroyed her."

"You've read Ms. Mandel's statement?" Joel asked coolly.

They were in the boardroom: Joel, Roxanne, and Howard
Haycraft. She'd recognized Haycraft at once from the photograph on the company's website. She had thought it unflatter-
ing, but his resemblance to a squirrel was even more striking in
the flesh. She half expected him to start nibbling at an acorn or
scamper up the wall. He was a stranger, but already she knew
his height and weight and spare-time interests, as well as the
names of his wife, his children, and his parents back home in
Cardiff. She'd followed the path of his career from his file. The
pay raises, the building society's request for a reference when he
moved to a new house in Richmond, his absence from work occasioned by an operation for a hiatal hernia. He was a
competent manager, his annual appraisals acknowledged, good
at getting younger, more charismatic salespeople to sell. His salary and benefits package were handsome. Yet there were stray
hints that he lacked initiative, some spark of imagination. Reading between the lines, Roxanne guessed that, although he had

reached a senior level and had a salary to match, he had not been going to rise any further in Thrust's hierarchy, even before the calamity which had led to his suspension.

"Pack of sodding lies!" Haycraft said loudly, waving his hand and knocking over a glass of water on the table.

Joel lifted an eyebrow. "Can we talk about the weekend, please? Gina Mandel says you approached her in the bar after the evening meal."

"We bumped into each other. I didn't plan it that way."

"You insisted on buying her drinks."

A trace of sweat made Haycraft's forehead glisten. His Welsh accent was becoming more pronounced as he talked. "I may have done that. Sort of goodwill gesture. It's not a hanging offense, is it? That's what these events are all about. Building team spirit."

Joel gave a discreet cough. "She says you kept brushing against her. She found it uncomfortable. Distressing."

"Look, it was a crowded bar. We barely had room to breathe. Like a tin of sardines, we were. As for distressed, you wouldn't have known it. She was still laughing and joking."

"She says she felt embarrassed by your behavior and decided to go to bed early."

"Embarrassed? Give me a break! I tell you, Gina Mandel was never embarrassed in her whole bloody life."

"Why did you follow her upstairs in the lift?"

"My room was on the same floor, for God's sake! What would you expect me to do? Climb up the fire escape?"

Joel said smoothly, "She says that as she got into the lift, you came running up and asked her to hold the doors."

"So what?"

"She says she was concerned by your manner. You reeked of alcohol . . ."

"Oh yes, and she'd been drinking tonic water? I don't think

so." Haycraft's cheeks were crimson. "Look, we chatted for a few moments and got out when we reached our floor. As we were walking down the corridor together, we were still talking."

"About what?"

"How do you expect me to remember? It was social chit-chat, that's all. We didn't get on to the meaning of life. She was flirting, perhaps, and I teased her."

"Sexual innuendo?"

"Nothing anyone could object to. Especially not her."

"She says you became persistent. She had the key to her room in her hand, and you kept badgering her. Inviting yourself in for a nightcap."

"Balls."

"Do you remember touching her?"

Haycraft hesitated. "Well, I did peck her on the cheek when we said goodnight. Is that a crime? I don't seem to remember her kicking up a fuss at the time."

"She says she was shocked by your behavior. She didn't know what to do. You were her boss, yet you'd abused your power. You rubbed yourself up against her as she stood outside her bedroom door."

"It's a lie!" The eyes were bulging again.

"She says you started by brushing your hand against her bottom. You tried to force your tongue between her lips and at the same time your hand crept up her skirt. She claims you were in an aroused state."

" 'Aroused state'! For crying out loud! She'd never use that turn of phrase. Gina's the kind who calls a spade a bloody shovel. That's lawyer-speak for you. Her brief has put words in her mouth."

Joel's eyes narrowed. No more Mister Nice Guy, Roxanne thought. The best advocates were always clinical when they went for the kill.

"Were you in an aroused state?" he demanded.

"Of course I bloody was," Haycraft said. "And all she said was that anyone could tell I was with Thrust."

"I thought your bloody boss was supposed to be on my side," Haycraft said half an hour later.

The evidence rehearsal was over, and Roxanne had taken Haycraft, at Joel's suggestion, to the Reading Room in Law Society Hall for a debrief. On the way, in the cab, he'd fumed about the injustice of it all and the way all the cards were stacked in favor of women with a grudge. Roxanne let him talk, an outpouring of self-pity. He was forty-four years old and had been married for eighteen years. How could he have imagined that Gina Mandel, by all accounts a pretty woman young enough to be one of his kids, would ever have wanted to seize the opportunity afforded by a weekend away and invite him to share her bed?

"He's on the company's side," she said, taking a sip of coffee. She was trying not to think about Tara Glass.

"I represent the company," he said in an injured tone.

"You're also under suspension," she reminded him.

He clenched his fists, breathing hard. "It's so fucking unjust!"

When Roxanne replied with a shrug, Haycraft said in a low voice, "Look, what's going to happen with this case?"

"It's early days yet."

"I know, but . . ."

"The company needs to make a decision whether to fight the case or settle. That's a matter for them. Joel Anthony will be reporting to them now that he's had a chance to evaluate your evidence."

"He thinks I'm a dirty old man, doesn't he?"

Roxanne said nothing.

"It was just a moment of madness. That's all! A moment of madness."

Roxanne exhaled, kept her eyes on the ceiling.

When Haycraft spoke again, his voice was choked. "Either way, I'm finished, aren't I? Not just with Thrust, but in the industry. I'm ruined. I'll never work again. My wife will find out, won't she? I haven't told her about this, not a word. Things are . . . difficult at home."

He buried his face in his hands.

In her mind, Roxanne heard Joel Anthony's voice. *Deep, deep trouble.*

When Haycraft looked up, she returned his gaze. She couldn't offer him any hope.

Pursing her lips, she said, "You must understand, it's for management to decide what action to take."

He blinked hard. She saw tears in his eyes. He clambered to his feet without another word and stumbled blindly toward the door. She watched him shove his way past a couple of young women lawyers, saw their expressions of distaste as he blundered on without offering an apology.

Roxanne gathered her papers together. She did not care for Howard Haycraft, but it had been cruel not to offer him a sliver of hope. She'd acted for too many employees with ruined careers and lives to want to inflict more pain. If only she hadn't let Tara Glass cut and run, perhaps things might have ended differently. Would it help to chase after him and try to calm him down, or would he see it as a sign of weakness? Never mind, she'd do it anyway. Hurrying down the steps that led from the main entrance to the pavement, she caught sight of Haycraft, weaving unsteadily along Chancery Lane.

She was about to call him when, without warning, he stepped off the pavement. A builder's truck loaded with cinder blocks was bearing down upon him. Roxanne put a hand to her mouth as she watched. Haycraft walked straight in front of the truck. Brakes squealed, a couple of girls emerging from a bistro screamed. The truck shuddered to a halt. For a split second, there was a moment of silence in the city. As if for an instant all activity had been suspended in a show of respect. Then people rushed forward.

Roxanne followed the crowd. A group of onlookers had gathered in the road. The traffic was at a standstill. A fat woman with a mobile phone called out that she was dialing 999. Roxanne could not see what had happened to Howard Haycraft. He had gone under the wheels of the wagon and that was all she knew.

A young man peeled away from the gathering. His face was white. He said, to no one in particular, "I think I'm going to be sick."

The fat woman seemed to be taking charge. Roxanne heard her say, "He just walked under the wheels. He never looked. There was nothing the driver could do."

Roxanne hesitated, then made up her mind. She turned on her heel and walked quickly back in the direction of Fleet Street. There was nothing she could do, either.

CHAPTER SEVEN

"I never even knew that Ella had a sister," Nic said.

Lea Valentine stroked her double chins with a chubby forefinger. They were in her office, a cramped and stuffy room. A fan whirred noisily and to no effect. "I have this picture in my mind of a kid at the funeral, throwing flowers on to the coffin as it was lowered into the grave. Amy Vinton. A slip of a girl, smaller than Ella and not quite as pretty. She kept blowing her nose. She didn't speak. People said she'd always idolized her big sister. She was in her first year of university at the time."

"I thought Ella had come back from the grave."

"Way I hear it, no actress could have impersonated her as well as young Amy did." Lea leaned back on her chair, wobbling dangerously. Her tent-like mauve top was complemented by vivid floral leggings that might have suited a skinny adolescent. Nic didn't know anyone brave enough to suggest that a skirt would be a better idea. She wasn't someone it was wise to provoke. She had a sharp tongue, and she wasn't afraid to use it. "No wonder you thought you were drunk or hallucinating. She already had the right build, the bone structure. Lifts in her shoes to give her the height. She'd kept Ella's clothes, her makeup even. End result—a doppelgänger."

"So she was trying to take on her sister's identity?"

Lea wrinkled her nose. "Bollocks to that. Take a tip from me and forget the spooky psychological stuff. She just wanted to scare the shit out of Dylan, and then make him pay for what

78

he'd done. It was all about vengeance."

"Perhaps she expected him to show remorse."

Lea opened a bag of shrimp cocktail potato chips that lay amid the clutter of her desk. The room was awash with faxes, scribbled notes, and sheaves of printouts. She and Dylan did their business away from here, visiting employer clients in their offices, chatting up jobseekers in discreet corners of hotel lobbies. They were as likely to be found here late in the evening as during the day, grabbing a snack while they updated their records. A musty smell of ramen noodles hung in the air.

"I could have saved her the trouble if she'd only asked. My late lamented partner had many qualities, but he lacked a sense of shame."

"He was a lawyer turned headhunter. What do you expect?"

"That's rich, coming from a lawyer turned crime buff. Next to you, Dylan and I are saints. Well, even if he wasn't, I fucking am."

She swore with a zest that would have made D. H. Lawrence blush. For a moment she treated him to a fierce stare, and then they both broke into laughter. Lea's parents had been a petty criminal and an occasional prostitute. She'd made it to college against the odds and drifted into recruitment as a way of making ends meet, only to find that she possessed a flair for screwing the rich that had always eluded her mother. She'd set up in partnership with Dylan, and the combination of her negotiating skills with his gift for making people feel good about giving him their business had earned them a lot of money. She spent all her spare time and cash supporting a cats' sanctuary down the road. On the evening of Dylan's death, while the kids were downing Bollinger at Westminster, she'd been out selling raffle tickets for an antivivisection campaign. She shared her home with half a dozen tabbies, and a whiff of them clung to her wherever she went.

79

She stuffed a fistful of potato chips into her mouth. "Never thought I'd say this, but I'm going to miss Dylan. I don't want to. I've cleared his stuff out already, as much as I can. That's why things are looking tidier than usual."

"Christ."

"People used to ask how we managed to stick together. We were both working-class kids, of course. Otherwise, chalk and cheese. I suppose it helped that we never screwed each other. He didn't go for fat women. I couldn't ever fancy anyone who didn't care about animals. But we worked well as a team. Dylan needed someone who wouldn't take any crap from him. People underestimated him because he was a Casanova, but he was smart. He took risks with some of the candidates he placed, but his instincts didn't often let him down."

"At the party, he was pushing the line that you and he were matchmakers."

"And I bet he had the kids swallowing it hook, line, and sinker, same as always. Me, I'm a realist. You can't say I haven't learned from my poor old mum's mistakes. I used to tell him we were more like pimps, flogging bodies to the customers with the biggest checkbook. Dylan wouldn't have that. He was a romantic, prided himself on it."

"How will you manage without him?"

Lea wiped her lips with the back of her hand. "I'll cope, don't you fret." She added, almost to herself, "I'm not saying it will be easy. Thing about Dylan, he understood what makes people tick. Me, I prefer cats. He loved gossip. It was his stock-in-trade. He talked a lot, but what most folk didn't realize was, he could be a brilliant listener, too. Like you."

"Flattery will get you everywhere."

She raised her eyebrows. "Oh yeah? Well, Dylan always knew who was unhappy at work, or ready for a move. Sometimes before they realized it themselves. People would tell him things, and afterward maybe regret it. Like he used to say, knowledge is power."

"He wasn't any sort of megalomaniac."

"No, all I'm saying is, he enjoyed being on the inside track. For him, it was a game. He loved finding things out. Another thing you and he had in common."

She was right. He'd always felt a connection with Dylan, perhaps because his friend reminded him of his own father. As soon as the thought struck him, he shoved it to the back of his mind. He didn't want to recall the past.

"Don't get me wrong," Lea said, "I'm not going to come over all sentimental about him. Many's the time I wanted to throw things at him when he misbehaved. Sometimes I did—see that stain on the wall behind you? Can of Budweiser. He'd two-timed one of our candidates, a pretty little probate lawyer, and she withdrew her instructions from the agency. Cost us a bloody mint. But that was Dylan for you. He was a commitment-phobe. He could never settle down and be content with one woman. He had to keep proving he was irresistible. In the end, that's what did him in."

He couldn't help yawning. "Sorry. Tired as a dog."

"Sleeping any better?" she demanded.

He shook his head. Since the killing, his insomnia had been as bad as ever. As bad as when it first began, all those years ago. He simply wanted to stop dreaming about Amy Vinton slashing Dylan's jugular vein.

"So you think that's what the murder was all about?" he asked. "Amy blamed Dylan for her sister's death and wanted to take revenge?"

"Isn't that what the police think?"

"Sure." Of course they did. They loved simple solutions every bit as much as he hated them. It had been the same when his mother had died. He'd learned then that it was a waste of time, trying to open up minds that were closed.

Lea put her head on one side, considering him. "What else? The grapevine says she suffered some sort of breakdown after Ella died. She couldn't cope, said it was all Dylan's fault. In her eyes, he'd murdered Ella. She dropped out of college, took one dead-end job after another. Her parents did their best to care for her, tried to sort out psychiatric help. They thought that this past twelve months, the scars had begun to heal. She'd been talking about going back to college, making something of her life at last. It didn't work out. For the past few months she'd been waitressing in a coffee bar next to Somerset House. Seems the hatred of Dylan got the better of her in the end."

"Was it fair to scapegoat him? Did Ella really kill herself because he was unfaithful?"

Lea puffed out air. "Don't waste your time acting as counsel for the defense of Dylan's moral fiber. It's a shit brief. He cheated on her, and she wasn't smart enough to figure out that she could never change him. They were looking for different things from each other. No prizes for guessing what Dylan was after. As far as Ella was concerned, on the other hand, he was a once-in-a-lifetime romance. Big mistake."

"Even though the affairs didn't mean anything to him?"

"Not much consolation when it dawned that she didn't mean much to him either. So off to the railroad tracks she went. Pity she didn't choose my route home—the eternity you have to wait for a train, she'd have had a chance to change her mind." Then, as if for once regretting a brutal turn of phrase, she added in a softer voice, "But fuck me, you'd have to be pretty tired of life to want to finish it like that, eh?"

"Dylan kept her photograph on his mantelpiece. He told me at the time he'd sworn to change his ways."

"Sure." Lea grimaced. "And so he did, till the next blue-eyed blonde with big tits signed up with us. The photo became part of his seduction technique, or so I heard. He could tell each latest conquest about the tragedy of a girlfriend who died young. Rewrite a bit of history—the suicide became an accident—then play for sympathy. He could be a manipulative bastard, could Dylan. For him, life always moved on. He was a survivor. Until the other night."

Nic bit his lip. "If only I hadn't been drunk. If only I'd—"

Lea leaned across the desk and seized his wrist. "Stop that, Nic. You've no cause to blame yourself, do you hear? You were nearly a fucking hero."

"People keep saying that. And you know something? It really doesn't make me feel better."

"Come on, Amy was determined to kill him. Look at how she conned her way past the flunkeys and into the party. If she hadn't made it that night, there would have been another chance, another day."

"Simple as that?"

"Yeah, simple as that. Hey, that's something Dylan used to say about you. That you can't ever bear to take the easy way out. You always love to make things complicated." She snorted with laughter. "You should never have given up being a lawyer. When it comes to making something out of nothing, you were a natural."

"I've been wondering. Why did Amy wait five years before murdering Dylan?"

"Who knows what the fuck was going through her mind all that time?" Lea shrugged, a seismic movement. She never bothered to conceal her contempt for excessive introspection. Animals appealed to her more than human beings. They concentrated on living rather than wasting their time worrying about things they could never change. "The hatred must have festered. Suddenly something blew inside her head, and she decided to kill him. Spur of the moment thing."

"Maybe."

"Going to make a mystery out of it?"

"I'm curious. You see, there's something else."

"Namely?"

"Did Dylan talk to you about the dead lawyers?"

She blinked. "What do you mean?"

"That's why I showed up at the party. After it was over, he was going to tell me the story."

The rich man who burned in Paradise. A giant who chopped himself in half. To say nothing of the boy who died of shock.

Lea heard him out, but as soon as he'd finished she said, "Load of crap, frankly. Mysterious deaths and some old flame he thought was living on borrowed time? He was winding you up, Nic. If not, then for fuck's sake, what was he talking about?"

"He never mentioned any of this to you?"

"Not a word." Lea pursed her lips. "Though maybe it's not so strange. He'd have known I'd send him off with a flea in his ear, told him he was letting his imagination run riot."

"Whereas I'm a credulous airhead?"

"Well." Lea rubbed her chin. "You do have this thing about unexplained deaths. Or deaths that don't have the right explanation, according to you. Like Crippen's missus. If I wanted to grab your attention, guess what line I'd spin?"

"Dylan was a lot of things, but he wasn't stupid. He wouldn't have wasted my time for no reason."

"He was getting carried away, as per usual. You should have seen his expenses claims. I never met a man with such a talent for make-believe."

"This woman he had the fling with at Oxford. Any idea who she might be?"

"Do me a favor. Even if I wanted to keep track of Dylan's love life, it wasn't possible. There simply weren't enough hours in the day."

"So he told you nothing about her?"

"We didn't waste time discussing his affairs. I worked on the premise it was better not to know what he was up to. That way, everything was deniable if the shit hit the fan. Although I knew something was going on. He'd been seeing an Australian girl who worked in radio. She found out he'd been two-timing her, and the balloon went up. I don't know the details. Now he's dead, of course I wish we'd talked more. Too bloody late."

By the look of her, Lea was not far from tears. Nic stroked her large, blotchy hand.

"The last thing Dylan said was, 'Why not jazz?' He whispered it. I'm not sure anyone but me heard. Any idea what he could have meant?"

"You're the one with the vivid imagination. You tell me. Maybe he was confused. He used to go to Ronnie Scott's, but why would that inspire famous last words?" She snorted with disgust. "You're trying to make a mystery out of nothing. Don't you have anything better to do with your time?"

"I owe it to him to figure out what he was talking about."

"You don't owe him anything. All right, take that look off your face. Go on, what did the police have to say?"

"I'm a writer, okay? So by definition I have an overheated imagination. The sergeant took a few notes and gave me rather more dirty looks. He obviously thought I was trying to work up a story."

"They showed no interest, then?"

He thought about his mother's death. "They never do. Not if it's something that contradicts their preconceived ideas. Anyway, I've disturbed you for long enough. Perhaps Dylan talked to someone else. Anyone I could speak to? This Australian woman, maybe?"

Lea shook her head. "Caron? You're wasting your time there."

Nic thrust his hands deep in his pockets. He wanted to make

his request sound casual, an afterthought. "You mentioned Dylan's laptop. He used to call it his life support, didn't he? If he'd been squirreling information about these dead lawyers, he'd have kept it in there for sure. He didn't take it with him to the House of Lords, so I presume he left it here. Any chance I can borrow it?"

Lea sighed and shook her head. "Sorry, can't help. He took it home."

Nic swore inwardly. He was aching from the weariness of nights with no sleep and wasn't in the mood to be denied. "Maybe I can take a look at his place. You have a key?"

"I do, as a matter of fact. But you're wasting your time."

"Look, I realize the laptop will be full of confidential stuff. But all I'm interested in is this stuff about the lawyers who died. Promise."

"God, I trust you not to download all our trade secrets. To say nothing about the dirt we gather on our candidates' private lives. That isn't the problem. Something else happened the day Dylan died. Caron took her revenge on him. He'd given her a key to the house and she went over there that evening."

Nic stared at her. "She trashed the place?"

"No, she's not a vandal. She simply wanted to get her own back. When she heard that he'd been killed, she rang me up and confessed. She was distraught, full of guilt. I promised I wouldn't tell anyone, okay? She wasn't to know what would happen to him that very night, was she?"

"So what did she do?"

Lea exhaled. "Just cut the arms off Dylan's favorite leather jacket and chucked his laptop into the river."

CHAPTER EIGHT

As she walked down the Strand, Roxanne felt guilt smothering her, like a blanket pressed against her face. She blamed herself for Haycraft's accident. If it was an accident. Maybe he'd meant to walk under the wheels of the truck. She could not be sure. More likely, he had ceased to care whether he lived or died. He'd realized that he was ruined. If he had not been run over in Chancery Lane, there would have been a tragedy somewhere else on some other day. Even so, she felt guilty. Haycraft was obviously at his wits' end. Joel Anthony had said the man was in deep, deep trouble, and she had taken a dislike to him, so she had allowed him to stare disaster in the face.

Five minutes after she arrived back in Avalon Buildings, Joel paused on passing her room to ask if she was okay.

"Of course." She didn't want anyone to know that she had seen what had happened. "Why do you ask?"

"It's just that—you looked a bit flustered, that's all." In the background, Roxanne could hear the ubiquitous piped music. Another lush ballad, "Make It Easy on Yourself." "Haycraft didn't try anything with you, I hope?"

"He was too far gone for that." The stud in Joel's ear gleamed under the fluorescent light. "You did a very good job on him."

As the door closed behind him, she swore to herself. Joel was sensitive to mood and atmosphere, more interested in what people were thinking than the other lawyers she had met. She was still afraid that he might start reading her mind.

Ben marched in a couple of minutes later. "Well, then, young Roxanne, how's it going?"

"One thing's for sure. I never expected to spend my first week at Creed trying to defend Ali Khan's empire from being punished for the sexism of some middle-aged manager."

"I'll let you into a little secret, Roxanne," Ben said, lowering his voice. "Just between you and me, all right?"

She could not imagine what was coming, but when he paused, she muttered, "All right."

"You've seen how much Haycraft is paid. His package costs Thrust a small fortune, yet he's a dinosaur. Snag is, it would take an age to sack him for poor performance without running the risk of a pricey unfair dismissal claim. So the main board had already given an executive search consultancy a tip-off about him."

"I don't understand."

"It's how companies offload their overpaid underachievers. An old trick. Management tips off a headhunter that one of their top executives may be on the lookout for a fresh challenge. The headhunter contacts him and, ego massaged, he's kick-started into considering a move. A prospective employer is then supplied with a reference trumpeting his achievements and—hey presto!—the problem is solved." Ben laughed. "Some third-rate managers spend their careers shifting jobs at regular intervals, accompanied each time by a testimonial that makes them sound like a cross between Bill Gates and Richard Branson."

"And?"

"Unfortunately, Haycraft interviews so badly that two of Thrust's main competitors have already turned him down. Then along comes Gina Mandel. A lucky break. Her claim could save our clients a small fortune. As a bonus, their equal opportunities enforcement record gets a boost. It's not every day a senior executive is sacrificed at the altar of the antisexism crusade."

Roxanne said, "So they can sack him, throw money at the girl to settle the claim, and then go back to making profits for shareholders. For Haycraft, end of story."

"Don't sound so shocked," Ben said. His tone was suddenly cold. "The law isn't a game, you know. This is the real world we're working in. Litigation is like warfare. You can't hope to avoid collateral damage."

The screensaver on her computer blinked at her. The legend read "Roxanne Wake." It helped if she constantly reminded herself of who she had become. A couple of right-on caseworkers at Hengist Street had made it clear that by joining Creed she'd sold her soul. The salary was amazing, and she wasn't embarrassed to take it. As soon as her first month's pay was transferred into her account, she would buy the leather coat she'd coveted in Selfridges. But the money mattered much less to her than it did to most. As for selling her soul—if only those other girls knew.

Her father had worked as a printer before competing technology bankrupted the company which had employed him for twenty-five years. He'd never worked again, and she'd watched him age before her eyes, spending money that the family could not afford in the Buxton pubs, rotting his life as well as his liver. Her mother was a nurse who supplemented her work at the local hospital with shifts at a private care home, which brought in a few extra pounds each week. The home owner took a fancy to her, and when she rebuffed his advances, she soon found herself made redundant in the interest of economy. Her husband urged her to take up a claim in the tribunal, but she'd refused through a combination of pride, ignorance, and fear of the unknown. Cassandra said nothing, but resolved that one day she would help people like her parents to regain the pride that a worthwhile job could bring.

Of course, things didn't turn out as expected. Her parents" marriage broke down and Cassandra's father finished up in public housing in Whaley Bridge. On her fourteenth birthday, he fell down a flight of steps in a drunken stupor and broke his neck. Cassandra's mother struggled to bring up a teenage daughter on her own, and tempers were often frayed. As Cassandra's interest in boys developed, her childish enthusiasm for wielding the sword of justice waned. And then she met Grant Dennis.

Later, Roxanne had time enough to reflect upon Cassandra's mistakes. Doors had closed during her lost years. She needed to make a complete break and strive to become someone else, so far as the rest of the world was concerned. Even if deep down she would always be Cassandra Lee.

One evening while flicking through the *Evening Standard* she'd seen a display advertisement in the "help wanted" section of the paper. A legal aid center in Hengist Street had an urgent need for paralegals. She'd fixed up an interview under the name of Roxanne Wake and walked straight into the job. Ibrahim was so desperate for staff that he'd probably have taken her on even if her CV had contained the truth, the whole truth, and nothing but the truth. He'd never shown the slightest interest in getting to know her better, nor had any of the other colleagues she worked with. In Creed, it was proving harder to guard her privacy.

Just how difficult became plain that afternoon. Will Janus rang and asked if she'd like to come up to his room in ten minutes. She prayed he wouldn't mention Buxton again.

His room was on the top floor, next to the boardroom where the partners met. He insisted on taking her in to see the vast round table and the Kandinskys on the wall.

"Very fine, don't you think?" Will said, as she remembered to express her admiration. "Kandinsky saw himself as having a mission. Messianic, almost."

Roxanne smiled cautiously. Before coming upstairs, she'd prepared herself by checking Kandinsky out on the web. All that she'd had time to discover was that he loved mumbo-jumbo. Typecast as a lawyer to the end of his days and beyond, that was poor Wassily.

He ushered her back to his own room, humming to the background music. "Bridge over Troubled Water."

Roxanne said, "You wanted me?"

"A bit of deviling, if you don't mind. I'm preparing a paper for the Council of Ministers, and I'd like you to let me have a précis of the latest judgments. My topic is surveillance at work. You're familiar with the current law?"

"In my last job I acted for someone who wanted to take a case to the Court of Human Rights. She discovered her boss had been taping all her phone calls in the office. Breach of the right to privacy. Clause Four of the European Convention."

"Clause Four, yes." He gave a satisfied nod, and she remembered that a celebrated lecture of his had influenced a radical overhaul of the legislation. "Did you win the case?"

"We couldn't get the funding. Our client was refused legal aid."

"Perhaps it's as well," Will said. "Your client would have lost if the employer had warned her he was monitoring her calls. As we do, for instance."

She stared at him. "I didn't know that."

Will Janus said pleasantly, "Haven't you read your office manual? It's all there on the intranet. Don't look so alarmed. We introduced monitoring as a routine precaution. For everyone's comfort. And security."

Back in her room, Roxanne took a deep breath. *What if they listen to the call Hilary made to me? She called me "Cassandra." I'm finished.*

Heart thudding, she checked the intranet. Sure enough, the monitoring policy was there, in print rather smaller than the office dress code. But the message was clear. *Big Brother is listening to you.*

So what? Thousands of reputable employers monitored calls, and the partners were simply covering themselves. Of course, it was good practice to put something in black and white. No organization she knew of systematically checked all calls made and received. The cost would be prohibitive. The tapes were kept for a few days and then recorded over. Why would they want to snoop on a newly recruited paralegal? All she needed to do was to keep her nerve, and the threat would disappear.

On Friday morning, Ben called her in to his room. It boasted an ego wall covered from floor to ceiling with framed cuttings recording his famous victories. Most included a photograph of Ben outside a tribunal building or the steps of a courtroom, punching the air in triumph or pumping the hand of a celebrity client. A recurring motif was the sheer awfulness of his taste in ties; an offense against human rights if ever there was one. One picture showed him looking on as a jubilant Ali Khan sprayed a bottle of champagne over a group of reporters outside the Royal Courts of Justice in the Strand.

"I have news for you," he said. "Howard Haycraft has been seriously injured in a road accident. He's still in intensive care. A broken pelvis is the least of his problems. He still hasn't regained consciousness. I gather it's touch and go whether he will survive. Even if he does, there's a likelihood of brain damage."

She didn't know what to say.

"It must have happened shortly after you left him," Ben

murmured. "He was run over in Chancery Lane."

"Uh-huh." Her past might be chequered, but it gave her one advantage: experience in telling lies. Only now did she see how well this had equipped her for a career in the law. "Terrible news."

Ben leaned back in his chair, arms folded, eyes glinting with amusement. He might have been a small ugly boy who had discovered how easy it is to tear the wings off flies. "You must have put the fear of God in him. According to eyewitnesses, he walked right under the wheels of the truck, as if he was in a daze. What on earth did you say to him?"

"Nothing! I can't imagine what—"

"Relax!" He laughed. "I was pulling your leg. It's not your fault that he didn't watch where he was going. Stupid fool. He'd been losing it for some time. This episode with the Mandel girl was just the latest in a long line of difficulties. One would not want to be callous, of course. But frankly, this is the ideal solution."

Five minutes later Joel looked in. His skin was glowing; he looked good enough to eat. Chloe had told her that all the partners had the option of a weekly manicure from Creed's in-house executive refreshment specialist. Power pampering while they worked, complete with a shave, exfoliation, and a camomile-soaked hot towel. Ben didn't take advantage of the service; no wonder, Chloe said bitchily, that his nasal hair was a disgrace.

A rub of the smooth chin. "I hear Howard Haycraft has been run over."

"Ben says the accident happened a few minutes after I interviewed Haycraft," Roxanne said carefully.

"What sort of mood was he in when you talked to him?"

Roxanne was conscious of Joel's keen scrutiny. She shifted in her chair. "He wasn't exactly full of the joys of spring. He realized his career was over."

"So you got the message across that Haycraft was in the shit?"

"What else could I say?" She hated herself for sounding rattled. "It was the truth."

"Of course," Joel said. "It sounds to me as though you handled the meeting perfectly."

Roxanne said, in a voice so low that Joel had to bend close to hear, "But Haycraft has finished up in intensive care."

"Not your fault."

She caught the faint smell of camomile on his flesh. "What if he meant to do it? What if talking to me hurt him so much that he'd stopped wanting to live?"

"You did the right thing. Believe me."

"I didn't intend to destroy his life."

Joel said sharply, "That's enough, Roxanne. You've nothing to reproach yourself for. Everything is under control. You did—what you had to do."

CHAPTER NINE

Nic understood Amy Vinton's suffering, knew what it was to be obsessed by past crimes. People coped with family tragedies in different ways. For Amy, time hadn't been a healer. Five years had passed before she'd made herself into an image of Ella, dressed in her sister's old clothes, and destroyed first Dylan Rees, then herself.

Needing the kick of caffeine, he went for a walk. Half an hour later he was ordering an espresso in the coffee bar where, according to Lea, Amy had worked. The place was crowded, but he managed to strike up a conversation with a plump Brazilian girl at the cash register. She was, he judged, Amy's age, and the name on her badge was Lani. Nic hinted that he was the brother of one of Amy's school friends. He soon learned that Lani had been fond of the dead girl.

"She was so quiet," Lani said in careful English. "Nice, but she never said much. Kept herself to herself, you know? She told me she'd been a student. When she first came here, she said she might go back to college. But she didn't like to talk about—personal things."

"She didn't mention Dylan Rees?"

"Uh-uh. I couldn't believe it when I heard this morning what she'd done. This man I'd never heard of . . ." She spread fleshy arms, her face a picture of bewilderment.

"Was she seeing anyone?"

Lani gave him a sly look. "Jealous, eh? She was a pretty girl.

95

You fancied her?"

"I was simply wondering . . ."

She turned to serve a customer. When she'd rung up the register, she murmured, "I guessed she had met someone. In the last few weeks. But I never knew his name."

"A man she met here, perhaps? A customer?"

"I don't know, honey."

An off-the-wall idea struck him. "It couldn't have been Dylan Rees, could it? The man she killed?"

"What kind of sense would that make? All I can say is that she changed."

He leaned close to her. "How did she change?"

She smiled at him, and he realized that she thought he fancied her. "She stopped talking about going back to college. This man she'd met, whoever he was, I guess she must have seen a lot of him. She and I had gone to the pictures a couple of times when we were on the same shifts. We both fancy Jude Law. But lately she'd been making excuses. Always too busy."

He inhaled the aroma of roast coffee beans. "Did she ever talk about her sister?"

Lani shook her head. "Not to me. She lost interest in the job. Started coming in late, not caring what happened. Only a week ago the supervisor gave her a final warning. Amy didn't seem to mind. I thought it was because of this man she'd met. He was generous. She didn't say much, but she told me once she'd been sent a bunch of flowers. Red roses, very romantic. If he had money, maybe she wasn't worried if she lost a crummy job like this."

"And now what do you think?"

A shrug. "Who knows, honey? Maybe I was wrong. Maybe all the time she was just dreaming of how she would kill him. The man who betrayed her sister."

★　★　★　★　★

Phil was packing a suitcase when Nic arrived back at the flat, cramming clothes in without caring whether it crumpled them. She was breathing hard, and there was a light in her eyes that he hadn't seen for a long time. A big new job, he guessed. The one thing guaranteed to turn her on more than fun and games with strawberries and cream.

"A double decker plowed into a parish hall up in Northumberland," she said. "I've been retained by the bus company. It's a catastrophe. One simple driver error and the police, the health and safety apparatchiks, and half the cabinet are on the warpath. My clients floated less than a month ago, and already the share price is down through the floor."

"Anybody hurt?"

"Oh, yes," she said, "loads. That's the big problem. They were all old people taking part in a whist drive. The journalists will hang my clients out to dry if we don't make the right noises."

After a few moments, he asked, "When will you be back?"

"No idea. Could be several days. The chief executive's worried about how the union will react, and the operations director is threatening to go off sick with stress. Tell me about it. Still, the fees are going to be fantastic. Every cloud." She paused in the act of trying to stuff a new pair of Levis into an overfull bag to add, "You'll have some time to yourself. You can make a start on the book."

"I don't think so."

She put the case down and planted her hands on her hips. "For God's sake, Nic. Don't you think it's time you started to get your act together? What sort of a writer do you call yourself? One who doesn't like writing, as far as I can tell."

"I'm not sure I do call myself a writer. Any more than I call myself a lawyer." He shrugged. "I'll write another book when I find something I'm desperate to tell the world. I'm not going to repeat *Crippen,* that's for sure. It's time to move on."

"And where exactly are you moving on to?" She was angry now, and her voice was rising. "On to your arse, basically. It's not enough, Nic. You'll have to shape up."

He folded his arms. "Or else—what?"

Pink spots appeared on her cheeks. "Or else—you can move on from here. I'm sick of all this. If you can't show me work-in-progress by the time I get back, I'm washing my hands of you."

He spoke gently. The anger had gone; he'd made up his mind. "This isn't working, is it?"

"Too bloody right, it's not working. And neither are you."

"So that's your final word, is it? I start a second book, or I'll be the one packing my bags?"

"If you like. An ultimatum. I'm so utterly pissed off with killing myself while you just hang around."

"Fine, I'll be gone before you get back."

For a moment she hesitated, as if about to tell him not to be so stupid. Something in his expression made hers harden. "When you go, push the key back under the door."

Once she'd gone, the flat was cool and still. A graveyard, the place where their affair lay dead and buried. He started throwing a few things into a suitcase, dropping her cards and letters into the wastepaper basket. Mustn't drown in sentiment's quicksand. He was better out of it. Phil, the flat, everything.

He walked over to Chancery Lane. At the top of Law Society Hall was Carmichael Webb's lair. If anyone could tell him who the dead lawyers might be, it was Carmichael.

"What can I do for you?"

Carmichael reminded Nic of an aging bloodhound. He sat in front of his computer monitor, scrolling through the archive records. For fifteen years he had been the Law Society's curator of records, and although the information technology at his disposal was supposed to be the best money could buy, no one doubted that the database he carried in his head was far more extensive than anything held on the computer network and much less likely to crash. Ask him who had been struck off for fiddling trust accounts in 1979 and he could recite the names without a second thought.

"I'm researching background. Perhaps for a book one day."

"So you are still set on writing for a living?"

Carmichael didn't understand why anyone would want to give up being a lawyer. All his life, he'd been fascinated by small print. The legal profession was tailor-made for him, but money had been tight and he hadn't been able to afford the premium that firms used to charge for the privilege of two years of drudging away as a trainee clerk. So he had worked in libraries and museums instead, until the opportunity of a job in Chancery Lane had come his way. To take it meant accepting cuts in pay and pension, but Carmichael hadn't hesitated. At last he was part of the legal world. Whenever they talked, it wasn't long before Nic felt a qualm of guilt. He'd thrown away a career for which Carmichael would have given his right arm.

"We all have to eat," Nic said. "I wanted to check on something Dylan Rees mentioned to me."

Bushy eyebrows rose. "A dreadful business. I heard that you tried to save him."

"Fine job I made of it, didn't I?"

"You did your best." Carmichael shook his head. "I hadn't seen Dylan Rees for a couple of years until he called in last month. Hard to believe that he's gone."

"What was he after?"

Carmichael frowned over his half-moon glasses. Together with his three-piece pinstripe suit, they made him look like a prewar family lawyer. He even kept a watch on a chain. When he put on a severe face, Nic imagined him advising an aged client against an unwise testamentary disposition.

"He gave the impression that Valentines were updating their records of the people they dealt with. He wanted to access our archives. Candidly, his manner struck me as evasive."

"That's not like Dylan."

"No, in my experience, he was always one to chat. We'd met several times when he was trying to ferret out the truth behind the gaps in the curriculum vitae of a candidate who had signed up with his agency. People who said they'd left jobs for career development reasons when in fact they had been sacked for failing their probation. That sort of nonsense. Straightforward detective work, and he enjoyed having a chinwag about it. He used to say the law is a people business. I always regarded that as nonsense. To my mind, it's a document business, slowly transforming into a technology business."

Nic refused to be diverted. "What did he do when he was here that last time?"

"He spent an afternoon tapping notes into his laptop, but he made it clear he wasn't interested in discussing what he was up to." Carmichael grimaced. For all his lugubrious demeanor, he was a sociable man and he expected others to respond accordingly. "As you might imagine, that piqued my curiosity, but I didn't make any headway when I asked him the odd question."

"So did you know who he was checking on?"

"After he'd gone, I did happen to notice the record on our system of the sites he'd visited on our database."

"And?"

"He was researching Creed." Carmichael raised his eyes to the heavens. "You'll have seen their advertisements and television commercials. There's no escaping them. *Lawyers who are different.* As if that's something to boast about! I presumed Dylan was targeting them for business. Though why he was checking details of their deceased partners, I can scarcely imagine."

"Deceased partners?"

Lesson one in cross-examination. Let the witness talk.

"He looked up the late Matthew Creed himself. And Bradley Hurst, who died in a car crash."

Nic racked his memory. "Creed died of a stroke or a heart attack or something, didn't he?"

"Natural causes, yes, but I don't believe the details were ever made public. Deference to the family, I presume. It was certainly very sudden." Carmichael wagged a finger. "Mind you, lawyering is a dangerous business. People don't realize."

"Oh yeah?"

"You may mock, young man, but this is rather a hobby horse of mine. Did you see the last annual report of the International Commission of Jurists in Geneva?"

Nic grinned. "Sorry, it must have passed me by."

"Do you realize they have identified five hundred cases where lawyers have been murdered, intimidated, or simply disappeared? *Five hundred!* You wouldn't want to be a legal representative in Turkey, Burma, or Brazil, I can assure you. As for Northern Ireland—"

"There was nothing unusual about the deaths of Creed or Hurst, was there?"

"True," Carmichael conceded. "But may I ask why you are so interested?"

"Something Dylan said made me curious, that's all." Nic tensed as an idea struck him. "By the way—Matthew Creed was worth a packet, wasn't he?"

Carmichael pondered. "Certainly. He founded the firm and even as it grew he kept a large slice of the equity. Didn't *Loophole*'s gossip column nickname him Croesus Creed? Rather unkind, if you ask me. Was it his fault if the legal aid fund and his trade union clients paid him hand over fist?"

"And Bradley Hurst?"

"A larger-than-life character," Carmichael said judiciously. "No restraint, of course. Think of that day at the High Court when he broke the nose of that barrister from a right-wing tabloid. Any other lawyer would have been fired but Will Janus made a joke of it and Bradley survived. What he lacked in IQ, he made up for with girth. He wasn't someone you'd willingly antagonize."

Nic leaned forward, not daring to reveal his excitement. "Bradley was a giant of a man?"

Carmichael nodded. "Six-feet-five and broad-shouldered, but overweight. I fancy he became too fond of good living in the latter years. If you wanted to be unkind, you might call him a fat thug, but I suppose you could properly describe him as a giant."

In the library, he checked out the newspaper archives and then took a look at Creedlaw.com. Naturally, the firm's website was state of the art, interactive to a fault. Visitors could download Plain English model contracts and personnel policies, subscribe to daily employment law updates, strike up a conversation in the chat room with other business-minded human resources professionals. No wonder entries in the guest book sang the praises of Will Janus and his mission to modernize the delivery of legal services for the new millennium.

A mini-biography of every partner was no more than a double click away. A history of the firm recorded its contribution to advancing the cause of fairness at work. Matthew Creed's career as a pioneering crusader of the industrial tribunals was noted, and there was page after page about Will Janus's achievements, including extracts from his books and major public speeches, as well as a chance to put questions to him directly about his views on ethical employment and human rights. An index search for Bradley Hurst came up with nothing. Nic wasn't surprised. Stuff on the net was like history. Written by the survivors.

Back in Clerkenwell, Nic found himself piecing fragments of a story together.

Matthew Creed had been the leading civil liberties lawyer of the late twentieth century, as well as the wealthiest. For several years his wife had suffered from motor neuron disease. Following the diagnosis, he'd led campaigns for increased health funding to combat the effects of the condition with the same energy he'd long displayed in acting for workers exploited by ruthless management. Yet he had predeceased her, and all the reports were vague as to the precise cause. There were references to his being struck down suddenly, and it was easy enough to infer a coronary or cerebral hemorrhage. Not the slightest hint of anything odd about his death. Yet in his head Nic could hear Dylan lilting the paradox.

The rich man who burned in Paradise.

He had discovered little about Bradley Hurst. An obituary in the *Law Society Gazette* hinted that the accident in which he'd been killed had been horrific. A female trade union official had been traveling in the car with him. The car had jackknifed on the M4 motorway. The woman had survived, albeit with serious injuries, but Hurst was killed instantly. No details as to what, precisely, had happened to him. Perhaps they weren't suitable to be read by those of a nervous disposition.

A giant who chopped himself in half?

Nic clenched his fists. He'd experienced it before, this exultation of discovery, when it dawned on him that Crippen might not have killed his wife, that there might after all be a plausible reason for the little quack's ludicrous, guilt-charged attempt to escape to America with his lover disguised as a boy.

103

But Carmichael hadn't been able to help him with the last line of Dylan's riddle. *The boy who died of shock.* Questions still outnumbered answers. He still did not have a clue to the meaning of Dylan's final words.

Why not jazz?

Dylan, the feckless friend whom he had failed to save. He owed it to him to make sense of that last question. He couldn't, he wouldn't, let go of this. All the more so as he had never discovered the truth about the crime that had turned his own life upside down. To himself, but no one else, he dared to admit the reason he couldn't dredge over the death and disappearance at Ravenscar all those years ago. He could not risk discovering that he had been wrong all the time and that his father was guilty of killing his mother, as everyone else believed.

CHAPTER TEN

On Sunday morning Roxanne took a walk across the heath and
oakland on the far side of Whipps Cross Road, which marked
the southern tip of Epping Forest. Since moving to Leytonstone, she'd grown to like Hollow Pond. Never mind that people
in the High Street shops dismissed the area as drab and depress-
ing, a haunt for flashers and adolescents sniffing glue. For her,
it possessed a subdued beauty.

As usual, old ladies were walking dogs, teenage couples
smooching, fathers playing football with their boys. None of
them would seek to challenge her privacy. Even the acned
adolescents who passed by seldom flattered her with a second
glance. She was wearing an Army and Navy Stores windbreaker;
nowadays she no longer dressed to impress. It did not trouble
her if she wasn't worth noticing; she'd already had enough attention lavished upon her to last several lifetimes.

She paused by a trash can and watched the people ambling
to and fro. No one, surely, could recognize her. No one, at least,
who did not study her at close quarters—and she had no intention of allowing anyone near enough to try. Altering her appearance had been the easy part. The hair was first.

"I love your hair," Grant Dennis had once whispered in her
ear. "It's very *you.*"

So it had to go. She'd opted for a black bob, styled by a
hairdresser she could not really afford; it gave her an efficient
look, perfect for a rising lawyer. Cassandra Lee had been so

proud of the silky blond hair that in her mid-teens she had allowed to curl down as far as her waist. She'd always loved touching it, feeling its silkiness against her fingertips. For years she had felt as though it helped to define her. To cut it off was an act of butchery, yet she'd understood, by instinct, that she had no choice. If she were to start her life again, the hair must go. The hair Grant Dennis so often caressed, it belonged to Cassandra Lee. It had no place in Roxanne's world.

Next, clothes. "I like a woman who dresses well," Grant had said. "Someone who thinks enough of herself to want to look her best."

Cassandra always looked good. She favored short skirts; her legs were slim and she liked showing them off. In summer she often wore shorts and tight-fitting cropped tops, even at work. Grant never complained. What he lacked in subtlety of taste, he made up for by always buying her the most expensive stuff in the shops. He bought her jackets by Versace and Janet Reger party dresses which showed plenty of cleavage. He liked sexy undies even more and insisted on her wearing garters and thongs, saying that they gave him something to think about when he was chatting up clients. In Roxanne's cupboard, there wasn't a single item of designer wear. She wore jeans at home and slacks to work, and her prim blouses didn't reveal an inch more flesh than necessary. Her lingerie came from British Home Stores, and when she put on the cotton bra and pants it was impossible to remember the thrill Cassandra always felt down her spine whenever she pranced around Grant's bedroom in her underwear.

Getting rid of Cassandra's stockpile of shoes cut three inches off her height; each pair had built-up heels. She'd thrown away the eye shadow and lipsticks and changed her perfume from Obsession to Yardley's. Finally she bought herself a pair of eyeglasses with plain glass, to wear when she wanted to seem especially studious or businesslike. As unlike careless, extravagant Cassandra as anyone she could imagine.

Her former self seemed like a separate person, a talkative, pretty, and vain young woman, like a character whose biography she had skimmed through long ago. The sense of distance between them increased as each day passed. Sometimes she found it hard to believe she had ever been someone else, someone whose tastes in magazines, music, and men she no longer shared.

She reached the edge of the pond and realized she was trembling. She picked up a stone and weighed it in her hand. Hilary's unexpected appearance in the Strand haunted her. She hated being at the mercy of another human being. Freedom meant so much to her. She would do anything to protect it.

A thought crept into her mind, unwelcome as an intruder breaking into her bedroom. Perhaps Cassandra was not dead at all, but merely sleeping. One day she might come back to life. Roxanne shivered. She feared nothing and no one—except the woman who lived within her still.

Returning home, she bumped into Dee, who lived downstairs, and always liked to stop for a chat. Dee said she was about to set off on a fortnight's holiday and asked her to take care of her keys and keep an eye on things.

"Are you due any holiday yet?"

Roxanne shook her head. "I've just started this new job, so—"

"Pity. 'Specially with this weather. You look as though you could do with a break. Or a 'mood induction experience,' as we say at the college."

"Sorry?"

Dee had a sharp chin and eyes that gleamed with excitement behind thick-lensed glasses. "It's something we're looking at on the happiness research project team. Pleasant activities therapy, that's the field we're engaged in at present."

"Oh yes?" Roxanne was edging away in the direction of her door.

"We reckon we're on the edge of a breakthrough, you know. One thing's for sure. Money doesn't buy you happiness."

Roxanne didn't ask how much time, expense, and intellectual heart-searching had been invested in coming up with this revelation. She offered a vague smile and started fumbling in her bag for her key.

"Objective conditions have little effect," Dee said, wagging a stubby little finger to emphasize the point. "Over the last half century, salaries have quadrupled, but there's been no effect on declared levels of happiness. The simple truth is, it's all a matter of perception. Especially when it comes to relationships. It's a question of how we interact with each other. Relationships are crucial, even if they are only with imaginary friends. That's why soap operas are so popular. We *love* it when we see someone worse off than ourselves. But the simple truth is, a human being can get used to almost anything. Win the lottery or lose your legs—after a while, your happiness level returns to pretty much what it was before."

Roxanne smiled, said nothing.

How little you know.

On Monday morning, she spent forty minutes stuck in a crush of commuters in the middle of a tunnel just outside Bank. Someone had gone under a train, and it took an age to clear the body from the line. Hardly anyone spoke, but she could see from the faces of her fellow passengers that they were cursing their bad luck. "Of all the times to pick," a middle-aged man muttered. "Why is it always the bloody rush hour?"

She arrived late and out of breath from running down the Strand. It was not until half past ten that she remembered to check her email. There weren't many messages. Advance notice of a seminar on age discrimination, and something from the mail room headed "Cassandra Lee."

Roxanne's stomach lurched. She never wanted to see Cassandra's name again. Holding her breath, she clicked on the message. It was a circular to all fee earners and comprised a single line.

Is anyone expecting a letter addressed to a Cassandra Lee? If so, please contact Rio at the post desk.

Roxanne's mouth was dry. Yet panic was pointless. She must think things through. She breathed deeply and leaned back in her chair with eyes closed, trying to decide what to do.

If anything. One option was to ignore the message. Keep her head down, pretend the name meant nothing to her. The email could be a trap. Someone in the office might be wondering whether she would respond and thereby confirm that she had concealed her true identity from her employers. If she toughed it out, would she get away with it?

Her heart was beating faster. She had to read this letter. Had to. The mail room was on the ground floor; she didn't want to wait for the lift, so she raced down the stairs. Rio was sitting at his desk, chatting to a junior with big eyes and long legs who had a sheaf of yellow faxes in her hand.

"Hi, Roxanne." Rio was no more than nineteen, but he was on first-name terms with everyone from Will Janus to the old witch who cleaned the telephones. He had learning disabilities, and his presence in the firm, and in a prominent photograph in its brochure, was a reminder of Creed's commitment to matching the words of their equal-opportunities policy with affirmative action. "And what can I do for you, then?"

"Your email." Roxanne hated herself for sounding breathless. "You said something about a letter for Cassandra Lee."

"Yeah, that's right."

"I'll take it off your hands." Roxanne saw Rio looking at her and wished she'd taken the time to think up a plausible reason for collecting the letter. "I'll—I'll make sure she gets it."

Rio fiddled vaguely with the pile of papers in front of him and, after what seemed like an age, he brought out a manila envelope. It was marked "For the Attention of Cassandra Lee— Personal and Private—Eyes of the Addressee Only." "Must be important," he said brightly. He had the envelope in his hand but did not pass it to her.

"Just the usual legal stuff," Roxanne said. "You know what lawyers are like. They always make things sound more important than they really are."

"Yeah, right. This Cassandra Lee's a client of yours, then?"

He smiled broadly, and for an insane moment, Roxanne thought that he was taunting her, that he had already unlocked her secret. She had to remind herself that he always enjoyed passing the time of day with colleagues. He loved his job, and already she'd heard him say more than once how glad he was that the firm had given him the chance to climb off the scrap heap. Every little thing about the legal profession seemed to fascinate him. She was desperate to snatch the letter from him and run off to some safe place where she could study its contents in private. But it would never do to upset Rio. There was no hurrying him. Everything had to be done at his pace. The last thing she needed was for him to tell people that she'd been rude to him when he'd given her a letter for someone called Cassandra Lee.

Roxanne gave an ambiguous grunt. "Anyway, thanks for notifying me that it had arrived. I've been waiting for this."

"All part of the service," Rio said, beaming.

She stretched out her hand and, obediently, he pressed the envelope into her palm. "Tell me, when did it arrive?"

He frowned. "Well, I don't know exactly. It was waiting when

I got back from taking an urgent delivery up to Ben."

She realized that he might be reading into her question an implied criticism, a suggestion that he should have been quicker to let her know that the envelope had arrived. "I mean, I'm just interested, that's all. I wasn't expecting it so soon. Otherwise I'd have warned you that it was for me."

Evidently she'd picked the right lie to tell, for he smiled again. "That's all right, then."

She glanced at the envelope. The words on the front were typed. No stamp or delivery label. "So it was handed in? Obviously not sent by courier. Who brought it in, do you know?"

"Soon tell you," Rio said. He lifted the phone and after a few words with one of the girls in reception, he turned back to Roxanne. "Funny. Mandy says it was found on one of the tables in reception. How it got there, she doesn't know. Maybe someone brought it in and then decided they wouldn't wait for a receipt or anything."

Roxanne couldn't think of anything else to ask. "All right. You've been a marvelous help."

"My pleasure. So how are you doing, Roxanne?" he asked, giving an elaborate wink to the office junior.

Roxanne smiled through gritted teeth. "I was just thinking when I arrived this morning. So far, so good."

She closed the door of her room, switched off the telephone, and ripped open the envelope. There was no letter inside, just a sheet of A4 paper bearing a single typed sentence:

You can change your name, but you can't change who you are.

The brutal simplicity of those dozen words hit her like a glancing blow from an iron bar. She felt dizzy, and there was a ringing in her ears. It wasn't just that her secret was out. The words barely disguised the anonymous writer's contempt for her. Her skin itched. She felt stained and frightened.

As if trying to crack an elaborate code, she stared at the message, but discovered no clues. A flame of anger began to burn inside her. It was so unfair, so fucking unfair. Sooner or later she would have to decide whether to give up the job before she was discovered and sacked—or fight back. At once she knew the answer. She would fight, as Cassandra Lee had fought.

"Penny for them!"

Chloe, who else? Peering round the door, wearing a grin which robbed her words of much of their sting. Roxanne pretended to yawn and said, "Sorry, my mind's wandering. I worked quite a bit of the weekend, sorting out these witness statements."

"Naughty. You know what they say about all work and no play!" Chloe sighed theatrically and started talking about her implants again. "Three hundred and fifty milligrams of silicone in there, believe it or not! You should have seen the bruises. The first time I looked, I nearly died!"

Roxanne already knew the story by heart: the operation had been the brainchild of a wealthy boyfriend. He'd footed the bill of a fancy Harley Street surgeon. Six weeks after the bandages came off, Chloe had dumped him. Girl power.

"Uh-huh."

"Sorry, I'm disturbing you, aren't I? You only have to say, you know."

Chloe sounded so hurt that Roxanne had an urge to grasp her hand and apologize for her brusque response. Before she could do anything, Chloe was glancing over her shoulder on her way out.

"Maybe," she said tentatively, "we could get together sometime. Go to a club together or something."

"Honestly, I have so much to do that—"

Chloe looked puzzled. "Don't you ever relax? Or it simply that you don't like mixing?"

Roxanne said carefully, "I suppose the truth is, I am a bit of a loner."

"I've noticed," Chloe said in an arch tone that Roxanne found unexpectedly menacing. "Quite mysterious."

The door closed, and she was alone again. Roxanne fished inside her pocket for the crumpled note and spread it out on the desk before her.

You can change your name, but you can't change who you are.

A statement of the obvious, frankly. But she must do whatever was in her power to ensure that it didn't wreck her life. No one had the right to do that to her. Her skin grew cold as anger seized her. It scared her, and yet she was glad that she could still succumb to rage if that was the only way to save herself.

Breathing hard, she started to shred the sheet, ripping the message with a relentless rhythm. She didn't stop until she had reduced it into bits too tiny ever to be put together again. Then, with her hand full of specks of confetti, she walked to the women's room and flushed them down the toilet. As the water gushed and swirled in the bowl, she felt a spurt of satisfaction. It was an act of physical defiance. When she caught sight of herself in the mirror, she realized that she looked a mess. But appearances meant nothing. She would never surrender to her unseen enemy. Cassandra Lee's spirit lived on.

CHAPTER ELEVEN

A legal charity was having a garden party on the North Lawns in Lincoln's Inn. It was an annual event, but Nic had never attended before. The Lawyers' Benevolent Society offered assistance to indigent families of deceased lawyers and others whom time had forgotten, but its social activities appealed to him no more than origami or folk dancing. On the other hand, Will Janus was chair of the society and sure to be there. Nic heard a distant trumpet as he walked down Holborn and quickened his pace.

The evening was dry and bright, the best part of the day after a rare flurry of afternoon rain had left puddles on the pavements. The gardens were filling as he arrived. The entertainment came from Brief Encounters, a quartet of lawyers, two men, two women, decked out in straw boaters and striped blazers. They were playing "Come Fly with Me" as if their lives depended on it.

The air smelled of damp grass. He accepted a glass of Pimm's and, walking past the makeshift bandstand, scanned the crowd until he caught sight of Will Janus, deep in conversation with Fergus McHugh.

Nic strolled across to join them. Will was relaxed and elegant in silk Richard James chinos and a hand-stitched alligator belt. He greeted Nic as an old friend, rather than someone he'd had three conversations with in his life.

"You know Fergus, I think."

Fergus McHugh said, "We were introduced at the Lawyers in the Media awards dinner."

He was a tall, softly spoken old Etonian. Nic had heard that his late father had been something important in the SAS, but Fergus had broken with family tradition by eschewing the army and opting to read politics at Oxford. The study of Nietzsche and Machiavelli proved an ideal training ground for a career in marketing and communications, and he controlled Creed's media relations with a military precision that would have brought tears of pride to his father's eyes. Even when he was flattering journalists, his voice always seemed to carry a note of menace. Unfavorable words about Creed seldom saw the light of day in the bitchy legal press. One reason was that Will Janus was squeaky clean. The other was Fergus McHugh.

"Quite a memory you have."

"Yes, I never forget."

The chilly blue eyes yielded no clue to his thoughts. Fergus was a gifted communicator who never gave away anything unless he wished to. Everything he did was aimed at getting results. And he did get them: Creed in general and Will Janus in particular were never out of the public eye. His flair for spinning a story would have made Aesop jealous. Journalists gave him their grudging respect. He wasn't simply one more no-brain bullshitter whose press releases had a natural home in the wastepaper basket. By and large, he gave the media what they wanted. It was more than most public relations people could claim.

"Shocking news about Dylan Rees," Will said in somber *I feel your pain* mode. "I read in the papers you were an old friend of his, going back to law school days."

"You knew him, I gather."

"Will knows everyone who is anyone," Fergus said quickly.

"Dylan did business with us," Will said. "He and I bumped

into each other now and then, but I can't claim to have known him well. A dreadful tragedy. Such a pointless waste of two lives. I hear you were quite a hero, by the way. You did your best to save your friend."

Nic shook his head. He couldn't forget that if he had moved a little quicker, Dylan would still be alive. "I don't understand why the girl kept biding her time for so long."

"The hate must have been there all those years," Will said. "Lurking beneath the surface. Ready to flare into vengeance at any time."

"But what lit the spark?"

"Who knows?" Fergus said with a shrug meaning "who cares?" "Ah well, life goes on. Another drink?"

Nic said, "Dylan once told me Creed was one of his best clients."

"We certainly paid him enough in fees," Will said. Affable to a fault.

"Your firm's had its share of bad luck," Nic said dreamily. "Dylan was talking about it, last time we spoke. The car crash that killed Bradley Hurst. Poor Matthew Creed."

"A lot of firms would have crumbled, losing people of that caliber," Fergus said, unfazed. "Not Creed. Stuff happens, but you have to move on. Look to the future, not the past."

Nic said, "Of course, you're right. I was looking at your website. So much progress in so little time. Even since Matthew Creed died."

Fergus jerked a thumb at Will. "Here is the man who's done it all."

Will laughed and made a few modest remarks about the joys of team-working. Fergus stood with his hands in his pockets; he might have been waiting for a wind-up toy to come to a halt.

"As Amy Vinton cut Dylan's throat," Nic said carefully, "he muttered a few words."

Fergus took a step forward. Their bodies were almost touching. He radiated physicality, a sense of power.

"What did he say?"

"It meant nothing to me." Nic paused. *"Why not jazz?"*

The others stared at him.

"Any idea what he meant?" Will asked.

Nic shook his head. "There was another odd thing Dylan said, last time we spoke. About Matthew Creed. I wondered what he meant."

"What did he say?" Will asked casually.

"He spoke of Matthew burning in Paradise. Strange, don't you think?"

Perhaps Nic had a playful streak. Certainly, he relished the reaction of his audience as he allowed his voice to trail away. It was worth dropping a stone in the pool and counting the ripples. Fergus was studying him, as if trying to see into his mind. There was a nervousness about Will's eternal grin, as if he couldn't decide whether it was wise to humor this flight of fancy.

"Dylan never dealt with Matthew," Will said.

"How did Matthew die, as a matter of interest?"

"In his sleep," Fergus snapped.

Brief Encounters had segued to "The Look of Love." A couple of eminent child-care lawyers who'd consumed too much champagne had started slow-dancing to the music, egged on by a group of braying friends.

Nic said, "Matthew Creed was scarcely an old fogey. Fifty-seven and a pretty active fifty-seven, by all accounts. Remember that time he cycled from Land's End to Hadrian's Wall in aid of trade union charities? Pink Lycra shorts and all. In the photographs he looked as fit as a flea."

Will tutted. "You're so right, yet what Fergus says is perfectly true. Poor Matthew died in his sleep."

He was so assured, he just had to be right. Impossible that

the great man could lie over something like this. What would be the point? Nic guessed that Will was telling the truth but not quite the whole truth. That was what lawyers did all the time.

"Heart condition, then?"

"I'm not an expert on the medical details. To be honest, I'm a tad squeamish at the best of times." Will smiled, ever self-deprecating. "Don't forget, Matthew's death came as a great shock to us. We were all pretty numb."

But not so numb, Nic thought, that he hadn't contrived to be anointed as senior partner within a couple of days. Ben Yarrow, his rival and at one time Matt Creed's heir apparent, had never stood a chance.

Fergus said, "You sound as though you're checking us out, Nic. Don't tell me you're planning to write about Creed for your next book?"

"That would be telling, wouldn't it?"

"We'd love it if you did," Fergus said unexpectedly. Nic caught the bafflement in Will's eyes, and Fergus's swift nod of reassurance. "I'm not talking about an authorized history, a piece of sanitized puffery masquerading as research. No, you're a serious writer. Tell our story as you see it. Warts and all. Have a look round the office, talk to people, make up your own mind as to how we've coped with the loss of Matthew and Bradley."

"Seriously?"

"Watch my lips," Fergus said. "We'd be thrilled to see you. Our shoulders are broad, our skin is pretty thick. We all read *Crippen*. We know you thrive on challenging received wisdom. Tilting at the establishment."

"And Creed has become the establishment?"

Fergus's satisfied smile reminded Nic of a conjurer who has pulled off an illusion before the audience's very eyes. "Remember our marketing. 'Lawyers who are different, a new kind of law firm,' blah, blah. Look at us with an open mind, that's all we ask. You can have the run of Avalon Buildings."

"Including freedom of information?" Nic asked, teasing.

"On a need-to-know basis, sure."

Fergus grinned. With a few words, he had twisted the conversation around. As if by magic, he was back in control. Will was keeping quiet, content to let Fergus have his head. Their expressions were inscrutable. But then, they all worked in the law, were past masters at hiding what they believed in their hearts. Assuming they believed in anything.

Nic glanced up at the sky. It had turned purple, like the choleric face of a gouty old colonel. On the bandstand, Brief Encounters were still giving it their all. As a chill settled on the North Lawns, they were playing "(They Long To Be) Close to You." They changed their tune so smoothly, you could tell that they were lawyers.

It had been like this with Crippen. He'd become possessed by the idea that the man might not have killed his wife. A sort of literary Stockholm syndrome. Taken captive by the little doctor, he had almost fallen in love with him—or rather with the dream of proving him innocent of the crime for which he had been hanged. He'd picked up fragments of information here and then, collected bits of memorabilia whenever they came along. Later, when the book was in the best-seller lists, he'd bought Crippen's turnip watch at auction, paying a huge price, not daring to tell Phil.

His theory was irresistible, if only because of its absurdity. Crippen had gone to his grave protesting innocence. What if he hadn't killed her? If the corpse in the cellar at Hilldrop Crescent did belong to Belle Elmore and her husband had told a web of lies before his desperate flight across the Atlantic, must that mean that he was guilty of murder? He obsessed about sex with Ethel le Neve, but hated meeting his wife's demands. Suppose he'd decided to give Belle an antiaphrodisiac. He was so inept, he might easily have given her an inadvertent overdose of henbane. His lawyers had rejected it as a line of defense, but suppose they were wrong? How would he have felt, what thoughts would have jostled in his mind as his world fell apart until at last he found himself walking out to the gallows?

Crippen was history. No one cared if Nic turned up ninety-year-old stones. Dylan had talked wildly of murder for pleasure, and less than twenty-four hours later he too had been killed. It suddenly came to Nic that in his heart he didn't believe Dylan's death was a coincidence. The answer lay buried in Creed, it must be. *Lawyers who are different*—no argument. Fergus was right. Nic wanted to find out just how different they were.

Creed was holding a breakfast seminar at the Cafe Royal, the theme "Dignity at Work," and Fergus had invited Nic along. While a girl at the welcome desk checked off his name, he cast his eye down the guest list. Government departments, local authorities, private and public companies galore were represented by senior officers. Will Janus had transformed his firm into a market leader, crammed with high-caliber specialists versed in acting on behalf of captains of industry.

Once it would have been unthinkable for Creed to attract such a blue-chip crowd. Bosses were seen as the bad guys by their traditional clients: the shop floor workers, the whistleblowers, the victims of workplace bullying. It was as if Robin Hood had opted to move with the times and focus on advising the rich about how to improve their ethical investment strategies.

Ten minutes after the last full English breakfast had been served, Will marched on to the stage and started talking about trust and confidence. This time he had on a Donna Karan navy shirt and taupe pashmina socks. His little Italian boots were of such soft leather that you could almost see his toes moving inside them. On the screen behind him, his enlarged image surveyed the scene, like a revivalist preacher surveying his flock. The law's gain had been the church's loss. His parents were missionaries, and during his teens he'd planned to follow in their footsteps before discovering there was more than one way of achieving an ambition to evangelize. He was multifaceted, and the facets were as carefully coordinated as matching furnishings at an ideal home show.

Nic, standing at the back of the room, turned and found himself gazing into the cold eyes of Fergus McHugh. "Glad I never had to fight a case against Will," he whispered. "It would have felt like blasphemy to suggest his client might be in the wrong."

Fergus smiled. "It's all about knowing the right buttons to press. So important in life, don't you agree?"

"Thanks again for your help."

"A pleasure," Fergus said. "I'm sure anything you write about us will be fair. And relevant, too. This old stuff you were talking about, poor Matthew and Bradley. I can't really see how digging over old ground will help. Frankly, we've done our mourning. It wasn't easy, but now it's time to move on."

"I want to understand what Dylan was talking about."

Fergus put his hands in his pockets and leaned back on his heels. "What's to understand? You're reading too much into a few stray words. Dylan was always a showboat, you know that better than anyone. The deaths were so tragic. They were private tragedies too, if I may say so. They involved real people, Nic, people like the poor woman who was injured in the accident that killed Bradley. Raking up the past can cause a lot of unhappiness. You had a good line in *The Innocence of Doctor Crippen,* simple but bang-on. 'It's not *right* that the innocent should suffer.' That came from the heart, I guess."

He'd chosen the best way to sting Nic, hinting at the way in which the press had treated Bryn Gabriel's guilt of murder as a foregone conclusion. He scanned Nic's face, checking for signs of damage, like a heavyweight boxing contestant admiring his bloody handiwork.

Nic felt himself coloring. "Yes, it did."

"Incidentally, you are sleeping better these days, I hope?"

Nic rarely spoke about his insomnia. He had no idea how Fergus had heard of it, but knowledge was power, and Fergus exuded power. He would have made a formidable advocate.

"You know the old line. I may have insomnia, but I don't lose any sleep over it."

Fergus sniggered as the applause thundered. "So, another triumph for Will power." There was affection in his tone, and something else. Nic thought he heard amusement and contempt. Like a ventriloquist singing the praises of his dummy. "Ah well, now the serious networking begins. I'll have to circulate. Hey, say hello to Joel Anthony here. Joel, this is Nic Gabriel, the writer. I told you, he's thinking of writing about Creed. Nic, meet Joel. Super advocate. A rising star."

"He's so sweet to me," the young man said, offering Nic his hand as Fergus slipped away into the crowd. "Actually, I recognized you from the photograph on the jacket of your book. I've heard a lot about you."

"How's that?"

"Well, I hear you've been asking questions about Matthew Creed and Bradley Hurst."

"News travels fast."

"Will and Fergus were talking about you before breakfast. I was intrigued. I suppose I'm a bit of a nosy parker. You know what lawyers are like. The worst gossips in the world."

There was an eagerness, a naïveté almost, about Joel that Nic found appealing. He said, "Dylan mentioned something strange. About Matt Creed burning in Paradise."

Joel stared at him. "What—what do you know about that?"

"Not as much as I'd like to."

Joel took a breath, as if making a decision. He hesitated, looked around. The room was emptying, no one could overhear. "I shouldn't say this."

An irresistible line, if ever there was one. "Go on," Nic said.

"It's true," Joel whispered.

Nic stared. "Meaning what?"

"This—this is off the record?"

"Nonattributable. Even if I use it. That's all I can promise."

Joel swallowed. "You'll find out sooner or later. If we don't come clean, you might think the firm had something to hide. Which we don't."

"If you say so."

"It's like this. Matthew was very good to me, gave me a lot of help when I was a young lawyer, just starting out. He had a rough time with his wife's illness. For all his success, for all his wealth, he was a lonely man. He needed—outlets for all that energy."

"Such as?"

"There was this sauna off Chancery Lane. He used to head off there after a day's work. Maybe after having a few drinks at El Vino's or somewhere."

"When you say sauna . . . ?"

"Massage parlor, brothel, whatever you like to call it. The ultimate pleasure palace, that's how they advertised it in the *Evening Standard*. Its name was Paradise. The girls would make you believe there is a God, after all."

"And?"

"One night, Matthew followed a tough day in the High Court with a few too many beers. He turned up and went into a cubicle on his own. Then he fell asleep." Joel paused, his voice barely audible. "An hour later they broke down the door and found him lying on the bench. Scalded to death."

Nic felt his gorge rising. He couldn't help picturing the scene in the pleasure parlor. Matthew Creed, drunk and aging, closing his eyes for a while as he acclimatized to the heat. Nic imagined the temperature rising, the smoky smell of burning flesh.

"Jesus."

"So you see," Joel whispered, "it is possible to burn in Paradise."

"None of this hit the press. There was a cover-up."

"That's harsh. Unfair. No one wanted Matthew's widow to suffer. She was a nice lady. Think of the hurt that publicity would have caused."

"To her? Or the firm?"

Joel colored. "I wasn't a partner at the time, but I can understand why they wanted to keep things tight. Like I said, it was a tragedy. No one's fault."

"Same as Bradley Hurst?"

"We didn't have much in common except for Creed. Even so, the accident came as a terrible shock. Bradley dead and Alice left in a wheelchair."

"Alice?"

"Alice Wythenshawe. Equal rights officer for one of our major clients and someone very definitely going places. At the party on the night when the accident happened, they spent most of the time in a corner, canoodling. We were all happy, we'd all put a lot of drink away, it was fun to see them getting it together."

"Why did Bradley drive if he was drunk? Wouldn't it have been easier to catch a cab?"

"Of course. That was the crazy thing. Half an hour before the pair of them disappeared, he said he might run Alice home. I told him not to be so silly. He'd already had a skinful. I thought I'd extracted a promise from him that he'd be sensible. Ben talked to him as well." Joel shook his head. "Something must have made him change his mind."

As a flunkey shooed them from the room, Nic asked, "Any idea what that something might have been?"

"None at all. I simply remember looking round later and noticing that they had gone. They must have slipped out of the party while the rest of us weren't looking. I'm not sure that they said goodbye. Mind you, I'd had a few myself by then, and I'm not used to drinking heavily. Especially not champagne"

"So what happened to Alice?"

"She had to sue, of course. I visited her in hospital. I felt a bit guilty—we all did. Somehow we should have stopped Bradley taking the wheel. I don't know how it happened, but I wanted to do anything I could to make up. I put her in touch with a good personal injury firm, and a deal was done. By that time she'd moved back up north."

They were standing alone on the landing, waiting for the lift. Nic said, "So why are you telling me all this?"

"Like I said, it's better to be upfront about these things. Others might disagree. Nobody likes washing dirty linen in public. But I'd rather you knew everything." Joel paused. "Here's the lift. You go down. I'll take the stairs. I don't want the other partners to think I've been talking out of turn. Fergus would go apeshit. But I suppose—it's about time someone like you asked a few questions. For all our sakes."

CHAPTER TWELVE

"Roxanne? News from the hospital." Ben Yarrow on the phone.
He had a rich voice; if she'd heard him before she'd met him,
she would have guessed at a Tom Jones type. Not only appearances that are deceptive. "Howard Haycraft died in the early
hours of this morning."

In her mind she pictured the accident in Chancery Lane.
Howard Haycraft had left her knowing that his career was over.
Deep, deep trouble. Joel had been proved right. It didn't matter
whether he'd meant to walk under the wheels of the truck or
had simply been too distracted to take care. The end result was
the same.

"All very unfortunate, of course," Ben said briskly. "As you'd
expect, the company is doing the right thing. Everything is
under control. Welfare counselors will look after the widow, and
there's a handsome death-in-service benefit package. A few
weeks on and he would have been out of a job and his family
would have been dependent on goodwill. This way, the insurance people will pay up. Every cloud, you know . . ."

"No silver lining for Howard Haycraft," she said.

Ben sighed. She had a vision of him, fiddling impatiently
with his mustache. "He had no one to blame but himself."

"He was a creep, but I don't think he ever meant to . . ."

"Roxanne, Roxanne. You know as well as anyone that his
intentions aren't relevant. This was a case of sexual harassment."

126

"Alleged."

"Quite," Ben said irritably. "But Gina Mandel says he made her feel uncomfortable. He would leer at her, make inappropriate remarks. Harassment is subjective, remember. Doesn't matter if other people say that you're making too much of things. Even if it's all in the mind, it's still real. Remember, bullying is all about the abuse of power."

Roxanne snapped, "I do know this. I've represented my share of applicants, remember?"

"Then why have you forgotten the lessons you've learned?" His tone was acerbic, reminding her of his crucifixion of Tara Glass. "Don't mourn Howard Haycraft, Roxanne. He's better off dead."

When Joel asked her to step into his office, he didn't waste time with preliminaries. "Ben's told you the news?"

She nodded, reluctant to trust herself to speak. Everything was falling apart.

He stroked the stud in his ear. "You think it was your fault, don't you?"

"Once he talked to me, he thought his life was over."

"You were only doing your job."

"Whatever the coroner says, I bet it was a kind of suicide. I don't know, perhaps I should have . . ." Her voice trailed away. She didn't know what to say, far less what she should have done.

He shook his head. "There's nothing to blame yourself for."

She exhaled. "Well . . . thanks."

"You did the right thing. I told you before." He was willing her to see things his way. "You did the right thing."

Nothing for it but to bury herself in her work. Any work. Ben had asked her to help tidy up a job for one of the privatized utilities. A reorganization scam. When people weren't performing, an employer had various options. One, Ben had explained, was the departure lounge. A Japanese idea—they called it the persona room. When you wanted one of your employees to go, you shifted their office to this bare little hutch next to the toilets and waited for them to get the message. Only problem was, a few introspective underachievers actually liked having nothing to do and minimal contact with their colleagues, so other measures became necessary. When large-scale disposal of second-raters was called for, the preferred solution was to redefine their jobs out of existence. A new set of tasks—or a list of old tasks with sexy new names—would be concocted and the underachievers required to apply for posts in the so-called new structure. They would be objectively measured against wide-ranging criteria, and if care was taken, not only would they fail to secure a job, but their resistance and morale would have been worn down so that even if they did bring claims of unfair redundancy, they wouldn't have a hope in hell.

Midway through the afternoon, Will Janus's PA asked her to come up to the senior partner's office for a conference with Will and Joel. Roxanne didn't know what to expect. The tune in the lift was "I Just Don't Know What to Do with Myself."

Joel said, "I hope you're not still worrying about Haycraft, Roxanne. That was no one's fault but his own."

"Haycraft?" Will said. "Yes, Ben told me he'd died. All things considered, perhaps it was for the best, actually. Fergus says he has been in touch with Ali about a suitable statement if there's any contact from the press."

"Where's the story?" Joel asked.

"There isn't one. I can't see the papers holding the front page. More to the point, Fergus agrees. Like he says, a middle-aged manager gets knocked down in the street, big deal. All the same, it pays to be prepared. Meanwhile, life goes on. We need to help Ali update the company's recruitment systems."

Roxanne shifted in her chair. Joel seemed to sense her discomfort. "Roxanne," he said, in his quiet persuasive tone, "we're pleased with the start you've made here. You realize Ali is an important client of the firm, but maybe you don't realize quite *how* important he is. Confidentially, we bill fifty percent more per annum to Thrust than any other client."

"It's not just about money," Will said. He'd frowned as Joel spoke, and Roxanne guessed that he didn't care to discuss billing figures with a new recruit, however good an initial impression she might have made. "Ali is a dear man. Like any high achiever, he has his share of enemies. Jealous, little people who would love to embarrass him in a tribunal. We need to protect him."

"What would you like me to do?" she asked.

Will reached for a thick file of papers on the coffee table in front of them and passed it to her. "Here's a rough first draft of the documentation. Think back to your days in the advice agency. Imagine you were consulted by a disgruntled job applicant who had applied to work for Thrust and been turned down. Read the company's paperwork. Search out the loopholes. On paper your client was the best qualified candidate. But— he's black. Or HIV-positive. Or she's a woman with epilepsy. Your client claims the company was only paying lip service to dignity-at-work and equal opportunities. What is your best line of attack? We want you to think the unthinkable."

"That's right," Joel said. "Think the unthinkable."

"You're ideally suited, with your background at the advice center," Will told her.

Joel nodded. "Poacher turned gamekeeper."

If only you knew. I'm not the hunter, I'm the prey. Roxanne picked up the file.

You can change your name, but you can't change who you are.

How could she hope to go on keeping her secret? It was suffocating her. She dared not confide in anyone. Certainly not Ben: she might owe him her job, but she was sure that he would have no qualms in sacking her if he discovered she'd misled him. Not Joel: he was sympathetic, but he was a partner and his loyalty must be to the firm. Not even Chloe: tempting, but too risky. She talked too much. Something she'd overheard at the weekend came back to her mind. There was another possibility, a way of confiding in others without destroying the career she'd only just begun. A long shot, but worth a try.

Decision made, she forced herself to concentrate on her work. Thrust Media wanted to employ the best people. Only the best. Ali Khan bragged about it in his introduction to the new draft staff handbook. People were the company's biggest asset, he proclaimed, as if sharing the secret of eternal life. Joel had highlighted the phrase in red and put a couple of exclamation marks in the margin. She liked Joel. He played the game, but he knew it was only a game.

The recruitment procedures seemed to go on forever. When it came to getting a job with Thrust, only the strong survived. If the psychometric analyses did not weed you out, the genetic testing would. And that was before the company graphologist was called in to express an opinion on every loop and curl of the requisite handwritten letter of application. Nowadays a loser like Howard Haycraft wouldn't even make it on to the bottom rung of the ladder.

Thank God for the way Ben Yarrow had relied on instinct in calling her in for interview and offering her the job. Amazing that he should be so casual. But she certainly wasn't complaining about that.

She left the office at eight, but didn't take her usual route for the station. Instead she traced a path through the warren of streets around Covent Garden. In less than ten minutes she found the place she was looking for, a tiny bar with the name *Sigmund's* scribbled across a green and white striped canopy. Hanging baskets full of fuchsias hung low over the pavement. She paused by the window and peered inside, brushing away a tendril from one of the baskets that seemed to want to twine with her hair. A wrought-iron spiral staircase in the center of the room led upstairs.

Click-clack, click-clack.

"So this is where you hang out, is it?" Chloe called. "Looks cozy. Can I buy you a drink?"

Roxanne spun round. Chloe was a couple of meters behind her. No mistaking her musky scent. There was something of the animal about her. Something predatory. And yet Roxanne felt her heart leaping at the sight of the other woman. The thought that she had followed her was scary. Her pulse raced. Scary, yes, but exciting.

"What are you doing here?"

"I was late, finishing a rush job for Joel, an expatriate's contract he wanted faxed to Hong Kong. I heard you shutting your door but by the time I was ready, the lift doors were closing on you. I thought you might fancy a quick drink, and I caught sight of you through the revolving doors, but you didn't head for Charing Cross. You obviously had a destination in mind. I couldn't help being curious."

"What's to be curious about?"

Chloe flushed at the abruptness of the question. "Sorry. I didn't mean to upset you."

"What's the idea, then?"

"Don't be cross. I spotted you leaving the office. I did wave, but you took no notice. You obviously had something on your mind. You crossed the Strand instead of making for the station. Before I knew what I was doing, I was trying to catch up."

"I don't understand why you're doing this," Roxanne said.

Chloe clutched her arm. "You look so lonely sometimes. You never mention any friends. Or family. And then, when I saw today that something was bothering you, well, I wanted to help. That's all. I like you, Roxanne. I really like you. And I haven't got anyone to go home to, either. Of course I shouldn't intrude if it bothers you. I know I keep doing it, but I never meant to infringe your privacy. If you want me to go, just say the word and I'll not bother you again. Promise."

She released her grip and looked down at the paving stones. Roxanne swallowed, then made her choice. "No, come in with me. It was just a shock, seeing you here."

"I'd have called out to you sooner," Chloe said, "but you set such a fierce pace. It was all I could do to keep up." She gestured towards the bar. "So this is one of your haunts, is it?"

"No!" Roxanne's denial was more vehement than she had intended. She regretted it at once. "I mean, I've never been here before. I overheard a girl in the supermarket telling a friend about this place. It sounded—unusual. I thought I'd give it a try. A spur-of-the-moment thing."

Oh God, now she was babbling. Fortunately, Chloe seemed not to notice. She was peering through the window, misting the glass with her breath. "Well, I'm intrigued. Can't see anything naughty in there, though. No whips, no stripping nuns, nothing but loads of people knocking back pricey cocktails. Very disappointing. Maybe there's a bit more action up that staircase? Oh well, in for a penny, in for a pound. So will you let me buy you that drink?"

Roxanne nodded and led the way inside. The ground floor was cramped, and she couldn't see any spare seats, even though one or two people were drifting up the stairs. As they waited to be served, she said, "You guessed right. It all happens upstairs."

Glasses in hand, the pair of them climbed the wrought-iron staircase. The final curve in the spiral led to the first floor. A man at a small table collected a fiver each from them and they moved under an archway to find themselves at the back of a gathering of fifty plus. They were sitting in a semicircle around a bald man with a tolerant smile and shoulders whose slope suggested a lifetime spent in study. He had a drinking straw in his hand and was twirling it around as if it was an aid to thought. A waiter navigated a passage among the audience while a woman with short blond hair and home counties vowels talked in the sort of jerky, high-pitched voice she might otherwise have reserved for issuing commands to a golden retriever.

"I feel so wretched, you see. Of course I regret what happened, of course I do. Now it's preying on my conscience. I mean, I betrayed his trust and now I have to put things right. Tell him what I did, beg him for forgiveness. That way we, you know, start over."

"You really think so?"

Moving to the side of the room, Chloe following, Roxanne had a better view of the man who asked the question. He chewed at his drinking straw, then put it down and stretched his hairy arms behind the back of his head. His name, she remembered, was Kobus. She'd overheard the girl in the checkout line saying that he was a top psychotherapist. Two evenings a week he forsook his rooms in Harley Street for a couple of hours at Sigmund's. The girl had raved to her bored friend about his insight, wisdom, and compassion.

The blond woman cleared her throat and said, "But we're getting married in a fortnight. I slept with his best man. On the floor of our kitchen, while my fiancé was out buying paint to redecorate our bedroom. Surely he has a right to know?"

A couple of men in the audience murmured agreement, but Kobus pouted. "Do you have a right to destroy his happiness? That is what you're asking me, make no mistake."

"You mean—it might be better if I were dishonest?"

"Let me tell you this, Sara. Honesty is the most dangerous prescription someone like me can write."

"So maybe I owe it to him to keep quiet?" She sounded hopeful.

"Truth lacks boundaries. What if he forgives your infidelity but asks you if his friend is a better lover? What if your candid answer isn't to his liking? Do you believe he will be grateful for your frankness? That it will contribute to the health of your life together? Show me the cupboard empty of skeletons and I will show you a wasted life. You have had an experience, Sara, that is all. Will you learn from it?"

Chloe whispered in Roxanne's ear, "So this is where you bring me. A confessional."

Roxanne gave her a wary smile, keeping half an ear on a young man stuttering through an account of his misadventures with the opposite sex. Kobus murmured encouragement with the relaxed air of someone who had heard much worse a thousand times before. The other people in the room were leaning forward in their chairs, whether out of sympathy or prurience Roxanne could not tell.

"Tell you one thing, though," Chloe murmured. "I'm not sure I'm up for baring my soul to a room full of strangers."

Roxanne paused, and then said, "Me neither."

"Some things are best done in private. Behind closed doors."

"Yes."

They were standing at the back of the room. There wasn't much space, since on one side they were up against the fire escape exit and on the other they had to leave a path clear for the bustling waiters. Roxanne felt the pressure of Chloe's hips against her own.

Eventually Chloe handed her glass to a passing waiter and wiped her lips. "I feel better for that. Fancy another?"

Don't loosen your tongue. She means well, but . . .

"No, thanks."

Chloe hesitated. "I suppose I'd better be going. This isn't the time or place to reveal my own innermost secrets. How about you?"

"No," Roxanne said, with what she hoped was a laid-back smile. "I don't want to tell all."

Chloe sighed. "I can understand why people come here. But it's not for me. Believe it or not, I only confide in someone I'm sure about. Oh, I know everybody thinks I'm an incurable gossip. But deep down, I like to keep myself to myself. Until . . . I really trust someone, that is."

"Uh-huh." Roxanne paused. "Sorry I bit your head off when you turned up here."

"No problem. I was just fascinated, that's all." Chloe giggled. She seemed to be about to add something, then thought better of it. "All right. Better get my beauty sleep."

She hurried down the spiral staircase before Roxanne could even say goodbye. Roxanne waited for a couple of minutes, but her limbs felt heavy and her eyelids were drooping. Time to go. She didn't speak to anyone else at Sigmund's, didn't have any wish to do so. And yet, the crazy thing was that she had actually contemplated the possibility of telling her story—minus identifying details, of course. She wasn't totally out of her mind—and seeking guidance from the guru. She'd been in a reckless mood. Thank God Chloe had turned up unexpectedly and made it impossible for her to open up on a whim.

Chloe's perfume lingered in the air. Lucky that she had decided to leave, Roxanne told herself. She hadn't let her defenses down too far. Tomorrow they would be back in place.

CHAPTER THIRTEEN

Lea Valentine put her feet up on the desk and said, "Suppose I tell you to piss off?"

"I'll keep asking," Nic said.

"You would, too, wouldn't you?" She chewed noisily. An empty box of Quality Street candy was propped against her pen organizer. The smell of ramen noodles still lingered in the stuffy atmosphere. "Why do you want to talk to Caron?"

"She was angry because Dylan betrayed her with this woman he met in Oxford. Maybe Caron knows something about her."

"You really believe there's something in that bullshit about the dead lawyers? And that they were Matt Creed and Bradley Hurst? Hey, I'd be really pissed off if you went around upsetting one of our best clients."

"All I want is a few answers."

"Bollocks. You just like asking questions."

He laughed. "Are you going to give me her number or not?"

"All right, you win. She works at Broadcasting House. Ask the switchboard for Caron Isley, and they'll put you through."

"Thanks." He paused. "I've split up with Phil."

"Thought so."

"What makes you say that?"

"You look great. Like a weight's been taken off your shoulders. So what are you going to do after you've interrogated poor Caron?"

"Find somewhere to stay, I guess."

She fished inside a desk drawer, took out a fat bunch of keys, and tossed them over to him.

He caught them one-handed, nonchalant as an Australian slip fielder.

"Don't tell me you're taking in lodgers now?"

She shook her head. "Don't get excited. When I said I almost fancied you, I was just being nice. Those are Dylan's keys to our place in Narrow Court. We bought it through the firm a couple of years ago. Part investment, part somewhere to put up candidates coming down to London for interview. Dylan decided he liked it better than that poky hole he used to live in at St John's Wood, but I didn't want to sell my share to him. Property prices in Limehouse were going through the roof, and it made sense for me to hang on. In the end he pestered so much that I let him move in and pay market rent into the business. We went back to putting candidates up in hotels. Of course, if you're spooked about living where Dylan . . ."

"No," he said, "that's perfect. Perfect."

At first Caron refused to meet him. She was alarmed that Lea had told him about her visit to Narrow Court. The police hadn't been to see her, she said. They must not know what she'd done.

"It was a mistake, okay?" Her voice conjured up images of long sandy beaches and the Pacific Ocean. "I'd had too much to drink, that's all, and it seemed like a good idea. Just deserts. Of course I never dreamed anything was going to happen to him . . ."

"I'm only asking for a few minutes of your time," he said.

"What is there to talk about?"

"It won't take long," he said. "Lunch? We can meet at the Langham Hilton, if you like. Then you can forget all about me. And Dylan Rees."

"I only wish I could," she said. "All right, I'll see you at twelve. Twenty minutes. No more."

Caron was waiting for him in the lobby when he arrived at the hotel, a skinny figure perched on the edge of a chair, rigid with tension. He recognized her by the Sydney Harbour sweatshirt; she hadn't mentioned the deep tan or curly shoulder-length hair. A loiter of businessmen by the check-in desk could not keep their eyes off her.

"I'm Nic Gabriel."

She said hello in a small voice as she fiddled with a hank of her hair. Nic ordered coffee, but when he suggested a bite of lunch, she said she didn't want any food.

"I'm not in the mood for eating. Since I heard about Dylan's murder, I've scarcely been able to keep anything down."

"You cared for him, then."

"I did once. In a funny sort of way I still do. Despite the way he shat on me."

"He had that effect on people," Nic said. "They kept on forgiving him."

"I'm not saying I forgave him," Caron said. "At least I didn't hate him the way that girl did. You know, Amy Vinton."

"Seems like she never forgave him for causing the death of her sister."

"Lea Valentine told me about Ella," Caron said. She stretched out her legs, starting to calm down. "Nice woman. She was kind to me. Surprise, surprise, Dylan and I were seeing each other for months, but he never mentioned Ella at all. He was good at amnesia, right?"

"To him, she was history," Nic said. "He didn't believe in regrets."

"Not all of us find it so easy to turn our backs on the past."

"At least when you decided on retribution, you didn't hurt anyone."

"Except myself," she said. "I thought it would do me good.

Catharsis, right? Instead, the night I took my petty revenge on him, someone else was cutting his throat."

"What took you back to his flat that night?"

"You haven't told me yet why you want to know."

"Dylan phoned me the night before he died. He mentioned the woman he'd slept with at Oxford. I told you, I'm a writer. She'd told him a story he thought would interest me. A story about dead lawyers. Does that mean anything to you?"

Her face was blank. "No."

"He was going to explain after the party at the House of Lords, but he never got the chance. I want to talk to her, but I don't know where to find her."

She cast an elaborate glance to the heavens. "Surely I'm the last person to be asking? I didn't interrogate Dylan, didn't want to be told the gory details. All I knew was that he'd screwed someone else. That was a no-no as far as I was concerned. You were a friend of his, you'll tell me I was an idiot and he was never going to be faithful to me. Well, for a while I thought different."

"How did you meet?"

"When he took part in a program about the recruitment business. I never thought anyone would ever sweep me off my feet, but Dylan did it. He had this knack for making me think I was the only thing in the world that really mattered to him. Bullshit, of course, but I fell for it. I still can't believe I was so stupid."

She moistened her lips, and Nic guessed she was on the verge of tears. He knew he ought to stop asking questions that would hurt her, but he couldn't help himself. He had to find out more.

"Tell me about Oxford—he went on his own, presumably?"

"Sure, for a whole weekend. He said it was a business thing. A meeting, a conference, I haven't a clue what he was up to. I thought it might be nice to have a look at the dreaming spires, but he told me we'd hardly have any time together. He had to schmooze. That was the word he used." As her voice hardened, Nic could hear the bitterness rising to the surface. "He was so open and casual about it, I never dreamed he had any intention of fucking the first woman whose path he crossed. The bastard. The utter bastard."

She fumbled in her bag for a tissue. As she wiped her cheeks, Nic said, "How did you find out?"

"It was a couple of days after he came back. He seemed distracted. I could tell there was something on his mind. I asked him about it, but he fobbed me off. I started wondering what he might have got up to at the conference. When he was asleep, I checked his wallet. On the back of one of his own business cards was a woman's name and an Oxford phone number. Purple ink, a woman's handwriting."

She lapsed into silence and took a sip of coffee. He said, "It might have been perfectly innocent."

A pitying look. "With two big kisses under her name? I think I was entitled to be a tad suspicious, don't you?"

"So you confronted him?"

"At least he didn't insult my intelligence by denying it. He said it was a one-off. You know something? If I'd believed that, I might, I just might, have given him another chance. But like I said, he'd not been himself after Oxford. I could tell she'd made an impact. Why keep a note of her number otherwise?"

"What did he tell you about her?"

"Not much. He said they'd both got drunk together and started doing what came naturally. He tried to say that he needed to keep in touch with her because of some information she'd given him. According to Dylan, she was a basket case. She'd tried to kill herself more than once. I didn't need to worry, he said. She was crazy about someone else, crazy to the point of obsession."

"Did he say who she was crazy about?"

"No, and I didn't ask. I said we were through. He pleaded for another chance. He was so well-rehearsed, it obviously wasn't the first time he'd said that sort of thing. I wonder sometimes why it took me so long to wake up to what he was really like."

"So you walked out on him?"

"Yes. I'd been staying over regularly at Narrow Court. Still kept my own apartment, though. Just as well. After I went back there, Dylan called me several times. I used to keep playing his voice back on the answering machine, listening to him saying that I didn't understand. Stupid bastard. I understood, all right. Too bloody well."

Her voice had risen, and a spotty young delivery man who had been eyeing her up from the concierge's desk glanced hurriedly away. Nic poured out more coffee.

"You never saw him again?"

Her face creased in self-disgust. "I made a mistake, right? He called me, asked if we could have a truce, offered me dinner. Afterward he asked me back to his flat and like a fool I said yes."

"And?"

"I was too suspicious for my own good. Early the next morning, while he was still in bed. I checked the last number he'd dialed. Guess what? It belonged to the lady from Oxford. This time I didn't bother to wake him up. I just scrawled a message on the steamed-up bathroom window. I'll spare your blushes. I won't repeat what I said. Not too ladylike, I'm afraid. Then I walked out. Out of his life forever, as far as I was concerned."

"Did he contact you again?"

"Sure, there were more calls. I never answered. I kept the machine on all the time. I couldn't bring myself to have a conversation with him. He was the original two-timing creep, and I didn't want to think about him anymore, but somehow I

141

couldn't help it. Each time he rang, it made me angrier. He kept saying it wasn't the way I thought. As if I was born yesterday."

"You decided to teach him a lesson."

"Yeah, well. It seemed like a good idea at the time. You remember that leather coat of his? He cared for it more than he ever cared for me, that's for sure. Same goes for his bloody laptop. I had this awful worry. What if he kept details of his conquests on there? It made my flesh creep even to think about it. I could just picture him, tapping in the data. Dates, times, places. Positions. Scores. Christ, he could be slimy. When it was over between us, I realized just what a sleazeball he was. I came to my senses. Shame it didn't happen earlier."

"So you decided to dump the laptop?"

"Sure. It had to go. I couldn't bear to think of our time together being reduced to entries in some sort of love rat's league table. So I went back to his place. It was too easy. I still had the key. The moment I started cutting up his coat, I began to feel better. Then I found his laptop locked away in a drawer. I could have hugged myself. I thought to myself: this is payback time."

Her eyes gleamed at the recollection. Nic could picture her, prowling from room to room, planning what havoc to wreak.

"I took a hammer from his kitchen cupboard and wrecked the bloody thing. When it was useless, I went out on to the balcony and chucked it into the Thames. It was a beautiful evening, and I felt as though I had my life back. I could start afresh. Dylan was done for." She sipped her coffee. "I hate myself now. It's as if I wished for what happened to him."

"You couldn't have known."

"It was childish of me. I wish I'd been able to put my relationship with Dylan down to experience instead of bearing a grudge. It isn't healthy."

"Thanks for talking to me."

"Sorry I can't help you any more. I don't know anything about this woman you're interested in. Not what she did, not anything."

"You could tell me her name."

"Didn't I mention it? It was Jasmine. Dylan called her Jazz, for short."

"Why not Jazz?" Nic asked himself as he paused outside Hamley's shop window. Inside, toy trains traveled in an endless circuit around a make-believe landscape of carefully painted papier-mâché. "Why not Jasmine?"

The question fizzed around in his mind throughout the long walk to Limehouse and his new home. Another scorching day in the city, and tempers were fraying. Taxi drivers leaned out of their cab windows to bellow abuse at jaywalkers, gridlocked cars hooted as cyclists freewheeled past them, panhandlers swore when camera-laden tourists ignored their pleas for loose change. Behind the dark glasses, his eyes were sore and the sun was burning his forehead. He felt sticky and overdressed in his tracksuit.

The house in Narrow Court provided a strictly functional contrast to the converted Clerkenwell schoolhouse. The decor was chain-store-bland, the solitary design flourish a small wrought-iron balcony overlooking the river. Dylan had made little effort to impress his personality upon the place. According to Lea, his older sister had come down from Porthmadog to collect his personal possessions. She had not left much: a hairy soap bar here, a tin of digestive biscuits there. Presumably she wasn't much of reader: Dylan's dog-eared paperback novels remained untouched, along with, improbably, a complete Shakespeare, book-marked with a taxi receipt at the end of the first act of *Othello*.

Traces of someone's existence soon faded after they were dead. From a cursory look in cupboards and drawers, it seemed that Dylan had left nothing which would cast light on his relationship with Jazz or the tale she had told him. The laptop had been his life-support. With that gone, there were no clues.

Nic didn't give up without a fight; it wasn't in his nature. Caron had told him which weekend Dylan had spent in Oxford, and when he rang Lea, she confirmed that her partner had booked in on a conference at Balliol on careers in the law. A check with the college confirmed that Dylan had registered there, but they had no record of a female delegate called Jasmine. She must have been a casual pickup. In the end he had to admit defeat—at least for the moment. Oxford might be a fraction the size of London, but to go there in the hope of tracking down an unknown woman, about whom he knew nothing but her first name, would be the ultimate fool's errand.

He stretched out on a sun lounger, sipping from a can of Stella Artois as the sun sank over the spiky skyline.

He wiped his mouth and started leafing through his battered contacts book, punching numbers into his cell phone. Time to acquaint himself with the dead. Thanks to Joel Anthony, he had a little more to go on. He hadn't expected such startling frankness, but maybe it made sense. Joel was smart enough to be aware that something was wrong, without knowing what it might be. Something that threatened the firm in which he'd recently been elevated to partnership. Something, he'd hinted, that might destroy everything he'd worked for—unless someone on the outside started digging.

Matt Creed, Nic soon discovered, had left no family; his wife had died six months after him, and they'd had no children. But Alice Wythenshawe had gone back to her roots and lived with her mother in Scarborough. A few short miles from the town that never was.

Time for a shower. He closed his eyes and let cold water jets hose away the city grime. Afterward he put on a fresh pair of boxer shorts and stretched out on the Ikea sofa in the living room. He lay there for a long time, gazing across the curving river. He'd ferried his things here before meeting Caron Isley, but had not had time to unpack. It made sense to keep most of the stuff in suitcases. He did not intend to stay long. Lea had announced her intention to put the place on the market, and she was happy for him to stay until it was sold, but he meant to move on as soon as he had worked out what to do with the rest of his life.

One option was to quit London, quit city life for good. In fresh surroundings he might even find a subject he wanted to turn into another book. He'd spent most of his earnings from *Crippen* as well as the proceeds of the sale of his houseboat, but he didn't need much to live on, and he could still make a bit of money from odds and ends of journalism until inspiration struck. If it ever did. Come what may, he would survive. To start again might be the best thing he could do.

Nothing bound him to the city except his hunger to learn what Dylan had meant to tell him about the dead lawyers. *Why not Jazz?* Dylan's last words had revealed bewilderment as he stared into the face of the woman who would kill him. He had believed Jazz was the one at risk. She had shared a secret with him, and she was frightened. Frightened of whom? Dylan had seen himself as her savior. To him it had started as a game, but he'd found himself believing that everything she'd said was true. Poor self-centred Dylan. He'd thought Jazz was in danger—he had never dreamed that he would be the next to die.

Chapter Fourteen

Roxanne met the postman coming down the path as she set off for work. He handed her a thin bundle of letters, which she stuffed inside her bag before breaking into a run for the station. Usually she missed the morning mail, but she'd overslept and was twenty minutes late. She'd fallen asleep the previous evening on the train home and missed her stop. It wasn't as if she'd had much to drink at Sigmund's, but so much had happened in such a short time. On arriving home at last, she had kicked off her shoes and flopped on the bed. Next thing she knew, it was ten to eight and she was lying sprawled over the duvet, still wearing crumpled office clothes.

She'd swallowed a mouthful of coffee, but there was no time for breakfast. On the train, she wondered if that was a mistake. The pangs in her stomach were familiar. They reminded her of what had happened all those years before. Hunger could be a sweet sensation. Seductive. She forced herself not to think about food, or starving herself. Things hadn't reached that stage, not by a long way.

At Charing Cross she took a couple of minutes to go to the washroom and give her hair another comb. Dark rings were under the eyes gazing at her from the mirror. She splashed her face with cold water. She must keep her wits about her.

Hurrying down the corridor to her office, she came face to face with Chloe.

"Mustn't stop," Roxanne said. She remembered the pressure

of Chloe's hips against hers at Sigmund's and hoped she wasn't blushing. "I didn't hear my alarm this morning."

"I overslept as well," Chloe said cheerfully. "I was shattered last night, though it's not as though we got drunk is it?" She lowered her voice. "Funny, isn't it? Even if you've only had one or two drinks, your inhibitions start to disappear. Embarrassing, really. Then the next day, you're afraid you may have made a bit of a fool of yourself . . . oh well, no harm done, eh?"

"No."

Roxanne went on her way. She'd dreamed of Chloe's warm body the previous night, but now it was all a jumble in her mind. It was no good. She mustn't start obsessing about Chloe Beck. Too dangerous. She had to bury herself in her work. There was no choice.

"You were working late last night," Ben remarked when he called in midway through the morning.

She shrugged. "It would have been an early dart for a corporate finance lawyer."

He smirked. "Maybe that's why I never wanted to be a corporate finance lawyer. How about you?"

"Employment law's the only subject I ever cared for."

"It's a hot topic. Political, economic, social overtones. Most of all, it's about real people, not subclauses and schedules in a dusty tax statute. Human nature, with all its imperfections. Think of Howard Haycraft."

"I'd rather not," she said in a low voice.

He wagged a finger. His mood was gleeful, and again she was reminded of a mischievous troll. He'd already announced that he'd received a reserved decision from a tribunal in Newcastle, the result of a battle he'd fought up there a fortnight earlier. It had been a tough and important hearing, a test case for a major redundancy program, but the panel had unanimously ruled in favor of his clients. Now they could safely proceed to close a factory at minimum cost. The shareholders would save a small fortune, and eleven hundred people would lose their jobs.

"Don't take it to heart. A lawyer should never get too closely involved. Detachment gives us our strength."

Something made her say, "Will Janus is involved with Ali Khan, isn't he? They go yachting together. Will's family stays in Ali's Tuscan villa."

"That's different. It's all about rainmaking, getting the work in. Staying close to the client, working out how he ticks, keeping him happy. We're like any other cutting-edge firm. We keep a database of people who matter to us. Clients and contacts. At the click of a mouse, Fergus McHugh can come up with the names of their wives and kids, favorite football teams, golf handicaps. We need to know them inside out, make sure they love us, so they won't take their business elsewhere. We have to give them what they want, all the time. It's called relationship management."

"I see."

"You sound disapproving."

Oh Christ. The last thing she needed right now was hassle from Ben. "It's just that it seems so—"

"Manipulative?" The ginger eyebrows lifted. "Is that what you're thinking?"

It was as if she were on the witness stand, like Tara Glass being cross-examined into a damning admission. "I suppose . . ."

"Roxanne, it doesn't happen overnight, acclimatizing to a firm like this. Your last job was different. We're not heartless here. It's just that we're advocates, very good advocates, the best around. Don't think of what we do as manipulation. It's simply a kind of persuasion."

She said nothing. It seemed safest.

He came and sat on the edge of her desk. "That's what

advocates do. We persuade people to say what we want them to say, to do what we want them to do. It's not trickery, it's technique. Almost like seduction, you might say."

He held her gaze for a few moments, then slipped off the desk. "Must get on. If you need help, if anything's on your mind, let me know. It needn't be between nine and five. Think it over, Roxanne. You only have to say the word."

It wasn't until early afternoon that she remembered the mail she'd collected from the postman and fished it out of her bag. There was more of it than usual. A phone bill, a handful of circulars, a polyethylene-wrapped mail-order catalog. Plus a large brown envelope bearing her address and the typed legend "Roxanne Wake—For the eyes of the addressee only."

With a frown, she ripped the envelope open, yanking out the folded sheet of paper it contained. As soon as she glanced at it, she froze. It was a photocopy of a press cutting, two folded pages from a newspaper: a tabloid's center spread.

The first thing she saw was a grainy black and white photograph of a young woman lazing on a beach. Her minute bikini revealed a skinny body, the outline of her ribs plainly visible. Lying on the sand beside her was a man with perma-tan. She was gazing at him as if mesmerized by the sharply defined features, the thick sensual lips. He was not looking directly at her, but rather surveying her slender figure. He wore the proprietorial expression of a man surveying a golf trophy or his new sports car, and with good reason. No one had ever possessed Cassandra Lee in the way that Grant Dennis had possessed her.

Snatching up the piece of paper, she crumpled it into a ball and hurled it to the other side of the room, but after a few moments she could not help going to pick it up. She'd never seen the piece before; she'd vowed not to read about herself in the press.

The door opened, and she bowed her head, hoping that whoever it was would take the hint and go away.

Click-clack, click-clack.

"Roxanne! What is it?"

Chloe. Who else?

"Nothing," she said in a muffled voice. She stuffed the cutting into a desk drawer. It must not be seen. "Just give me a few minutes, will you?"

But Chloe advanced into the room and folded her arms. "Don't you think you'd better tell me what's going on?"

"Leave me. Please."

"How can I? For goodness sake, your eyes are red, you look as though you're about to burst into tears."

"It doesn't matter. Really. I'll be fine."

"Please. Don't treat me like a child, Roxanne. I'm not stupid. It's not the work, is it? You may be new, but you can take that in your stride. Someone's upsetting you. Why don't you talk about it?" A pause. Roxanne could almost hear Chloe's mind working. "Hey, is that why you went to Sigmund's last night? To unburden yourself—and then I showed up and stopped you? Oh shit. Roxanne, I'm so sorry."

"It's not your fault."

"Listen, you can't keep it all inside."

Roxanne gritted her teeth. "Can't I?"

"No, you're strong, but you're not invulnerable. No one is. You're ready to share—whatever it is that's bothering you. You wouldn't have gone to Sigmund's otherwise. I want to help. I don't like to think of you crucifying yourself over something and nothing."

"It's not something and nothing."

"Well, whatever. Even if it's a calamity, isn't it better to talk it over with someone, instead of sobbing quietly over your computer keyboard? Let's take half an hour off, shall we? We could pop up to the restaurant."

"No," Roxanne said. The harshness of her tone caught her by surprise. "I mean, we can't talk here. Not in the office."

"But we can get together?"

Chloe held her gaze. Roxanne couldn't look away. "Maybe," she said in the end.

"When?"

"I don't know. I want to get my head together first. Have a walk in the fresh air. On my own."

"Suit yourself. After work, then? Fine. I'll see you here at six-thirty."

Leaning over the fence of the pedestrian walkway on Hungerford Bridge, staring into the unfathomable river, listening to a boat guide imparting factoids about the London Eye to a group of Japanese tourists, Roxanne wondered what story to tell. If Chloe talked out of turn, Roxanne would have to give up the job. If she was quick enough to resign before being sacked. Wasn't it a criminal offense to give a false name on a CV? People lied to get work all the time; newspapers and magazines were stuffed with jokey articles about how to improve one's career prospects by adding in a few extra qualifications. But every once in a while, someone was found out and sent to prison for obtaining a job by deception.

"Despite what many people say, the London Eye is correctly described as an observation wheel, *not* a Ferris wheel," the guide explained. "It's a mistake often made, but you shouldn't believe everything you are told."

She had not shared her secret with anyone since breaking up with Hilary, but discretion had not kept her safe. Although she'd planned to start afresh, Hilary had tracked her down in no time. And now Hilary—it must be her, surely?—was playing cat and mouse with her, taking revenge for betrayal by sending the anonymous note and press clipping. Even if she didn't talk to Chloe, would it make any difference?

The big wheel was turning on the opposite bank. Passengers moved round in their air-conditioned capsules, listening to the commentary and watching the closed-circuit television screens. For a while they would see everything from a different perspective. But they always finished up in the same place they'd started from.

At six-thirty Chloe came for her. Even though she hadn't finished drafting weasel words for Ali Khan's dignity-at-work policy, she was sick of the task and allowed herself to be led to a bar off St. Martin's Lane. It was called the Yellow Jersey, because it was owned by a cyclist who had once done well in the Tour de France. The walls were festooned with posters extolling pedal power, and the place was supposed to be a sort of unofficial headquarters for an anti-car anarchist cell. A group of teenagers and twentysomethings with studs in every visible bit of flesh were huddled together in a corner, talking in whispers about reclaiming the streets. As Roxanne and Chloe came in, a couple of the people shot glances at them before looking away, satisfied that the newcomers were not journalists or undercover police officers. As if.

All the stools and tables were made out of bits of bicycle. Stylish, distinctive, and bloody uncomfortable. Chloe didn't seem to care, and the pair of them perched precariously in a quiet corner drinking lager and lime.

For an hour Chloe chattered away about all manner of things—soap operas, clothes, the never-ending saga of her implants—as if intent on putting Roxanne at her ease, not fussing or pressing her for confidences. There wasn't much for Roxanne to do other than laugh dutifully at the jokes and exclaim in sympathy at each suitable opportunity.

"Cheers," Chloe said on returning to their corner with replenished drinks. "To friends in need?"

They chinked glasses. "Friends in need," Roxanne said.

Her stomach still felt empty, but she liked the sensation of lightness. She sipped greedily and blushed as she realized Chloe was watching her. "The booze is doing me good. I'm beginning to understand why so many lawyers end up in Alcoholics Anonymous. First warning sign, eh?"

Chloe touched her hand. "You deserve a bit of time off for bad behavior."

Roxanne cleared her throat. No one could go on forever, keeping the past locked inside them. She needed to share a little, and she wanted to share with Chloe. Chloe was interested in her; soon she'd find out how interested. She was a lawyer, so she would do what lawyers do so well. Compromise. Fudge it. She'd tell Chloe the truth. But it wouldn't be the whole truth.

"It's difficult for me to say this," Roxanne began.

Chloe studied her fingernails. "As it happens, I can guess what's been going on. Even though you've denied it. It's Ben, isn't it? He's made a pass at you, and you're afraid to say no. Afraid that's why he took you on, afraid that if you turn him down, he'll take revenge. Kill off your career before it's started. Don't worry, it's—"

"This isn't about Ben. I can handle him."

"But I thought—"

"Oh, he's sent me one or two not-very-coded messages lately, but he's wasting his time. I'm not just another of the Creed chicks. By the way, I've noticed that while most of the lawyers in the firm are women, hardly any of them ever make partner. But I never had any intention of sleeping my way to the top. I'm not interested in him. Or any other man."

She hadn't meant to add that last sentence, and the moment the words slipped out, she heard Chloe's intake of breath. Averting her gaze, she swore inwardly at her lack of legal caution. Hilary had once advised her that it was a mistake to come out too soon. First you had to make sure of your ground.

"I see."

Roxanne was gazing at an aging poster on the wall. Eddy Merckx, head down and pedaling furiously on the final stage. "You can go now if you want to."

"Don't be silly."

Roxanne felt her friend's hand covering her own, lingering there. Warming her. When she turned to face Chloe, she was greeted by a smile.

"I'm not shocked. For goodness' sake, this is London, not some backwater in the sticks. We're in the twenty-first century. To tell you the truth, I'm not even surprised."

"Am I that transparent?" *Jesus, I hope not.*

"There's something about you . . . I don't know." Chloe's hand pressed down more firmly. "You're different."

"I suppose I should feel flattered."

"Yes, you should." Chloe hesitated. "So—this upset you've been going through, you've split up with someone recently?"

"A while back, but the other day she came here looking for me. I told her again we were finished."

"So that's why . . ." Chloe nodded to herself, as if confirming a theory. "You were together a long time, then?"

"She helped me through a bad patch. And she encouraged me to learn about the law, told me I was bright enough to make it my career, in spite of all the evidence to the contrary. She believed in me, did Hilary. I owed her so much, but it wasn't enough, not to keep us together. She was so possessive. If ever she thought I expressed the slightest interest in someone else, man or woman, she became jealous. In the end, it was too much to bear. I had to make the break."

"So you have been interested in men—in the past?"

How much do I say?

Roxanne bowed her head. "Yes."

Chloe leaned across the table. "What happened?"

"He was the only man I ever thought I loved. His name was Grant Dennis. I met him when I was sixteen years old."

Roxanne paused and studied her friend. Chloe was on the edge of her chair, holding her breath, awaiting revelations, giving no hint that the name meant anything to her. Well, it was all a long time ago.

"He was my first lover. Until I met Grant, I'd lived in what seemed like a small little world. We lived in Derbyshire, on a hilltop outside Buxton. That's where I met Grant. He had a cottage there. A bolt-hole, he called it. One day we bumped into each other. It was a chance encounter. He was an agent for football players. He struck up a conversation, and it was all I could do not to swoon. He was tanned, handsome, sophisticated. When he talked about it, even football became entrancing."

"God," Chloe giggled, "he must have been special."

"He asked if I'd like to work for him, and I jumped at the chance. For a while, everything was perfect. He'd diversified, he had a stake in a couple of radio stations and owned a share of a glitzy restaurant. Soon I was living with him in a house the size of a stately home."

"So what went wrong?"

Roxanne fiddled with her bracelet, remembering. "I could put up with Grant's cocaine, even though it never did anything for me. I even turned a blind eye to his other women. But the first time he asked me to look after one of his favored clients, I didn't realize what he had in mind. When I found out, and made it clear that my duties didn't extend to giving blow jobs to a Premier League striker, things turned nasty."

Chloe's eyes widened. "Shit!"

One of the studded kids at the other table threw them a

glance. As if satisfied with what she saw, she turned back to her murmurings with her fellow conspirators.

"Later, he told me he'd thought I was happy to do anything. No limits. And I won't pretend it was all his fault. That was how I behaved, Chloe. I'm not proud of it, but I won't deny it. In my early days with him, I acted like a whore. But we all have a point where we draw the line, and I wasn't interested in anyone but Grant. Trouble was, the footballer was livid. He was one of Grant's best clients, and Grant wasn't happy. He'd wanted to watch. So he took his anger out on me."

In her mind, Roxanne could still see the yellowing bruises he had left on her body. Nothing that ever showed. He always liked her to look immaculate. A trophy to match any of the medals his clients had won.

"Funny, I'd never seen that side of him until then. He kept it hidden in the early days. Later, I saw more of it. Familiarity bred contempt as far as Grant was concerned. One client was Dutch. He kept Grant well supplied with hard-core porn. Nothing was off limits. Nothing, Chloe. And yet, when he'd finished enjoying himself, he could turn around and be sweeter than ever."

"Bastard," Chloe hissed.

"He started nagging me about my weight. I've always had a sweet tooth. He said I ate too much chocolate, that he didn't want me to turn into a fat ugly sow. It sounds stupid, but I'd always been desperate for his good word. I'd maybe put on half a stone since we got together, no more than that, but I went on a diet and discovered I could lose a few pounds without too much trouble. It didn't stop there. I knew I was in trouble when I passed a display of chocolate in a shop one day and the smell of the stuff made me want to puke. At first, Grant fancied the waif look. It turned him on. He wasn't so keen when my boobs disappeared. I went too far." She paused. "That's my problem,

Chloe. I always go too far."

Chloe moistened her lips with the tip of her tongue. "What happened?"

"He arranged for me to check into a private clinic. Soon, I was eating again. But as soon as I began to look a bit like the old me, he started up again. I was his slave."

"Oh God," Chloe whispered.

"He stole my self-respect. I should have fought harder, but I didn't know how. I never got back to my old weight. I started to love being thin. It wasn't a matter of seeking his approval any longer. Anorexia gave me a kind of power. If only because Grant didn't want a dead girlfriend on his hands. I was addicted to thinness, the way he was hooked on nose candy. Let's not talk about those days any more, okay? I want to forget what it was like. When—feeling hungry was an aphrodisiac."

"It turned you on," Chloe breathed.

"Yes, it turned me on."

Roxanne closed her eyes. *Time to change the subject. Now, before it's too late.*

She felt a touch on her cheek. Rouged lips brushing against the softness of her skin.

Afterward, Roxanne couldn't remember whose idea it had been to spend the night together. She had a hazy recollection that Chloe had suggested that she come home to Greenwich with her. She hoped it wasn't simply because Chloe felt sorry for her. Or drunk; they had both been unsteady on their feet by the time they left the Yellow Jersey, and it wasn't just out of mutual affection that they had leaned on each other as they made their way to the station.

Nothing much happened when they took off each other's clothes and climbed into Chloe's comfortable king-size bed. It was as if they were in unspoken agreement that there was no need to go too fast too soon. For Roxanne, it was enough to be able to fall asleep with another warm body next to hers. Since Hilary there had been no one. At times she persuaded herself that she did not need anyone else, but in her heart she knew it wasn't true.

Chloe's radio alarm was set for six. Twenty minutes later, she reappeared in the bedroom, bearing a breakfast tray, while Roxanne was still wiping the sleep from her eyes and trying to remember everything she had said the previous evening. She was never at her best on waking; it took her time to come round. Hilary had been a lark, rather than an owl. Judging by her bright smile, Chloe was equally incompatible.

"A treat," Chloe said. "For a special occasion. It's been a while since I last served anyone with breakfast in bed."

Roxanne made an effort and sat up. For some reason she felt self-conscious. Despite her confession and the kisses and cuddles they had shared in the small hours, she pulled up the duvet so that it covered her breasts. Chloe noticed, and colored as she handed over the tray. She had on a toweling dressing gown; her own famously expensive boobs were no longer on display. Already she'd found time to make up and douse herself in that musky perfume.

"There's something I ought to say, Roxanne. Last night was my first time—you know, with another woman."

Roxanne felt a stab of guilt. "Look—I didn't mean to—"

"No, no," Chloe said quickly. "Don't apologize, for Christ's sake. No regrets, all right? It's just that—it takes a bit of a mental leap, that's all."

"Don't feel bad about—about you and me," Roxanne said on impulse. "It just happened."

"I don't feel bad about it," Chloe murmured. "Just strange."

It was strange for Roxanne, too, waking up in an unfamiliar room. The furnishings were trim and Scandinavian, the aroma of essential oils hung in the air. Chat magazines were scattered around. Chloe wasn't much of a reader; Hilary had been passionate about Jeanette Winterson and Virginia Woolf, but Chloe's library comprised a single shelf of chick-lit. She had opened the curtains a little, allowing Roxanne to gaze out toward the sunlit river. The flat was on the tenth floor of a new complex on the waterfront opposite Canary Wharf. To the east, over the roofs of factories and houses, she could glimpse the angled masts of the Dome.

"I like this place," Roxanne said.

"Me, too. I was very lucky to get it."

"How did you . . . ?" Roxanne suddenly realized that her question might seem tactless. Creed paid its people well, but she wouldn't expect a personal assistant to be able to afford such a swish apartment.

"My last boyfriend had some pull with the landlords. He did a deal with them on my behalf."

"Same boyfriend who paid for your op?"

"You know something?" Chloe's cheeks had turned pink. "I think deep down you're just as inquisitive as me."

"Sorry, I didn't mean to—"

"Oh, forget it. I shouldn't be so tetchy. Besides, you have much more reason to be angry with me."

"I don't follow."

Chloe bit her lip. "I have a confession to make."

Roxanne felt a chill and pulled the duvet tighter around her. "How do you mean?"

"I've been checking up on you. I found out Roxanne Wake isn't your real name."

Jesus. Roxanne caught sight of her face in the mirror on a chest of drawers. Her features had frozen in disbelief.

"I'm sorry, I'm sorry, I'm sorry. I should never have done it, but I couldn't resist. I was just—fascinated by you. You seemed

159

so cool and remote and beautiful—and unhappy. I wanted to find out more about you. So I accessed the recruitment file on his computer. It's supposed to be confidential, even from me, but Ben is careless about his passwords." Chloe was talking fast, barely pausing for breath as the words tumbled out of her. "I guessed Ben had taken a fancy to you, but that didn't explain why you weren't more forthcoming. So I rang up the Hengist Street center and spun them a line. It turned out they knew nothing about your past. You said you'd worked in a welfare rights bureau in Manchester, but no one seemed to have heard of you. You'll never believe this, but I was so obsessed, I checked with Public Records. The date of birth you gave—there's no record of a Roxanne Wake being born on that day."

"No," Roxanne said faintly. She couldn't move. It was as if Chloe had given her a paralyzing injection. "No, there wouldn't be."

"You must have been so terrified of him," Chloe said. She put an arm around Roxanne's shoulder. "I know what it's like, to be with a man who possesses you. At first it's exciting, later it's creepy. But with me it never got so bad that I not only ran away but had to change my name."

Roxanne dared not speak. Chloe pulled away and looked her in the eye.

"Don't worry. Of course I won't give you away to that vicious bastard. My lips are sealed, cross my heart and hope to die. But you must tell me one thing. Who are you?"

Now for it. "My real name is Cassandra," Roxanne muttered. "Cassandra Lee."

Chloe considered, no flicker of recognition on her face. The name must mean nothing to her. "I prefer Roxanne," she said and kissed her lightly on the lips.

Roxanne felt the tension ebbing out of her. Chloe wasn't angry or scornful. She had worked out her own happy ending.

CHAPTER FIFTEEN

"I suppose you think I'm bitter?" Alice Wythenshawe's weathered cheeks flushed. "Of course I'm fucking bitter! What do you think I am, some kind of martyr? A heroine?"

She wheeled her chair a little distance away from Nic and stared out across the small back garden. It had been adapted for her, with no lawn but waist-high troughs of begonias, geraniums, and impatiens bordering the paths. She moved in the direction of a pergola covered in wisteria and climbing roses. After a few moments he followed, inhaling the perfume of the flowers as he joined her. Alice picked a pair of pruning shears from the top of an upturned pot. She started cutting furiously at deadheads, as if inflicting punishment, dropping the old leaves into an aluminium bucket already half-filled with buttercups and dandelions.

Under the pergola was a small wooden bench. He sat down, so that they were on the same level, and said, "I didn't mean to upset you."

She coughed. "Oh, take no notice of me. I fly off the handle sometimes. Always did, but now people are more tolerant. Good excuse, isn't it, having your spine shattered? Don't tell me I ought to count my blessings. I already know that. There's a chap I see down at the Center, he's quadriplegic. Needs a transmitter just to breathe, has to drink through a straw, but he never utters a cross word. A fucking saint. He makes me feel guilty for not being the life and soul of the party."

Gray streaked her hair. She didn't bother with dye, or with makeup to cover the lines around the mouth and eyes. The sun had burned her freckled cheeks deep brown. She smelled of compost, and her hands were grubby from weeding the densely planted troughs. Nic detected no trace of self-pity in the large dark eyes. She might have passed for fifty, but he knew she was a dozen years younger. He couldn't imagine that she'd ever been a beauty; her mouth was too wide, her chin too sharp for that. Yet even in her wheelchair, breathing noisily as she reached out to prune the roses, she struck him as strong and full of energy.

He nodded toward her bungalow, a neat stone building with a ramp leading from the back door. "You bought this house for your sister and yourself with the compensation money?"

"The insurance coughed up in the end. We settled out of court. I took a lower payout to sort it quickly. They were going to say I was partly to blame, that I should never have let Bradley drive me, he was so obviously drunk. Funny old world, isn't it? My life may have been wrecked, but I'm worth more than I've ever been." She put down the pruners and bared her teeth in a fierce grin. "An upstairs flat wasn't much use to me after I came out of the hospital. It was time to come home. At least I survived. Which is more than you can say about poor Bradley."

"He was killed instantly, I suppose?"

A casual question, but he held his breath for her reply. *A giant who chopped himself in half?*

She swallowed hard. "He wasn't wearing a seat belt, you know. Bloody fool. I ought to have said something, but I'd been drinking as well. But I'd put my belt on and that saved me. He went straight through the windshield when we crashed. The impact—it ripped him apart. I mean, it literally tore him in two. The only good thing was, it was quick. Happened in an instant."

For a while neither of them spoke. Nic found he was clenching his fists.

"How could you bear it?" he asked hoarsely.

"Well, I'm not denying there have been days when I've thought he was the lucky one. I don't like being a cripple, Mr. Gabriel. Actually, I hate it. When I was active, I campaigned on behalf of disabled people, but I never dreamed I'd become one of them. Lucky we can't see into the future, eh?"

A bee hummed around them, moving from petal to petal. When it came too close, Nic brushed it away with his hand, but it kept coming back. He couldn't help admiring its persistence. Alice Wythenshawe took no notice, as if she'd been stung once and had nothing more to fear.

"Bradley worked for the union himself, didn't he?" Nic asked.

Alice nodded. "He did things the hard way, left school at sixteen and went to work in a factory. Before long he became a shop steward. He was ambitious, and he became hooked on the law. Beer and sandwiches weren't enough for him. He always had a fancy for the high life. He liked to dress well, drive a big car. You can't fill your wardrobe with Savile Row suits and keep a couple of Mercs in your garage without a bit of cash in the bank. Working for the union, he was never going to make a fortune. So he decided to catch up on the education he'd missed and won a scholarship to Ruskin. Once he had a degree, he moved into the legal profession and joined Creed."

"How did Bradley and Will Janus get on?"

She grunted. "Will Janus was a winner—and winners can be forgiven anything. That's what Bradley used to say. I thought Will was patronizing, he was using Bradley simply to pretend the firm still had union roots, but Bradley didn't mind. Will's fan club, now, that was a different matter. Bradley couldn't stand them. Fergus McHugh played tennis with Will and always let him win. As for young Joel Anthony, Bradley said if he stuck his head any further up Will's arse, it would have come out the other side."

Nic smelled the roses, felt them brushing his hair. "Bradley was married, wasn't he?"

Alice examined her fingernails. The gardening had left them grubby. "Yes, he was married. She was a childhood sweetheart, the old familiar story, of course. Successful middle-aged man whose wife doesn't understand him meets younger woman and fancies his chances. Mo had been a hairdresser. He got her pregnant when she was seventeen, and they were married before the baby was born."

She reached out to a climber that bore rich red roses and tore off a couple of leaves spattered with black spots. "You know, someone like Will would never see the disease; he'd rather preach about the beauty of the flower. It's his gift, when you think about it. He's a lucky man."

"And he likes his partners to be pure as the driven snow?"

"Sure. He pays lip service to everyone being human, loves to come over as just a regular guy, but he simply isn't. Committed to equal opportunities? Don't make me laugh. He'll never understand that tucking into chicken tikka marsala isn't enough." Her voice was trembling with anger; her breathing was jerky. "The idea that Creed, the firm—the *brand* as that turd Fergus would put it—could be contaminated by scandal and sleaze, it would be anathema to him. Will is Mister Perfect. A tough act for the rest of us mortals to live up to."

"What if partners slept with clients?"

"Perk of the job, Bradley used to say." She made a visible effort to calm herself, gave him the tightest of smiles. "Only joking."

"Did anyone in the firm know about your relationship?"

"Ben guessed eventually. Bradley was what Ben would have liked to be. Tall, broad-shouldered, full head of hair. It didn't help when I sent him off with a flea in his ear."

"He tried it on with you?"

"I wasn't flattered. Imagine a garden gnome in heat, that was Ben. I suppose I wasn't tactful. No wonder he held a grudge."

"What makes you think so?"

"There was a big equal pay claim. Millions of pounds were at stake if our members won. It would mean that all the pay rates of shop floor workers in one of the country's biggest retailers would have to be uplifted. Needless to say, the employers hired the best City lawyers money could buy. It was a high-profile case, name of *Smethurst*, you might remember it."

"I do," Nic said. "You won. Won well."

"We did." A faraway look came briefly into her eyes, and he guessed she was transporting herself back in time to the final triumph of a career cut so short. "Yes, it was a marvelous result. But all the way through, Bradley felt people in his firm were sniping at him."

"About what?"

"Silly things, mainly. Fergus was angry because Bradley wasn't keeping him up to speed, so he couldn't brief the press with a good news story. Ben was twitchy about the funding of the claims. I'd been instructed to drive a hard bargain. Paying by results. Ben's attitude was: no win, no fee, no bloody profit. Bradley kept saying the case was a winner, but Ben favored doing a deal. I tried to reason with him, but it didn't do any good. All that happened was that he asked Bradley if there was anything going on between the two of us."

"How had he cottoned on?"

"I suppose we weren't as discreet as we thought. Bradley gave him a load of bullshit. That was his forte, but Ben wasn't fooled. Things started to get tense. We were both under pressure. It was always important to win, but then Bradley found out that Ben was plotting against him."

Nic reached out absentmindedly and tore one of the petals

off a rose. "Tell me about it."

She glared at him. "This is off the record?"

"I haven't even taken out my notebook, have I? Like I said on the phone, I'm simply trying to get background for a book about the firm."

"Joel Anthony came to see Bradley one evening. He was working closely with Bradley on the case. I took a liking to him. Anyway, he told Bradley that he'd been wrestling with his conscience. Bradley's first question was to ask what a lawyer was doing with a conscience."

"So why was Joel's conscience pricking?"

"Ben had asked him to keep an eye on Bradley's handling of the case and to report to him about it. Joel was Ben's spy in the camp, and it bothered him. He'd been put in a no-win situation. He was careful how much he said to Bradley, but the message wasn't hard to make out. Ben expected the litigation would go pear-shaped and that would give him a chance to stick the knife into Bradley. If the union ditched the retainer with Creed, that might have been grounds to force him out of the partnership. Joel had been promoted after Matthew Creed's death. Ben was grooming him, someone close to Will, but someone he thought he could control. A way of strengthening his own position within the firm."

"How did Bradley react?"

"His instinct was to laugh it off, but I warned him to take care. I didn't trust Ben. Thanks to Joel, we were on our guard, all the more determined to make sure the litigation was a success. And it worked out for the best." She coughed. "Or did it? I suppose that if Ben had got his way, Bradley would still be alive. He might have left Creed—Christ, he might even have left his wife. The two of us would still be together."

Nic put his hands behind his head, stretched out his legs, and waited. The old advocate's trick, after picking up clues that the witness wants to talk. Bury your urge to know; just relax. Don't be too anxious: have the courage to sit back and let the truth come tumbling out, all in its own good time.

She shifted around so that she was facing him, her eyes boring into his and yet not, he thought, seeing him. Her mind was back in London, and the past. "Mum never asked me about that night, you know. I'm sure she was trying to be kind, not wanting to upset me by bringing back the memories. That's the problem, though, Mr. Gabriel. Memories are all I've got."

"*Smethurst*," he said softly. "It's in all the books on equal rights. The leading case on the interpretation of that particular subsection of the Equal Pay Act."

"Weird kind of fame, isn't it? To have helped to rewrite a paragraph in a dusty legal tome."

"The compensation changed your members' lives. Not to mention all the others who have benefited since."

"That's what I ought to cling to, isn't it? That case did make a difference for people. I'm proud of that, Mr. Gabriel. The moment judgment was delivered, I'll never forget it." Her eyes shone as she relived the triumph. "We'd worked so hard, Bradley and I, fighting to get that result. Fighting the big battalions, to say nothing of the folk who should have been on our side. Oh, I know that it was a team effort, but Bradley and I drove it. Without us, that case would have been lost. We made the difference. We believed in the cause, you see."

Nic closed his eyes. For a few seconds, he was an advocate again, heart thudding against the walls of his chest as he opened his final submission. Consumed by the urge to win, experiencing the adrenaline rush. Twisting the strands of the case into a thread of reasoning that no one could unravel. When he spoke, he had to believe in his case with a lover's passion. He *made* himself believe; he knew no other way. Once it was over, he invariably stayed on his own while his witnesses returned to the sanctuary of the waiting room. His shirt would be damp against his chest as he stood in the corridor, listening to the footsteps of clerks echoing in the silence, shifting from one foot to another as he kept checking his watch, wondering if delay was a good sign or bad. During those lonely minutes, nothing in the world seemed to matter more than the verdict of the court. Defeat was unthinkable.

"Yes," he said, "I do see."

"Bradley decided we must celebrate. Everyone who mattered was there. People from the union, partners from Creed, sundry hangers-on. Fergus was rushing out media releases, proclaiming a famous victory. Ben showed up, needless to say, hoping to claim some of the credit. We held an impromptu press conference, though it was Will who finished up on the nine o'clock news, not Bradley."

"Somehow that doesn't come as a complete surprise."

"He did pay generous tribute to Bradley. He's brilliant at that, so skillful at creating the feel-good factor that you forget he's actually climbed on board your bandwagon and grabbed hold of the steering wheel. Anyway, we all finished up drinking champagne in a bar. It's all a bit hazy in my memory. I was drunk, of course. At one stage, I think I sat on Bradley's knee. If anyone hadn't known about our affair beforehand, the cat was well and truly out of the bag by the end of the evening. Bradley was even talking about us booking in together at a hotel in town. No expense spared, typical Bradley bravado. He said something about a suite at the Savoy."

Her eyes glistened. Knowing that she was about to weep, Nic swallowed hard. Again he was transported back to the old days, confronting a witness whose nerve was about to break. The decent thing would be to hold back, to refrain from putting the final question that would cause the tears to flow. To continue would be cruel: but a cross-examiner had no choice but to pursue his cause to the bitter end.

"Why did you decide that he would drive you back to your flat? Wouldn't it have been easier to call a cab?"

"Of course it would have been fucking easier!" She choked back a sob. "Oh Christ, I don't know. It cropped up in the conversation. Both of us were fuddled with the booze, especially me. I suppose I had a vague idea that I'd invite him in and we'd complete a perfect day with a session of wild lovemaking. Utter crap, naturally. Bradley was quite a man, but I doubt if even he would have been able to keep me satisfied after all he'd put away that night."

"You were happy to go with him?"

"At one point I even offered to drive. I was pretty far gone and someone dissuaded me. It didn't cross my mind to protest that Bradley was too drunk to take me home safely. We said our goodbyes, there was a lot of kissing—and that was that. I must have fallen asleep in the passenger seat. First thing I knew, there was this almighty noise, as if a bomb had gone off. The most terrifying sound I've ever heard. The car jackknifed and we hit a fence, a barrier or something, Christ knows what. I never wanted to know the grisly details. I was in so much pain all of a sudden, and Bradley—well, I told you what happened. Then the pain became too much, and I passed out. When I woke up, I was in a hospital bed and a doctor was telling me I'd never walk again."

Ahead of them, the ground dipped and there was a gap in the row of shrubs and trees that marked the boundary of the garden. Nic halted to gaze at the Spa, the Esplanade, and the harbor and castle in the far distance. Landmarks from his childhood. The familiar salt smell was in the air.

"See where the land falls away?" Alice said. "A hotel used to stand there. One night, the land started to slip away, and soon the cliff collapsed. The hotel fell into the sea. A place which had stood for many years—vanished in a trice."

Nic nodded, remembering shots from the television news. Scarborough's moment of national fame. A bizarre incident, like something from one of his father's tales about Camelot.

"Like Bradley, I suppose. He achieved so much, and yet with a few drinks too many he threw it all away."

The sun was beating down on the garden. Nic undid a couple of shirt buttons and shifted his position on the bench. "I'm sorry," he said again.

"You're not really," she said. "You're simply doing your job. Or so I suppose. Which makes me ask one question, if it's my turn."

"Go ahead."

"Just what is this all about?" She rested her elbows on the arms of the wheelchair and gazed steadily at him. He was conscious of her burning intelligence, the flame undimmed by the breaking of her body. She could never have been conventionally pretty, but in that moment he understood perfectly what had attracted Bradley Hurst to her. "I mean, someone else rang up to ask me about the accident, not long ago."

"Dylan Rees."

She stared. "Right first time. You know him?"

"We were friends. He died recently."

"I read about it. Some woman stabbed him. Is that why you're here? I mean, I don't buy the line that you're simply researching background for an in-depth profile of Creed. This doesn't have the smell of Fergus about it. As far as he's concerned, Bradley's death was a PR disaster and I'm just an embarrassing reminder of it. So why would an outsider like you be interested in old news?

"I owe you an explanation, I suppose."

"You do, really."

Jazz must have sworn Dylan to secrecy. As soon as he had

decided to spill the beans, he'd died. Coincidence, no doubt, but perhaps his tall story was one that people weren't meant to know. Alice might not find ignorance bliss, but at least it was safe.

"Sorry. I'll have to disappoint you."

She clicked her tongue, but he could see she wasn't too angry with him. She had more sleep to lose over than conundrums about the life she'd left so far behind.

His next destination was a few miles up the coast. He told himself it would not be much of a detour. There was time for him to take a look at the place where his life had changed forever.

Soon he was following the winding road signposted to Ravenscar. How long since he had last traveled this way? As a boy, sitting in the back of his father's Rover, this had sometimes seemed like their own private drive. Summer tourists didn't count, and houses were few. This afternoon, there were more cars on the road than he remembered, but that was true everywhere.

Ravenscar should have been a popular destination as a bustling resort perched on the cliffs overlooking the sea. Instead, there were only rolling fields and scattered buildings. As Nic drove into the village, he saw that the National Trust had put up an information center. The hotel and golf course were still there, but the markings of the old roads were scarcely visible.

A hundred years ago, entrepreneurs had conjured up the idea of building a town at the midpoint on the new railway line linking Scarborough and Whitby. Boulevards were laid out, sewers constructed, plots of land sold to townies seduced by the idea of living at the seaside. But the developers had failed to do their homework. The shore was inhospitable, and in winter the weather was wild. The company folded as war broke out, leaving a network of broad streets and a handful of houses that seemed oddly out of place, stuck in the middle of the country-side. The station was abandoned, and the track became a bridle path.

The Gabriels had lived in the house nearest to the cliffs, optimistically named Sunny View. During a gale, Wuthering Heights would have been nearer the mark, but although the site was exposed to the elements, Nic did not care. He had relished the isolation, the sense that he was set apart from other children. For him, the only cloud had been his father's absences. At least when Bryn Gabriel came home again, there were always fresh stories about Arthur and his knights of old, and the long wait for his return had suddenly seemed worthwhile.

The house was still there, a solid and ugly stone building, aggressively asymmetrical. It even boasted a small turret with a single window. Once it had been the playroom. Nic had kept his boxes of Legos there, and his train set. Now the house doubled as a sort of shop. A brightly painted signboard at the gate promised "Pine Furniture at Knockdown Prices, Fine Art Bargains, Household Knickknacks."

He pulled up by the gate, and a middle-aged woman in t-shirt and jeans who was pottering about outside the front porch turned and waved at him. She gestured for him to wind his window down.

"Come and look round." She didn't sound like a native. Mancunian, at a guess. "We've just had a stock of bedside cabinets delivered. Going cheap."

The sight of the house made him dizzy. He'd pictured it so many times in his mind. It was smaller than he'd remembered, not in the least bit Gothic in design. He could feel his heart thudding. One thing he knew for certain. Even after all this time, he could not bear to go back inside. It would be too much.

"Thanks, but I'm just getting my bearings."

"Suit yourself."

The garden was neatly kept. Someone had built a rock garden and populated it with heathers tough enough to survive the blast of winter. When he had lived here, the grounds had been wild and overgrown. He remembered the sweet fragrance of the untamed honeysuckle that had clambered along the broken-down fence at the back. His father always used to say that one fine day he would landscape the garden, perhaps put in a little pool, but he preferred telling stories to his son to do-it-yourself projects, and the place had remained ramshackle. For all that, Nic had loved living here and had never imagined leaving. Not, that is, until the day when he came home from school and found his mother dead. His father was missing, and Nic never saw him again.

As a boy, Nic worshipped the father he seldom saw. Bryn Gabriel traveled the world. He was some kind of journalist, but Nic knew little about what he actually wrote. His father never discussed it in his presence. It didn't matter, because his father brought back presents from all four corners of the globe. A model of the Empire State Building, wonderful in its detail. Sweatshirts from Moscow and Johannesburg, a set of toy cars and an armful of comics from Sydney. Nic lived for the short spells when his father returned from overseas and made up for lost time by spoiling his son rotten, buying him things, playing soccer and cricket on the unkempt lawn that ran down to the cliffs, taking him on trips across the snow-covered Goathland moors in the depths of winter.

Bryn Gabriel was nothing like other fathers. Doing the unexpected was what turned him on. It was exciting simply to belong to him. One summer day, the year before the murder, he turned up without warning after a month abroad and took them out for a drive. Only when they arrived at the airport did he show them the flight tickets for Florida. He'd grabbed a late booking, and the three of them were together for a dizzy Disney fortnight that Nic would never forget.

Above all, Bryn Gabriel was a storyteller. He claimed it all came down to his Welsh roots. As a student, he'd spent a long hazy summer at Harlech Castle, entertaining tourists with tales from the *Mabinogion*. He knew a hundred legends by heart, and those he didn't know, he made up. Romances of Arthur and the Otherworld, populated by shape-shifting necromancers, beautiful women who turned into snakes if kissed, and knights whose armor changed color in the blink of an eye. He painted word pictures of a miraculous kingdom, where brave men claimed swords from stones floating on water, chess pieces were moved by invisible hands, and ships sailed by themselves. The boy drank it all in, the tales of true love and chivalry and the promise that the secrets of immortality were waiting to be found, if only one knew just where to look.

His mother was slim and blond; physically, Nic took after her. She was quiet, content to remain in her husband's shadow. When she wasn't occupied in looking after Nic and the rambling old house, she liked to go on long walks along the cliffs. She did a bit of freelance copyediting for the publishers she'd worked for before her marriage; her favorite hobby was reading, and every nook of Sea View was crammed with her paperbacks. When Bryn was away, she would read aloud in her soft cool voice, stories by C. S. Lewis and Tolkien. She was calm and well-organized and never seemed to worry about a thing. Except, perhaps, her husband's absences. One night Nic had heard his parents talk about them.

"We need you here," his mother said, her low voice drifting up the stairs and in through the open bedroom door.

"And I want to be here, too. Give it time. It will happen. Promise."

A sigh. "How many times have I heard you say that? I just feel sometimes—that things aren't ever going to change."

Of course, she was proved right. Nothing did change in the town that never was, until the day Nic came home and found his world destroyed.

A warm afternoon; he'd stuffed his blazer and tie in the saddle bag. As he wheeled his bike into the courtyard at the end of the drive, he caught sight of his father's Rover parked by the kitchen wall. Bryn had been abroad for the last six weeks, and he wasn't expected home for another fortnight. Joyfully, he abandoned the bicycle and ran to the open front door.

"Dad! You're back! Somehow I *knew* you would be. I dreamed about it last night, believe it or not. How's that for ESP?"

The silence of the house was strange and unexpected. Usually when he came home, his mother was pottering about, singing old Beatles songs to herself. This afternoon, there was nothing. He felt butterflies in his stomach, wondering if something might be amiss.

He shouted again, "Dad! Mum! Are either of you around?"

Nothing. They must be outside. He wandered into the garden, but he felt suddenly cold and his legs had begun to shake. The gate leading onto the cliff path was swinging open. The thought sprang to his mind. *It's better not to know. Things are never going to be the same again.* Yet he had to keep going, force himself to see whatever there was to be seen.

He peered over the edge of the cliff and saw, far below, a crumpled figure. His mother, spread out on the rocks like a broken puppet.

The days and weeks that followed were a blur in his memory. All Nic knew was that his father had come home and then disappeared. At first the police said they were seeking him in their inquiries in connection with the death of his wife. They never found him. Nic did not understand what had happened. Part of him did not want to understand. Nothing could bring his mother back to life. All he could hold on to was the belief that his father was innocent. Inconceivable that the devoted husband could have killed the woman who meant so much to him. He might have embroidered Arthur's battles and the search for the Grail, but when he told his wife he loved her, as he often did, it was no less than the truth. Nic had faith in that, a diamond-hard certainty that the family's life together had not been a lie.

From the day of the murder, he had suffered from insomnia. He was cared for by his aunt and uncle, who were childless. They and the doctors suggested a hundred so-called cures, but none of them worked for long. When he did sleep, one dream kept visiting time and again, like an old movie repeated endlessly on late-night television. He played the detective and discovered who had killed his mother. Having proved his father's innocence, he tracked the old man down and brought him out of hiding to reunite the family. When he woke up, the program changed. Everyone thought—he knew this to be true, although *no one,* not one single person, ever said it to his face—that his father had committed suicide after killing his wife. Probably he'd hurled himself into the sea after weighting his body down so that it could not be washed up again. The police said the case was not closed, but Nic knew they were sure about the identity of the culprit. He'd tried to talk to them himself, but they had been kind and sympathetic and not taken a blind bit of notice. How could he know more than they did?

Of course, once he was grown, he could always investigate for himself. Time without number he picked up the telephone to make the first call that would set him on the path to unravelling the knots. In his late teens, at university, as a trainee lawyer and after qualifying, he had said to himself that nothing was worse than not knowing. Self-deception: he needed to cling to the faith that he had. If he discovered the worst, he would lose more than sleep. The mystery of his mother's death and his father's disappearance were like the legend of the Questing

Beast—they were meant to tantalize, never to be solved.

Half way down the M1, on the way back to London, Nic's cell phone rang.

Fergus McHugh said, "About tomorrow. Will has confirmed you're to have the run of the place, and who am I to quibble with the senior partner? Especially in the light of today's news."

"What news?"

"Haven't you heard?"

"Surprise me."

"Only this. It was announced this morning that Ali Khan has been busy again. Keeping our commercial people out of mischief." A chuckle. "Thrust has taken over Huckerbys. They are your publishers, aren't they? I gather you have a two-book contract with them, and delivery on the next manuscript is seriously overdue. No problem. I'm sure Ali will make sure you have plenty of leeway. Have no fear. He has no intention of influencing editorial policy."

"Oh yeah?"

"Yeah." Fergus sounded pleased with himself. "Ali has always been a great believer in the integrity of the creative process. You'll love working for him. Love it. Two o'clock tomorrow, then?"

CHAPTER SIXTEEN

Scrolling down her customized daily legal update on the internet, Roxanne found her mind wandering. Over the past seven years she had tried to squeeze Grant Dennis out of her mind like water out of flannel. At first, numbed by the horror of all that had happened, she had made herself dizzy and weak from lack of eating. Later, as she grew stronger, the memories jostled back into her consciousness. She would wake screaming, the t-shirt she slept in damp with sweat, after his face loomed up in her nightmares. His handsome, mocking face, distorted by hatred and fear.

"Busy?" Ben asked. She hadn't even heard him walking into the room. "Glad to see you keeping up to date."

She nodded, said nothing. He tugged at the hairs sprouting from his right earlobe, as if they had provoked him to retribution. "You've made an excellent start. I'm delighted. Relieved, as well, frankly. I can say this, now that you've bedded in, so to speak. We obviously took a big chance on you."

"I want to make the most of it."

"I'm sure you do." He smiled, leaned a little closer to her. "If you ever need help, you will sing out, won't you, Roxanne?"

"Of course," she promised.

As he closed the door behind him, she returned to her computer. A thought that had stowed away in the back of her mind came to the surface. Might he be the rich boyfriend whom Chloe had dumped? If so, she didn't care. The time to worry about Ethics Man was when he thrust a love contract under her nose for signature. Not before.

She was wearing the clothes she'd worked in yesterday, apart from a fresh pair of borrowed pants, but although she felt grubby, she didn't care. She couldn't stop thinking about Chloe, wondering if tonight they would go home together again. They had dodged the subject on the way in from Greenwich. Roxanne wasn't sure what she wanted, couldn't guess whether Chloe was simply experimenting with her before taking up with yet another unsuitable boyfriend. For her part, Roxanne wasn't ready for another heavy relationship. Between them, Grant and Hilary had done this to her: she couldn't imagine ever sharing her life with someone else forever. Of either sex. She wasn't even sure whether her time with Hilary had made her aware of her real self and her most deeply rooted desires, or whether she'd merely taken a woman for her lover to help extinguish the memory of Grant Dennis.

The moment she caught sight of Chloe, she realized something was wrong. The other woman looked up as the door opened, and then cast a quick glance at her screen. Her face was scarlet, her lips compressed. Roxanne flinched. She had never seen Chloe so angry before.

"What is it?"

Chloe pointed at the screen. "I've been surfing the net. Doing a little more research. Better late than never, eh?"

Roxanne's mouth dried. She guessed what was coming next. "Oh yes?"

"You didn't tell me everything last night. Or this morning."

"Listen to me." Roxanne leaned over Chloe. She wouldn't lie down and allow herself to be trampled over. "I never pretended to be a saint."

"Amazing what you can find on the web. Especially when you want to look up a *cause célèbre*. There's a good deal of material about Cassandra Lee, you know."

"I've never checked."

"You should. If you have the stomach for it."

Roxanne took a step back and folded her arms. "I didn't lie to you."

In a muffled voice, Chloe said, "So you were just economical with the *actualité,* were you?"

"Something like that."

Tears were starting to drip down Chloe's cheeks. She wiped them away with a furious swipe of the hand. "I don't know how you can stand there and look so calm. After what happened."

"I'm not proud of it," Roxanne said quietly.

Chloe's gaze had been drawn back to the screen. She was like someone with a toothache, unable to resist the urge to probe the tender place. When she spoke again, she didn't seem to be talking to Roxanne, but rather to herself. She muttered, as if in wonder at her folly, "And to think that last night . . ."

"Yes?" Roxanne's own temper was rising. "Last night? What are you saying, Chloe? That if you'd known the whole story about Grant Dennis, you wouldn't have touched me with the proverbial?"

The tears were flowing freely now. "Oh, God knows what I'm saying."

Roxanne moved toward her, but Chloe put up a hand, as if warding away an evil spirit. "Just leave me alone, will you?"

"Chloe—"

"Did you hear what I said?" Her voice was choked with emotion. "Fucking well leave me alone! It's true—I would never have let you touch me if I'd known—if I'd known what you're capable of."

There was no reasoning with her. Roxanne went back to her room. She could hear Chloe through the wall, sobbing her heart out. She couldn't face the pious maunderings of the Thrust dignity-at-work policy, so she tried to immerse herself in other files, but the trick didn't come off. She found herself rereading the same paragraph three, four, five, half a dozen times. A single phrase glared at her from the text. *Breach of trust.*

At five o'clock, she heard Chloe's door slam. Easy to guess that she was meant to hear it. The door banged with such force that the partition dividing the rooms shook. She had to *do* something. Grabbing her bag, she raced down the corridor; never mind logging out of the computer system or tidying up the documents on her desk. Too late: the lift doors had closed, and Chloe was gone. Roxanne did not want to wait for the lift's return. Better to keep moving. She made for the staircase, crashing down the steps two at a time, as if the fire alarm was shrieking.

This wasn't like her. It wasn't cool to chase someone, the way Hilary had chased her. Besides, there was the risk of rejection, the risk of being hurt. For once, none of that seemed to matter. Strange. She had not known Chloe long, and the two of them didn't have much in common. Yet somehow Chloe had slipped under her skin. If she'd set out to seduce her, she couldn't have done a better job.

On the first-floor landing, Roxanne paused. *Had* Chloe set out to seduce her? No, she couldn't salve her pride so easily. Perhaps Chloe wasn't only angry because Roxanne hadn't told the whole story about Grant Dennis. Maybe, in part, she was lashing out because she was embarrassed and ashamed about what had happened between them.

Chloe could destroy her if she wanted to. All it would take was a word to Ben. Even if she did not want to be vindictive, she was emotional, someone who did things without thinking them through. It was dangerous to follow her, but Roxanne couldn't help herself. This was her old failing.

Roxanne hurried through the revolving doors and looked up

and down the Strand. Chloe was twenty meters away. She turned her head and saw Roxanne. Averting her gaze, she stumbled past a couple of passersby in the direction of Charing Cross.

"Chloe!"

Roxanne raced after her. Chloe quickened her pace, but soon Roxanne caught up. They were side by side in the middle of the rush-hour crowd. Roxanne was puffing hard at the sudden exertion, wishing she'd paid more attention to the yoga tape. She grabbed Chloe's arm, yanking it harder than she had intended to attract her gaze.

"We need to talk."

"Nothing to talk about," Chloe muttered. She pulled away. "Leave me alone."

"Just give me a chance to explain."

"I'm sorry, Roxanne."

Was it imagination, or did she detect a softening in Chloe's tone? No hint in her stony expression of a willingness to relent. Try again.

"If we can only have a conversation. Five minutes, that's all I ask. You know the case for the prosecution. What about listening to a plea in mitigation?"

Chloe pushed her hand through her hair. "Oh, I don't know."

"Five minutes, not a second more."

Chloe gazed skyward for a moment. "Okay."

"Shall we go to a bar? A café?"

"Not likely," Chloe said, her face a mask. "Let's sit out in St. James's Park. The world may pass by, but no one will bother to eavesdrop. And we don't want this to be overheard. Do we?"

Soon they were sitting next to each other in the park. The grass was parched and wouldn't stain their clothes, but Roxanne didn't care either way. Only that morning she had woken up with this woman's warm body next to hers. Already it seemed a lifetime away.

"So," Chloe said. "You're going to tell me your side of the story?"

"If you're willing to listen."

"I'm here, aren't I?"

"I didn't lie to you about the lead-up. If anything, I understated how vile it was. I felt like some weedy heiress in one of those nineteeth-century novels where the wicked uncle pens her up in the remote stately home. Except that I wasn't consumptive. I just had anorexia."

"Tell me about the fifteenth of December," Chloe murmured.

Roxanne winced. Her friend's research had been thorough. "He took me out for dinner. When I wouldn't eat, he got cross, and I fainted with the lack of food. There was a palaver in the restaurant. Grant hated being shown up in front of other people. He couldn't bear the thought that people might be pointing the finger at the man with the skinny girl who wasn't taking care of herself. He was furious, said I'd embarrassed him in public and I'd have to be punished."

"What did he do?"

No matter how she'd tried to blot it out, that night had haunted her for the past seven years. She could recall every moment. "We were in the parking lot, outside the restaurant. I'd had a couple of drinks, but my strength had gone. I had to lean on him for support. When he opened the trunk of his BMW, picked me up and put me inside, there was nothing I could do. Not even scream."

Chloe clutched at her throat. "Oh God."

"I thought I was going to lose my mind. The darkness was impenetrable. It was the most terrifying hour of my life."

Words couldn't describe it. However many times she relived that journey, she could never capture the smothering horror of it all. The way she retched whenever she thought of the sauce-coated duckling she had left untouched in the swanky restaurant. The taste of vomit on her tongue. And all the time, the question that didn't have a certain answer: *will he free me before I pass out again—or am I going to die here, alone and afraid in this black airless tomb?*

Grant had driven as if he meant to crash the car. He'd always had a lust for speed, but now the car careered along as if tonight he meant to break every last rule. The brakes howled as he spun round corners, and in the back Roxanne's head had banged against the trunk lid, bringing tears to her eyes. The trunk smelled of motor oil, and her legs were wedged against a set of tools whose sharp edges dug into her flesh. She was sure he hadn't taken the straight route home. He meant to squeeze the rage out of his system by taking her on a journey to hell.

"Torture," Chloe whispered.

"Oh yes, that's what it was. When he thought I'd had enough, he headed for home and let me out, but even then he wasn't finished with me. It was late, and he'd had a lot to drink. I didn't want him to touch me. I was on the verge of passing out, but he handcuffed me to the railings on the stairs. He was into bondage, always had been. Then he had sex with me, made me mimic the poses from those magazines sent by his pal, the Dutch porn king."

She paused for breath, recalling the steel cuffs cutting into her wrists, the sweaty smell of the man forcing his way into her, the stink of whiskey on his breath. The memory of her prayer to a God in whom she did not believe. *Please end it.*

"It wasn't so much the pain as the humiliation. There was nothing I could do. The man I'd been crazy about had turned into an animal. I remember closing my eyes while he was on top of me and wondering if I should kill myself after it was over. An overdose, perhaps, or putting a plastic bag over my head."

Chloe reached out and started stroking Roxanne's hand.

Gentle, rhythmic movements. Her fingers were long and cool. Roxanne didn't move.

"When he was finished, I wept long and hard. He unlocked the handcuffs and dried my tears, then he took me upstairs. Once he'd shown me who was boss, he could afford to be kind and gentle. He fetched a fresh bottle of Glenfiddich, poured himself a generous measure, and smoked a couple of cigarettes. I didn't say a word. I was too full of self-loathing. Even then, I made my decision. I wasn't going to destroy myself or let him destroy me. After a while he fell asleep. I can still picture him, lying there on the black sheets. He looked good naked, and he knew it."

Roxanne closed her eyes. She was back in the bedroom. It was warm and stuffy with the windows shut, and she could see his reflection in the mirrors on the walls and ceiling. Grant liked watching himself perform. For a moment she struggled to remember how she had once lusted after him. But all that belonged to the past. It was over.

"I had to make sure he would never hurt me again."

"But the method you chose . . ."

"I wanted to pay him back. I wanted him to—to experience agony. The way I had."

She'd found his matches, and as he slept, she'd picked up the bottle of Glenfiddich. With infinite care, she'd poured its contents over him. He'd groaned and shifted position on the bed, but he had not woken up. Dead to the world.

"You turned him into a torch." Chloe swallowed hard. "You doused him in whiskey, lit a match, and set fire to him."

"He didn't notice me. If I thought about it at all, I supposed the house would burn down, too, and that would end it for both of us. Our funeral pyre.

"The room had a balcony overlooking the garden, and he managed to get through the door in a sheet of flame. Outside it was pouring with rain, perhaps he thought that might give him a chance. So he threw himself off the balcony." Chloe's voice was hoarse. She was making a visible effort to repeat word for word what she had learned. "Everyone assumes he was aiming to land on the grass, but if so, he miscalculated. He landed on the York stone patio. A cruel sort of blessing. His head smashed to a squishy mess before he could burn to death.

"Don't ask me what I did next. I can never get the sequence straight in my head. At some point, I went into the bathroom and turned on the shower. I wanted to wash every part of me that he'd touched. Cleanse myself. Afterward, I sat down and wondered what to do. I suppose that in a muddled way, I must have thought at first that I might get away with it. Then it began to dawn on me that it wasn't so easy. Forensics are so complicated. I decided to run away. Not such a smart idea."

"You may not have been mad, but you certainly needed your head examined. Of course, you couldn't escape. From what I read, you'd never even passed a driving test."

Roxanne nodded. "I took his car and some money, but five miles away a police car flagged me down. I put my foot down, but they soon caught up with me. Defective tail light, of all things. As soon as they started asking me questions, I broke down and wept. Within ten minutes, they knew everything."

Chloe was staring at Roxanne, couldn't seem to take her eyes off her. Fascinated, yet repelled. Roxanne's flesh itched. She felt like a specimen on the dissecting table.

"Even then, there might have been a way out." Roxanne's voice was dreamy as she cast her mind back. "That's the thing about murder cases. You can say whatever you like about the dead and not be sued for slander. I could have come up with a cock-and-bull story. Only one problem."

"The video." Chloe's voice was trembling.

"You read about that, too? Yes, the video." Roxanne shook

her head. "I didn't know Grant as well as I thought I did. He'd concealed a video camera set up in the bedroom so that he could tape our greatest hits. All he managed was to create the evidence of a cold-blooded murder. Right up to the end, he screwed me." She shook her head. "Or should I say, he screwed Cassandra Lee."

Chloe was still looking at her, as if in a trance. "So you took your punishment."

"I hate what I did," Roxanne said. "The judge was right. No matter what I had been through, it was an act of wickedness. I didn't have to kill him, let alone—incinerate him. There was a price to pay and, God knows, I've been paying it every day since Grant died."

Chloe cradled her head in her hands. "Your timing was lousy. The Home Secretary was launching a campaign about personal morality the same week that the papers were stuffed with articles about what you had done. A young gold digger had leeched on to a rich businessman whose only crime was that he liked a pretty face. People said you were evil."

"I was crazy in those days. I've never denied it."

Chloe pulled a face. "Mad, not bad?"

Roxanne shrugged. "Plenty of discussion about that, both before the trial and in court. When it came to possible defenses, I was spoiled for choice. Self-defense, provocation, diminished responsibility. You name it. Trouble was, what I did to him was too dreadful to be a proportionate response to his behavior. That was counsel's opinion. There wasn't much evidence of provocation, only my word. People in the restaurant said that Grant had been solicitous. Witnesses said what a caring guy he was. The police even dug up an ex-girlfriend, someone I'd supplanted, to say he never harmed a hair on her head."

"I read about it. She said he was besotted with you from day one."

"Oh yes, it was a fine revenge. Everyone decided I was a prize bitch. I was sick. I still wasn't eating. Diminished responsibility was the best card I had, but I refused to play it. I'd done wrong and known it was wrong. In court I came across as a sullen cow. I couldn't take in that all this was happening to *me*. The judge and jury took against me, and the prosecution lawyer did his job perfectly. He was a good cross-examiner. I realized that even as I let him goad me into screaming at him. The judge rebuked me. My counsel put his head in his hands. I'd proved to everyone that I had a wicked temper. When I'd calmed down and realized it was too late to save myself, I contented myself with admiring his advocacy. I wondered what it must be like to be in total command of a brief, to have the facts at your fingertips, every argument marshaled to perfection. He convinced me of my own wickedness, and I threatened to sack my own lawyer if he didn't let me change my plea to guilty to murder."

"So you were sentenced to life."

"It was the *waiting* before I set him ablaze that did for me." Roxanne could not keep the bitterness out of her voice. "I picked my moment. I didn't strike out in the heat of the moment. That was unforgivable, so far as the prosecution and press were concerned. Unsporting. Killing a man when he was asleep and stark naked. Not playing the game."

There was a long pause before Chloe reached across and put her arm around Roxanne's shoulder.

Roxanne looked at the other woman. "Sorry. I've taken up more than five minutes of your time. Thank you for listening. You can run for it now."

Chloe tightened her grip and slowly shook her head from side to side.

They went for a meal to a Vietnamese restaurant on Wardour Street. The fates had tested them, and they had come through.

Roxanne was in the mood to listen, not talk, and so Chloe told her the story of her life, starting from her years as the youngest in a large family in Thanet. She'd always fantasized about working in a big city firm and marrying a millionaire, she said, giggling uncontrollably.

Roxanne said, "One more ambition bites the dust, eh?"

Suddenly Chloe was serious. "Was Hilary—your first time with a woman?"

Roxanne said softly, "Don't forget, I spent years inside a women's prison. Things—sometimes happened. Soon over and done with. For me, they meant nothing."

"Uh-huh." Chloe was taking care not to seem shocked. "And Hilary? She was your defense lawyer. How come you and she got together?"

"I told you, she was only an assistant when I was put inside. She'd turned to the law late after years as a social worker. I barely noticed her at the trial, I was in such a daze." Roxanne paused. She'd thought that she would never get over what had happened. Yet here she was, at liberty just seven years after Grant Dennis's death. "After she qualified, she joined another firm and got in touch. She told me she thought I'd suffered an injustice, that more could have been done to persuade me to plead diminished responsibility. The judge was biased, and the publicity didn't help. The jury should have been given better direction."

"It took ages to persuade you to challenge the verdict."

Roxanne shrugged. "Most of the time I was inside, I was doing my best to starve myself. I didn't have a handle on my life. One thing I could control was my weight. The first kindness Hilary did for me was to persuade me to start eating again. Next, she convinced me I should appeal my conviction. She kept saying I'd punished myself enough."

"And it worked."

"Yes, the wizened old appeal judges decided the conviction was unsound. They weren't ecstatic about it, any more than the tabloid hacks who'd helped to convict me in the first place, but what could they say? The press didn't want me suing for libel after I'd walked free with supposedly not a stain on my character. After I was released, Hilary asked me to move in with her. I said yes because I couldn't think what else to do. It took me long enough to get my head round the idea that I was not guilty in the eyes of the law."

"In the end, you dumped her," Chloe said.

"Ruthless bitch that I am."

"I didn't mean that!"

"It's the truth," Roxanne said, "whether you meant it or not. Without Hilary, I'd still be inside. Without Hilary, I'd never have rekindled my interest in the law. She really cares about justice. She made me care about it, too. Who knows? If she hadn't kept pointing out to me how much she'd done for me, I might never have wanted to escape from her."

"You don't believe that."

"Maybe not." Roxanne paused. "Ever read *Trilby*?"

Chloe's brow furrowed. "I thought it was a hat, not a book."

"No, no. Sort of a Victorian classic. I caught up on my education while I was inside. 'Specially my reading. It's a book about a model who is trained by this man Svengali to become a singer. He controls her. When he dies, she can't escape his spell. Her voice fails, and she ends up dead herself. Well, sometimes I think there was a parallel between poor Trilby and Cassandra Lee. Even with Grant Dennis gone, Cassandra simply couldn't make sense of being free. After the last few days, I'm not sure Roxanne Wake is any different."

"Hilary promised she wouldn't wreck the new start you've made."

"Who else would have sent the anonymous note, the press cutting?"

"You can't let her do this. You have to stand up for yourself."

"And how exactly do I manage that? Make a clean breast of everything to Will Janus? A preemptive strike before I'm outed? What do I say? 'I did something rather disagreeable as a young person, but it was a long time ago. Besides, the wretch is dead.' Call in Fergus McHugh for a bit of advice on good PR?"

"No," Chloe said quickly, "It wouldn't be a good idea to shout it from the rooftops. The fewer people who know about you and Grant Dennis, the better. Obviously."

Roxanne considered. "Maybe I should have a word with Ben Yarrow or Joel Anthony. They took me on. Perhaps I owe it to them."

"No, don't make a snap decision. What you need is a bit of space. A chance to make your way without people looking over your shoulder. Don't worry about me. I'll tell no one. You can depend on it."

Roxanne leaned forward and gripped the other woman's hand. "I do depend on it, Chloe. Believe me, I do."

Later, they wandered drunkenly back to Charing Cross and caught a train to Greenwich. Neither of them said much. There did not seem to be any need. Soon they were together in Chloe's bed. It wasn't like any lovemaking that Roxanne had known before. Chloe was wild; there were no longer any taboos. Roxanne, engulfed, found herself helpless, unable to do anything more than surrender.

Afterward, Chloe propped herself up on her elbows and looked into Roxanne's eyes. "Tell me about it. The murder, I mean."

"I told you." Roxanne was drenched with sweat, but suddenly she felt cold.

191

"No, that's not what I mean. Not a rehash of the facts. Not what I read on the screen. What I want to know is how you *felt.*"

Roxanne closed her eyes. "Why? Why would anyone want to know?"

"Because," Chloe moistened her lips, "I need to understand. It's important to me. I want to have some clue about what went through your mind."

"My mind was a mess." A pause. "Besides, that was Cassandra Lee. I'm Roxanne Wake."

"Oh, darling, of course you are." Chloe kissed her on the lips. A chaste kiss, as if the last hour had not happened. "But that's not the point. Cassandra is part of you, deep down inside. We are who we are. So I want to get to know Cassandra as well as Roxanne. Share in the bad times as well as the good. Does that make sense?"

"Not really."

Chloe let out a sigh. "So you won't tell me any more?"

"Not won't. Can't."

"Oh, all right." Chloe didn't disguise the hurt in her voice. She closed her eyes again and edged away a little.

Roxanne kissed the thick red hair. "I'm sorry, darling."

Chloe buried her face in the pillow. "Doesn't matter."

It did matter, of course, and Roxanne knew it. She stretched out, her hair brushing against the headboard. She wanted to tell her lover everything. It was an instinct that she had not experienced before. Yet she did not trust herself to be honest. Even now, even after their reconciliation in Soho, it would be so easy to blow the whole thing apart. It could happen, it could easily happen. If Roxanne described what she recalled, as she saw Grant Dennis on fire, listened to his screaming. The dizzying sense of being in complete control. She had seduced a man and then destroyed him. She had played God, wielded the power of life and death. And, for a few moments before sanity returned, she had exulted in it.

CHAPTER SEVENTEEN

Nic watched the day break from Dylan's bedroom window. Even if he'd never suffered insomnia in his life, he would have found it too hot to sleep. He opened the window wider and stood naked at it, listening to the slap of water against the wharf. The tide was flowing out, leaving stones and bits of brick on the shoreline. When he'd first lived in the houseboat, he'd been startled by the speed with which the tide turned. He'd never been so aware of the phases of the moon, of the way in which the world worked.

"The estate agent never mentioned the bodies," Dylan had once complained. Murder victims and suicides alike washed up on what he liked to call his private beach. "Funny thing, their arms are always spread out, like they were modeling for a crucifixion. Talk about pollution. They all have bits of polystyrene in their hair. I have this neighbor. He compares them to Ophelia with weeds and flowers in her tresses. Pretentious, or what?"

Mail tumbled through the letter box. Most was junk, not worth adding to the pile awaiting onward transmission to Dylan's family, but one envelope caught his eye. A phone bill. On impulse, he tore it open and scanned the list of itemized calls. Nothing with an Oxford code, but a dozen times Dylan had rung the same cell phone, and almost every time he'd been on the phone for less than a minute. Someone giving him the brush-off?

Nic dialed and held his breath.

"Hello? Hello?"

A woman's voice. Edgy, as if she'd been waiting for his call, but expecting bad news.

"Is that Jazz?"

A pause. "Who is this?"

Yes. He'd guessed right. Her tone was suspicious. On guard.

"My name's Nic Gabriel. Dylan Rees told me about you."

He could hear the intake of breath. She was scared, no question. Hissing her question down the line.

"For Christ's sake, what is this? What are you trying to do to me?"

"Can we talk? You—"

The line went dead, and he redialed. A polite disembodied voice told him the phone was switched off. "Please try later."

Every ten minutes for the next couple of hours he tried again, but Jazz wasn't answering.

"Please try later. Please try later."

"Shit, shit, *shit.*"

He stomped around the kitchen, furious with himself. For a few seconds he'd had the chance to win her trust, to persuade her to tell him what she'd told Dylan. And he'd blown it.

"Have you visited Avalon Buildings before, Mr. Gabriel? Here is your visitor badge. Please read the safety and fire instructions for your security and comfort. May we offer you a drink? Caffe latte? It's a pleasure. Would you like to take a seat? Fergus McHugh will be with you shortly."

The receptionist's smile made him wish he'd remembered his Ray-Bans. She chanted the welcome refrain with so much conviction that he could imagine her being hurt if he failed to take note of where the emergency exits were situated on each floor. She and her colleague at the desk had flawless skins and voices like the chorus singers fluting in the background. Graduates of intensive training at Stepford.

The sun was burning high above the Strand, but inside the lobby the air was cool and cleansed of all impurities. The coffee smelled rich and tasted mild. In the background, Noel Harrison sang about the windmills of your mind.

Nic picked up a newspaper. Headlines warned of a big demonstration planned for the day after tomorrow. Protesters were threatening to bring London to a halt. They wanted justice for the people. Whatever justice was. Whoever the people were. Politicians kept saying the way to protest was through the ballot box, priests appealed for calm, pundits recalled student riots of the sixties. All police leave had been canceled.

"Strange, very strange," Fergus McHugh said.

Nic stood up and tossed the paper onto the table. As they shook hands, Fergus nodded at the photo-spread on the open double page. Pictures from the protests on the day that Dylan had died. Men and women in balaclavas, cops in riot gear, the home secretary nibbling at his fountain pen.

"These people may have a legitimate argument, but breaking the law isn't the answer. Anyway, good to see you here. Will is delighted you've come to have a look at us."

"He's not seen what I'm going to write yet."

Fergus beamed. "We're in your hands."

"And I'm in Ali Khan's. So I have something in common with the partners of Creed. We're all in hock to him."

Fergus frowned. "He's a good client, that's all."

"I ran a few checks. He owns Avalon Buildings, doesn't he? I suppose the firm took it on a cheap lease. He's your paymaster, isn't he?"

A shrug. "Someone has to be. Now, let's look in on Will before he becomes even more snowed under. He took a call from Downing Street this morning. I'm not at liberty to tell you more, sadly. Let's just say that the client base keeps expanding. And please be nice about the Kandinskys in the board room."

Fergus had the knack of seeming to impart confidences without giving anything away. It was not so much what he said as the way he said it. A grimace, a shrug, a glance toward the heavens, all were part of his stock-in-trade. Nic remembered his father's tales about Merlin: seer, shaman, the wise man who advised the king. The magician who dwelt in the shadows yet who kept so close to the throne that jealous enemies called him the devil's son.

Soon they were on the penthouse floor. Nic glanced through an open door into a room containing a vast circular table. The room was smaller than St. Paul's Cathedral and the decor didn't quite compare with the Sistine Chapel, but the atmosphere was of calm and contemplation, far from the hurly-burly in the world below. Each wall was festooned with framed whorls, blots, and squiggles. At the far end of the room, sliding glass doors opened onto an outside sitting area and roof garden overlooking the Thames.

"The boardroom," Fergus said. "Where our partners meet."

"The fellowship of the round table," Nic said softly. A phrase his father had liked to roll off his tongue.

Fergus gestured outside. The centerpiece of the roof garden was a tall and tangled work in iron. "It's an original, created by our sculptor-in-residence. Inspired by Islamic calligraphy and saplings in Vermont."

"Yeah, I should have guessed."

Fergus gave a sly grin. "Will likes it very much. Come and say hello."

They moved next door, and Will Janus bounded forward from behind his desk like an eager Labrador. For a moment Nic thought he might have his face licked.

"Welcome, welcome. Does coming here make you pine for

the days when you were in practice? You'd like to record our chat, I presume? Super. Fergus will tape us as well, if you don't mind. We don't want any misunderstandings, do we?"

The bonhomie was like chloroform. Will suggested that since the weather was so heavenly, the three of them might sit outside. They returned to the boardroom, and Fergus opened the sliding doors. Even before they stepped outside, it was as if they were in the open, with the room itself transformed into a shady part of the terrace. Recliners were arranged between the potted plants and the three of them sat out in the sun, with trailing fronds from the hanging baskets tickling the backs of their heads. Eden in the sky.

Nic asked about the firm, and Will talked. The firm had come a long way in a few years, but there was still so much to do. At last the law of England and Wales was shaking off the shackles of precedent, following the European philosophy that the *purpose* of laws was paramount, so that justice was done in each and every case. The Internet was transforming the delivery of legal services, offering the firm plenty of scope for eye-catching initiatives. Through the innovative use of technology, Creed's clients would have access to the best advice twenty-four hours a day, three hundred and sixty-five days a year. But at the end of the day, the law was not about virtual reality but about real people. Flesh and blood. Human beings, with all their imperfections. People, Will reminded Nic, like you and me.

At last Nic had the chance to put his second question. "You weren't the most senior lawyer in the partnership after Matthew Creed. How was it that you took over when he died so suddenly?"

Will's expression wrinkled into earnestness, tinged with modesty. He was in his shirtsleeves, his preferred style of dress, businesslike yet easy-going. He spread his arms, palms open, nothing to hide. "You tell me, Nic. It was just something that happened, seemed to gain a kind of momentum of its own. When Matt was taken from us, one or two people came to see me. We'd made so much progress, everyone was anxious that we shouldn't skip a beat."

"Was that peaceful? You overtook Ben Yarrow in the pecking order."

"It was very peaceful, actually." Will gave a lucky-me smile. "I couldn't have asked for stronger support. I lean on Ben. You can quote me on that."

"What about Bradley Hurst?"

Fergus's grimace said *so what about Bradley Hurst?* Will shook his head sadly. "Bradley was Bradley. We miss him a lot. He was the salt of the earth. One of a kind."

"A bit of a dinosaur, surely?"

"Not a bit of it!" Will dismissed the suggestion with a flip of the hand, as if wafting away an importunate mosquito. "He'd been in the trenches. Served his time, paid his dues. His heart was in the right place."

"Ah." Nic folded his arms. "Past his sell-by date, then."

"You're disappointing me," Will said sadly. "There's no cause for cynicism. They don't make lawyers like Bradley anymore, you know."

A choking noise. Fergus, stifling a giggle.

Ben Yarrow said pleasantly, "I never like to speak ill of the dead."

Nic said, "But?"

Ben shrugged. He'd made it obvious from the start that he was only seeing Nic to humor Will's spin doctor. "Bradley was a maverick. When Will took over, he expected all the partners to row in the same direction. Bradley didn't like to toe the partnership line."

"Bradley's heart was in the right place, Will said."

"Faint praise, don't you think?" Ben pulled his mustache so

hard that Nic half-expected him to pull a chunk of hair out by the roots. "No point in beating about the bush. Bradley was fine when it came to thrashing out deals with shop stewards in smoke-filled rooms. Ask him to put a case together on a technical point of European law, and it was something else. He had to rely on sidekicks deviling for him. Smart young chaps like Joel Anthony. They soon saw through him, realized the simple truth. Poor old Bradley was no rocket scientist."

"Tell me about Matthew Creed. I heard that he fell asleep in a sauna after he'd been drinking. It made me wonder."

Ben's head jerked as if on a string. "What did you wonder?"

"If he'd spent the evening with a friend, having a few beers. I wonder if his drinking companion knew he was going to Paradise. Why didn't he say something? Everyone knows it's dangerous, taking a sauna if you're drunk."

"I don't know what you're talking about."

"The grapevine reckons you might have succeeded him."

"Will was an outstanding candidate."

And you hate his guts. "What if Will moved on? Went into television, say? Would you throw your hat into the ring then?"

"The question doesn't arise. Will isn't going anywhere."

"Learned anything of interest?" Joel Anthony asked. Sunlight streamed through the window, making his ear stud twinkle.

Nic took a seat. "When we talked at the Cafe Royal, you gave me a lot of useful information. To be frank, much more than I would have expected. One snag, though. You hinted that I ought to keep digging. But you refused point-blank to tell me what to dig for."

Joel spread his arms. "Maybe your guess is as good as mine."

"So you're not giving me any clues?"

Joel considered his lovely fingernails. He seemed to be trying to make up his mind. Suddenly the door opened behind Nic, and Joel's head jerked up. Nic turned and found himself staring into a woman's face. A beautiful face, and a face he recognized, yet from some other context. A face he associated—a stab of shock at the realization—with crime.

She held his gaze for a moment. He saw fear creeping into her eyes. She was smart. She could tell he'd recognized her—and for some reason, that scared her.

"Sorry. Bad time. Sorry." She handed Joel a document, stumbling over her words. "I didn't want to interrupt. I'll—I'll come back later."

Within a moment, she had gone. Joel blinked and then wiggled his eyebrows in a comical fashion. "Do you usually have this effect on pretty women? What's your secret?"

"If she finds me irresistible, she has a funny way of showing it."

Joel grinned. "Starstruck, maybe. Perhaps Roxanne has read your book. I had the impression she recognized you."

"Who exactly is she?"

"She joined us recently from a legal aid center. Very clever. It's a surprise that she's never qualified."

"What else can you tell me about her?"

"I don't think she's married, if that matters."

Joel gave him a knowing wink. It was custom and practice, and accorded with precedent, for lawyers to sleep with each other. That had been a tradition long before women entering the profession outnumbered the men. The divorce rate for lawyers was high, but never mind: if a first marriage didn't work out, there were always plenty of other lawyers in an eligible income bracket. Dylan used to say Nic didn't know what he was missing, but the point was that he did. When he wondered out loud why lawyers fell for each other when they knew, none better, that all the love talk was rhetorical bullshit, Dylan shook his head and told him not to worry: "At least if two lawyers are in a relationship, then for once they're not screwing the rest of us."

"I don't want to shag her," Nic said. "I'm just curious."

"Oh yeah?" Joel chuckled. "Sorry, can't help. She was one of Ben's discoveries. He was on the other side of a tribunal case she was conducting. He came back and said he'd met a paralegal who was as smart as a whip. Rapturous praise, from Ben. He's usually too busy sticking the stiletto in between his opponents' shoulder blades."

"And if the opponent looks like Roxanne?"

Joel chortled. He might have been sixteen years old. "I'm sure Ben would never allow himself to be influenced by inappropriate considerations. Good young advocates are hard to find, whatever they look like. I must admit she impressed me at the interview. She didn't give much away about herself, but she obviously knew her stuff and was burning to make a success of her career."

"So you made her an offer?"

"One a paralegal in an advice center could scarcely refuse. Not that her CV mattered. We don't tolerate elitism here."

Nic couldn't help saying, "Even though most of the partners are Balliol men and African-Caribbean workers are underrepresented everywhere except on the cleaners' night shift?"

Joel reddened. "Even in the most enlightened firms, change takes time."

Nic left it there. Sooner or later it would come back to him, who the woman was and why she was afraid of him. For the first time since Dylan's murder, all the stuff about the weird deaths seemed trivial in comparison to the puzzle of Roxanne Wake.

By the time Nic had finished, it was after six. His head had begun to ache. It was time to get a bit of air. As he approached the lift, he saw Roxanne Wake and his heart skipped a beat. She was already inside, homeward bound. She caught his eye, and her cheeks reddened.

The guilt reddening her cheeks as the doors closed was enough to prod his memory. It all came back to him now. He would have recognized her much sooner, if she hadn't taken the trouble to alter her looks. She could change the cut and color of her hair more easily than those high cheekbones.

He'd followed her case in the papers, along with millions of others. She was the woman who had doused her boyfriend in whiskey and then set fire to him. She'd been rescued from prison by a stubborn lawyer who had taken her case to the Court of Appeal. She was—now, what was the name? Yes, of course. Cassandra Lee.

CHAPTER EIGHTEEN

When Roxanne dreamed, it wasn't Grant Dennis's face that filled her mind, but Chloe's. After they woke, Chloe gave her a lingering kiss, as if to say that all was forgiven. Roxanne reached for Chloe's hand and held it until the radio alarm switched on, greeting them with news of another scorching day and the prospect of record temperatures in the city.

They took a cooling shower together before setting off for work. Chloe's idea. Roxanne felt light-headed. The previous night she had drunk too much champagne and hadn't had enough sleep. Her limbs ached. As she soaped Chloe's bony shoulders, allowed her lover to tip her head back and shampoo and wash her hair, her mind was drained at last of the fears that had haunted her since her first day at Avalon Buildings. She had found someone she could trust.

"You know, it's funny," Chloe said as they toweled each other dry. "We've only just got together, and yet I feel I understand you better than I've understood anyone. Maybe better than you understand yourself. Does that sound stupid?"

"It sounds wonderful," Roxanne said. "But I'm not sure even I understand myself at all."

This wasn't like life with Hilary. Hilary had fought for her, but in the end the relationship had become a second prison. Hilary had fallen for Cassandra Lee, whereas Roxanne Wake was the one Chloe cared for. Chloe wanted her to relish freedom. As they gulped down coffee in the tiny kitchen, Roxanne surrendered to the urge to talk about this, but it was difficult to find the right words. Soon Chloe was shaking her head.

"That's where you're wrong. You see Cassandra and Roxanne as different people. They aren't. They are just two different sides of you."

She tried to laugh it off. "I'm not sure that's what I like to hear."

"Listen." Chloe's voice dropped, as persuasive as any trial advocate's. "You'll never be happy until you stop being ashamed of the past. Face up to it, and be proud. You were Grant Dennis's victim, not the other way round. No one can blame you for trying to reclaim your own life."

"Plenty of people blamed me."

"Not me, not now I've heard the whole story. At first I was shocked, but you did what you had to do, that's all. I'm proud of you."

Proud of a murderer? Roxanne let it go. She didn't want another argument, one she couldn't win. Thank God Chloe could not see into Cassandra's head, could not imagine the buzz that killing Grant had given her. Already she was falling into the same old trap, keeping yet another secret. If she was not to scare Chloe off, there was little choice.

On the crowded train, they stood next to each other, back to back. Chloe was wearing a summer dress, thin as gauze, and Roxanne felt her lover's buttocks rubbing against hers in a determined rhythm.

She'd borrowed a cotton top and trousers from Chloe, and although they didn't fit well, Roxanne didn't care. They were late for work, but she didn't mind that either. The job no longer seemed to matter so much. She said something of the sort as they fought their way through the crowd at Charing Cross and was taken aback by Chloe's reaction. She stopped short and seized Roxanne by the wrist, almost causing her to lose her footing.

"Of course the job matters. More than anything." Her voice rang out through the din from the passersby and the metallic drone of the departure announcements. "This is what you've worked for, dreamed of. At Creed, you're accepted for yourself. Everything you ever wanted is within your grasp. It mustn't be ruined for you. It *mustn't* happen."

"But—"

The concourse was a blur of tired faces. Only Chloe's seemed alive. Her brown eyes bored into Roxanne's. "Never mind what may have happened years ago. You've started again. I won't let you give up on this. Not me. Not the job. Not anything."

Chloe squeezed her wrist so hard that it hurt, then released her grip. They gazed at each other in silence, oblivious to sharp elbows and the people jostling past.

They raced down the Strand and into reception together. Before long, if things carried on like this, people at the office would realize that the two of them were involved. So what? No one would mind about the sexual orientation of two junior members of the staff. Creed's equal opportunities policy preached sympathy and understanding and made it clear that the partners would not tolerate any hint of discrimination or harassment.

For the first time since Roxanne's arrival, her work seemed tame. The redundancy files needed tidying up. Millions of pounds were at stake, and hundreds of jobs, but Roxanne was beginning to believe that in each case the outcome was preordained. Creed's clients would win, must win, because that was what they paid for. The unions might huff and puff, rival law firms would be allowed to portray a face-saving settlement to their clients as a victory for common sense, but the bottom line was always the same. Money talked. People with money bought the best advice and made it pay. All that had happened at Creed was that those who held the purse strings were no longer those whom the firm had been created to serve all those years ago. Nothing stayed the same forever. One had to move on.

During the afternoon, Joel rang and asked her for an update on the Thrust staff handbook.

"Would you like a report from me now?"

"Give me five minutes."

She walked to Joel's office and pushed open the door. Someone else was in there, a man she'd never seen before. He turned and looked straight at her. She saw the dawning look in his eyes and felt her gorge rise. For a moment she thought she was going to throw up. She stammered something and escaped. Hardly daring to breathe, she stumbled back to her own office and shut herself in, taking deep gulps of air. One thing was for certain. Somehow the man had recognized her. He knew she was Cassandra Lee.

A couple of minutes later, Chloe came in, carrying a cup of coffee. "Thought you might like a drink. It's—hey, what's up? You look as though you've seen a ghost."

"There's someone here," Roxanne said. Her breath was coming in little gasps. "He was in Joel's room just now. He's maybe thirty. Fair hair, black eyebrows. I'm sure he knows who I am. I mean, who I really am."

"Are you serious?" Chloe stared at her. "Okay, you're serious. He's with Joel, you say? Jesus. Haven't you asked the girls at reception who he is? All right, leave this to me."

"What are you going to do?" Roxanne had worked long and hard at being strong. She found it strange to be sitting behind a desk with her head in her hands while Chloe took charge.

"Find out this man's name, of course. Who he is, what he's

doing here. We have to know the situation we're dealing with here, right?"

"I suppose so." She hated the tremble in her voice.

"I'm sure so." Chloe leaned over the desk and stroked the back of Roxanne's hand. "Look, I'll be discreet. Promise. I can be very subtle. People don't realize. Let me ask one or two questions, that's all I mean to do. Then I'll report back to you. Okay?"

Roxanne nodded, hardly trusting herself to speak.

"Don't worry. We'll sort this out. One way or another. Nothing's going to mess up your career, I swear."

Roxanne felt Chloe's nails dig suddenly into her flesh, and for a moment it was as if Chloe were the single-minded one, Chloe the woman with murder on her mind.

"Chloe, we must be careful."

"Trust me."

Roxanne nodded. She did, she had no choice.

Twenty minutes later, Chloe returned. Her features were set in a somber expression, as if she were visiting a patient in a hospital ward and the doctor had taken her aside to break bad news. She moistened her lips, a nervous gesture suggesting uncertainty about how much of the truth she believed it safe to reveal.

"I found out who he is. Ben and Fergus McHugh were discussing him at the coffee machine, so I did a bit of eavesdropping. His name is Nic Gabriel. He's a writer."

Roxanne swiveled on her chair, soaking up the information. She hadn't been able to touch her work since their last conversation. The screensaver was up on her computer screen, black letters flitting across a red background. *Roxanne Wake, Roxanne Wake, Roxanne Wake.*

"What does he write?"

"For a start, a book. Now my memory's been jogged, I think

I've seen it in the shops. Apparently it was a number-one best seller."

"What was it about?"

Chloe bit her lip. "A murder case."

Roxanne closed her eyes. "Oh fuck."

"Hush, hush," Chloe said softly. She might have been a mother comforting a small child. "It may not be as bad as you think. The book was about Doctor Crippen. Not exactly topical, huh? That's the good news."

"And the bad news?"

"I'm not sure it's a great idea to tell you this, but you'll find out anyway sooner or later. Gabriel is supposed to be an expert on crime. Someone who likes to reexamine old trials and come up with ideas the authorities missed at the first time of asking."

Roxanne let the news sink in. Ibrahim used to say that it was a mistake to react too soon to fresh information. One should always weigh it, test it, make the sort of dispassionate judgement lawyers were supposed to be good at and yet which so often seemed elusive.

"I don't want you to panic," Chloe said. "There's no need. Honestly, there isn't. This could be just an amazing coincidence. The Crippen case was different, wasn't it? Old stuff. The people are all dead and buried. What—what happened with you, there's no comparison. I can't believe this man would ever want to write it up."

She meant to be helpful, but her words of consolation troubled Roxanne more than anything else she had said. There was no hiding the truth. Chloe was afraid for her. The death of Grant Dennis would always be a *cause célèbre*. It had everything: money, sex, and savage violence. No wonder the media had lapped it up. A skilled writer could bring it all back to life. He could reinterpret past events with the benefit of hindsight, coupled perhaps with a bit of poetic license. There was a book in it, for sure. His publishers would make a splash. Press interviews, radio, television. He might sell the rights to a film company.

Even in the air-conditioned sanctuary of her room, Roxanne felt hot and sticky. The borrowed top was itchy and uncomfortable.

"Suppose he's known about me for some time. Suppose it wasn't Hilary who sent me the note, the press cutting?"

Chloe came round the desk and took Roxanne's hands in hers. "Darling, it's going to be all right. I promise."

Someone knocked on the door, and Chloe sprang away as if she'd received an electric shock. Glancing up, Roxanne saw the gnome-like shadow of Ben Yarrow through the narrow glass pane in the center of the door. He didn't usually knock. She guessed he'd glanced in and seen Chloe comforting her. All at once, everything was falling apart.

The door opened. "Is something wrong?" Ben asked. "If you could spare me a minute, Roxanne, I have a client who needs advice on a new dress code policy. Sorry to interrupt."

He couldn't quite keep the mockery out of his voice. Roxanne knew then that she'd been right. He'd seen Chloe holding her hands. The sight seemed to have put him in an excellent humor. Perhaps it would make him feel better about Chloe rebuffing his advances. Now he could put it down to her being a lesbian rather than any lack of charisma on his part.

"Roxanne's feeling a bit off color," Chloe said. "Must be the heat. I was saying, she ought to take it easy."

Ben stroked his mustache as he considered this. "Of course, you're right. This weather is taking a toll on all of us." He treated Roxanne to a philanthropic smile. "Forget about the dress code. Go home if you need to. Recharge the batteries. You've taken a lot on already, considering that you're acclimatizing to a different way of working. Don't overdo it."

Roxanne promised that she would soon be fine. After he'd gone, she turned to Chloe and said, "Thanks. I don't know what I'd do without you."

"You don't need to be without me," Chloe said simply. "I'm here for you, Roxanne. That's what friends are for. I won't let Nic Gabriel destroy you."

"But how can you stop him?"

"I'll think of something," Chloe said. She moved toward the door. "Are you coming back to mine, tonight?"

"I need to get a few more oddments. I can't keep borrowing from you."

"We can buy them after work. Retail therapy, eh?"

Roxanne mustered a smile and nodded. But she knew that it would take more than a little shopping to take her mind off Nic Gabriel.

They arranged to meet at six-thirty in Covent Garden. Roxanne hauled herself away from her desk and made her way to the lift, she pressed for the ground floor, and she heard footsteps coming down the corridor. They quickened in pace, and Nic Gabriel appeared round the corner. When he saw her, he paused in mid-stride. She ground her teeth. She would not surrender to panic. Lifting her chin, she looked straight at him. Their eyes locked for a few moments as the doors closed, and then his pale face finally vanished from view. She was on her way down.

Her breath came in short jerky gasps. Lucky she was alone in the lift; anyone seeing her would have thought she was having a seizure. Yet she wasn't ill, simply shocked. This time she was sure she had seen a strange light in his eyes. Something she remembered from the day when she first met Grant Dennis. The sight of her had excited Nic Gabriel: somehow she knew it. She was sure that he wasn't turned on by her looks, but by the realization that she was at his mercy.

She blundered along the pavement, uncertain whether she was heading in the right direction, passing shops which sold maps and jewelery, clothes and kitchenware, fitness equipment and books. She halted and retraced her steps. A branch of Waterstones. She could not help going inside and searching out the true crime section. A row of shelves that, until now, she would never have gone near.

The titles on the spines, picked out in gaudy lettering on a background of black, were enough to set her teeth on edge. *Deadly Children, Inside the Brain of Ian Brady, A History of Unusual Executions.* She pulled one from the shelf. It promised hitherto unseen illustrations. Snapshots of decomposed bodies and bloodstained weapons. A rare photograph of a hooded murderer strapped into the electric chair. Or "Old Smokey" as, the caption said, the device was affectionately known.

This is my world, she thought as she stuffed the book back in its place. I belong in a freak show, just as much as bearded ladies and elephant men. My place is with the killers and the slain, trapped between the pages of a finger-marked paperback, ready to be gloated over by the innocent reading public. This is where Nic Gabriel will pigeonhole me, and I shall never escape. I may not meet the same fate as Crippen, Ruth Ellis, or Hanratty, but the Grant Dennis murder will be crawled over for fresh clues for as long as I live. Feminists will use my name as shorthand for the oppression of my sex. Armchair Freuds will speculate about my state of mind when I killed Grant: bad, mad, or simply sad?

Suddenly she saw the name of Nic Gabriel. It was like a slap on the cheek, knocking all the melodrama and self-indulgence out of her. She was burning with curiosity as she lifted the book. The artwork was subdued. This wasn't meant to be crime-as-porn, but a serious piece of writing. The quotes on the front were lavish in their praise of the author's insight. The *Times*

Literary Supplement raved about the way Nic Gabriel had woven familiar material into a new and striking fabric. The *Literary Review* said that he made Crippen seem like one of us: a man defeated not by his own evil act, but by the vagaries of fate.

On the back cover was a black and white photograph of the man she had confronted twice that day. He was staring over his shoulder, as though he had heard someone call his name at a time when he thought himself to be alone. The lines of his face were straight, but she did not find them cruel. That might have been easier to cope with than what she saw in the picture, what disturbed her so much that it made her clutch at a shelf for support. She saw a man on an endless quest, a man who would never give it up, whatever the cost.

Moistening her lips, she began to turn the pages. As she read, she was startled to find herself appreciating the limpidity of the prose, the bleak sympathy with which the author traced his subject's fate. Other shoppers passed to and fro, but she paid them no heed. She was hypnotized by the picture painted of the timid little American who fell for the girl who worked in his office. Perhaps it was true that he had not meant to murder his wife and that the prosecution case was built upon sand.

"So that's his angle," she murmured to herself. "I may end up not a monster but another victim."

Scarcely a morsel of comfort. So Gabriel was a serious writer, not a peep-show merchant, but in a way that made things worse. He wouldn't focus on what she had done, she guessed, but on how she had felt. He would rob her of the last shreds of self-protection. Even in the darkest days, when she had felt like a beast in a zoo, she had at least been able to conceal her thoughts. She had talked to psychiatrists, chaplains, doctors, lawyers, a hundred and one experts in hearts and minds, but not one of them had penetrated her defenses. She'd cut adrift from the rest of the world while she'd starved herself in a muddled attempt to find a kind of peace. Now she was fit and free, she was easy prey for Nic Gabriel.

He wanted to speak to her; she had read that in his face before the lift doors closed. He was fascinated, not repelled, and she guessed that he was already planning an approach to her. She wondered what he would say, how he would sell it to her. The prospect of collaboration, perhaps; a share in the proceeds. Distinguished writers did that sometimes. They made deals with murderers, all in the interest of understanding the evil that men do. Men and women, rather.

"How long are you going to stand there, putting yourself through hell?"

Roxanne looked up and saw Chloe on the other side of a table stacked high with new paperbacks. She showed her the cover of the book. "Nic Gabriel."

"Uh-huh. I've been watching you for ages. I thought I'd do a bit of window-shopping before we met, then I caught sight of you coming in here. Honestly, you looked as though you were in a world of your own. If I didn't know better, I'd swear you were on something. I followed you, saw you checking the plan of the shop, scouring everywhere for his book. I guessed what you were after right away. I've worked out what you're like, Roxanne. You simply can't stop punishing yourself."

"It's a dirty job, but someone has to do it."

"Let's go home. We need to talk."

"Wait a minute." Roxanne fiddled in her bag, searching for her purse. "I need to make a purchase."

"Oh, Roxanne." There was no mistaking the alarm in Chloe's eyes. "Don't buy the book. Please. Don't let him do this to you."

"Don't you see?" Roxanne asked. "If I'm to look after myself, I need to know what I'm up against."

"I'm not with you."

"I've decided that you're right," Roxanne said. "I can't give everything up and run away. Even if I did, this man Gabriel would track me down anyway. It's his will against mine."

Chloe's eyes had begun to gleam. "You mean . . ."

"I mean," Roxanne said, "that Nic Gabriel is never going to write about me. I won't let it happen."

They were lying on the rug in the Leytonstone flat, Roxanne stroking Chloe's breasts. As soon as they had arrived back home, they had undressed each other and made love hungrily. Afterward, they sent for a takeout and polished off a couple of bottles of wine before making love again, slowly this time, luxuriating in the intimacy.

Chloe traced a finger along her thigh, the tip of the nail scraping against the skin. "Roxanne, you're gorgeous. I'm not the only one who thinks so. Chances are, Nic Gabriel wants to screw you. Any normal man would."

"That's crazy."

"It's the truth. You know it, I know it. Why pretend? You're so gorgeous, I can hardly believe we've finished up in bed together. I bet Gabriel would do anything to swap places with me. He's not married, and he's a bit of a hunk himself. Face it, Roxanne, this is complicated. I bet he fancies the pants off you."

A few minutes passed, with no sound but Chloe's sighing whenever Roxanne's fingertips touched her nipples. Eventually Roxanne said, "You're not jealous, are you?"

After a pause, Chloe said, "So what if I am, a bit?"

"No need."

"Easy for you to say."

"It's true. This man scares the shit out of me. I'm not likely to drag him off to bed, am I?"

"That's the recommended course, when someone sexy turns your life upside down."

"I don't find him sexy."

Chloe hauled herself into a sitting position. "You bloody liar."

"You know what I mean. I'm serious. He terrifies the living daylights out of me. I wish he'd go to hell. I wish he didn't exist."

Chloe caught her breath. Her eyes were wide as she looked down at Roxanne. "Oh God, darling," she said. "Don't even think about that."

Chapter Nineteen

Nic walked through the door of the house in Narrow Court and dropped his briefcase on the hall carpet. He'd stuffed it with books and sheets of A4 that told the story of Cassandra Lee. Old news stories printed off from the internet, a couple of dog-eared paperbacks he'd picked up in a quick trawl of the secondhand bookshops in Charing Cross Road. He made himself a pizza and read as he ate.

The press had taken against Cassandra from the first. It wasn't simply what she had done to Grant Dennis that outraged journalistic sensibilities. Far worse, she had offered no explanation for her crime, let alone an apology. The columnists who guarded public morals loved admissions of shame and promises of atonement; with luck, a five-hundred-word sermon would write itself. Cassandra hadn't lifted a finger in her own defense, and that kind of contempt for law and order was beyond the pale.

One news agency picture of her dominated the front pages. An anorexic, washed-out Cassandra, her cheeks hollow, her hair tangled, and her eyelids drooping with fatigue. It had become the standard image, just as the mug shot of Myra Hindley in her peroxide phase demonized her forever. The Cassandra in the photograph was a far cry from the temptress who had been Grant Dennis's fashion accessory. A once-beautiful young woman, made ugly by her own act of savagery. There was a lesson there, and the pundits were eager to teach it.

Coverage of the appeal, years later, was subdued and grudging. The press resented being cheated of its hate-figures. Even the reports of her acquittal used the old photograph. She did not sell her story, so there wasn't even one paper to take up the cudgels on her behalf. The lawyer who had fought for her refused to do more than make a terse public statement thanking the court and expressing the wish that Cassandra should be allowed to pick up the pieces of her life in private and without hindrance from the media. Talk about hope springing eternal. A couple of newspapers hinted that Hilary Metcalf's interest in her client was more than purely professional.

After that, the media trail grew cold, but not because Cassandra had been content to settle down in decent obscurity and seek to rebuild her life. On the contrary. She had created a new identity for herself. New name, new career, new job. A murderer reinventing herself as an ethical employment lawyer. A woman who had listened to her lover's screams as he burned was alive and well and advising blue-chip companies about how to sack staff and still keep on the straight and narrow. He had only to pick up the phone and half a dozen tabloid editors would be wetting themselves with excitement. Especially those who had been forced to settle Ali Khan's libel claims and were itching to cut Will Janus down to size. Rehabilitating offenders was fine and dandy, but hiring a killer to help make hundreds of hard-working factory hands redundant was guaranteed to provoke well-chosen words of condemnation in the leader columns.

Nic stretched out on the sofa, clippings in his hand. Could there be a connection between her presence and the deaths of the people from Creed? The coincidence troubled him, but he couldn't make sense of it. He remembered Roxanne's stunned look each time she'd seen him. She must be convinced he intended to give her game away. Either she had realized from the start who he was, or she had been responding to something in his own expression. What had that revealed?

He stared again at the old cruel photograph. Roxanne was so different, not just from the sick girl accused of murder but also from the slinky plaything pictured in some of the stories printed prior to the trial. She'd had her hair cut and dyed. Lipstick and mascara were things of the past. Even her eyes were a different color. No wonder it had taken time to work out who she was. Yet some things did not change. Roxanne, he thought, was gorgeous.

The shattered face gazed back at him from the photograph. Her eyes were beseeching, as if pleading for rescue. How had he never noticed that before? She'd worn the same look today, as the lift doors closed on her. It was somehow irresistible.

"So, Roxanne," he said to himself, "what do I do about you?"

While he wondered about her, he made himself a coffee and started flicking through the *Evening Standard* he had picked up in town. Same old stories: hospital waiting lists up, crime detection down. He was about to toss the paper aside when a line tucked away in the late news caught his eye.

The naked body of a woman of forty-seven had been found in her Oxford flat that morning. Foul play wasn't suspected. Big deal: the piece was only a couple of sentences long and wouldn't have made it into print had the tragic victim not worked for a famous London firm. She was an editor with the Aldwych Press, a tiny but venerable publishing house, and tittle-tattle about Aldwych always made good copy.

Aldwych had a distinguished reputation for its backlist of legal and philosophical books, but it owed its high public profile to a recently developed niche in literary erotica. As Nic recalled, Will Janus had once written for Aldwych, although in recent years he had signed up with a mainstream publishing house and kept well clear of embarrassment by association with exquisitely phrased porn. But it wasn't the Creed connection that caused

Nic to sit up straight and read the story a couple more times.

It was the woman's name: Jasmine Delahayee. That and the mention of Oxford. Nic forgot about Roxanne. What if she was the Jasmine who was called Jazz for short?

He called in half a dozen favors, phoning up everyone he could think of who might be able to tell him something about her. He'd guessed right: she was Jazz to everyone. Zack Flowers, an acquaintance he'd met through Dylan, had worked for Aldwych Press before moving to review rock music for the *London Lawyer.* He turned out to have known her for years.

"Yeah, I only just heard. Hanged herself, hasn't she? Fucking awful news."

"Tell me about her."

A pause. "What do you want to know?"

"Everything."

"Jesus, where do I begin? At first glance, you'd say she was someone who'd spent too long at Glastonbury and Woodstock. A bit of a hippie. Long reddish hair, didn't look her age, didn't act it. I liked her a lot. Totally off her head, of course. But then you'd have to be, wouldn't you, working for old Mickey Aldwych?"

"You met at Aldwych Press?"

"A dozen years back, right. She lived in Oxford and traveled in. She was the legal series editor. Eventually Mickey realized that dirty stories in polished prose made even more money than ripping off legal authors and law library budgets. He started with unexpurgated translations of Catullus and Aristophanes. You know that line in *The Acharnians,* "What tits! How firm, like quinces!"? That really tickled old Mickey; he had the quote framed and hung over his desk. Later on he moved into contemporary smut, stopped commissioning so many worthy monographs on judicial review. In the end Jazz went freelance. Money meant nothing to her. She wasn't one for the real world, wasn't Jazz." A pause. "Sounds as though that's the conclusion she just came to herself. Shit, shit, shit."

"If she told what sounded like a tall story, would people take her seriously?"

"Depends on who she told, I guess. What's all this about, by the way?"

"She knew Dylan, didn't she? I heard he had a fling with her."

"Could be. It's ages since I last saw either of them. If their paths crossed, they'd probably have hit it off. Are you suggesting she killed herself because her heart's desire had been murdered?"

"I'm not suggesting anything. Tell me, did you and she—?"

"No, no." Zack sighed, perhaps remembering long-ago opportunities, now lost forever. "We never did. Circumstances, you know. Besides, I was five years older, and she had a yen for toy boys."

Zack couldn't tell him anything else except for the names of a few friends of Jazz Delahayee. Even with all the windows open, it was still hot and sticky, and Nic took a midnight bath. As he soaked in the round tub, he was thinking of the man who had lived here. Dylan had been proved right in the end. Jazz was destined for sudden death. Pity Dylan hadn't realized that he was ahead of her in the queue. Typical. He loved himself and supposed everyone else did the same. He'd probably forgotten all about Amy Vinton, never mind guessing that she hated him enough to kill first him and then herself.

As he dried himself, he glanced again at Dylan's copy of Shakespeare, scanning the bookmarked final scene of the first act of *Othello*. Iago, now, there was a man. A skilled advocate, expert at manipulating others so that they did his bidding.

When Nic first trained in the law, his principal once asked him to name the most successful advocate of the twentieth

221

century, and when Nic offered a couple of wild guesses his boss had burst into laughter.

"Not even close," he said. "How about Adolf Hitler?"

Advocacy was like heroin, and as dangerous as the drug that had destroyed Tara Glass. It was so easy to get hooked on the power of persuasion. The rush you got when the words came out right and you swayed a judge or jury—nothing like it. The case became your whole world. Everything. All you wanted was to win. It was so much more than an intellectual challenge. People talked about the logic of the law, but the best advocates knew they must conquer the heart and soul as well as the mind. Advocates were supposed to be actors, a trite metaphor, but the best were *storytellers*. Yes, storytellers as mesmeric as Bryn Gabriel. They spun yarns with a difference. Rather than telling others what they wanted to hear, they urged their listeners to do what they themselves wanted. Which was not the same as encouraging them to believe in what the advocates believed. Belief simply didn't come into it.

Wild ideas kept jumping around in Nic's brain, but by a miracle he managed a couple of hours' sleep. A good night; his best since Dylan's murder. He was on the road early, heading for Oxford. Another hot day; he'd forgotten what clouds looked like.

Jazz Delahayee's flat had occupied the second floor of a Victorian villa in a leafy crescent near the Parks. An elderly widower who lived below had been the one to find her. According to a pal of Zack's, the old man fancied fifteen minutes of fame and had tipped off the press the moment he'd hung up on the emergency services. He proved to be a diminutive halitosis sufferer with an accent straight out of *Coronation Street*. He wouldn't have looked out of place wearing a flat cap and limping across a townscape by Lowry. He'd had no time for Jazz and wasn't bothered about speaking ill of the dead.

"Daft as a bloody brush, she was. Miss Floppy, I called her. Never wore a brassiere, y'know. My late wife would never have given a woman like that the time of day, and that's a fact."

They sat in a kitchen smelling of tobacco and burned toast, on either side of a table with a chipped Formica top. Nic remembered the frightened woman who had slammed the phone down on him. A short while later, she had been dead.

Brusquely, he said, "You said you overheard her on the telephone?"

"It was a scorcher, yesterday," the old man said, folding his arms as if to defy contradiction. "I opened that window as soon as I got up. She'd done the same upstairs. I wasn't eavesdropping. I just couldn't help hearing her."

Of course not. "What did she say?"

"There were two calls. The first on her cell phone, I think. It didn't last long. Then the phone in her room rang."

Nic wanted to punch the air, but he'd told the old man he was a journalist undertaking background research on Jazz's death for a piece in the *Oxford Mail,* and he wasn't ready for his cover to be blown.

"What did she say?"

"She was getting herself upset. Raising her voice. Like I said, I couldn't help hearing. Obviously it was a boyfriend on the line, giving her the heave-ho. She kept saying she loved him, that she'd never let him down. Why didn't he trust her? He ought to know she'd never betrayed him." A reminiscent chuckle. "Soft soap. It never works. He was on his way, all right, and there was nothing she could do to talk him out of it."

"What else was said?"

"I got the feeling he was trying to calm her down. Saying they could still be friends, or summat like that, I suppose." The old man paused in theatrical style. "She said, 'I loved you and you destroyed my life.' Then she banged the phone down and started banging about like a bull in a china shop, the way she always did when she was in a state. I heard her cell phone go. It wasn't a long conversation, maybe a wrong number, I dunno. Five minutes later I heard this crash. As if something had fallen over. After that, everything went quiet. For a change."

Nic ground his teeth. *When she picked up the phone and heard my voice, she was praying it was her lover. Instead, I gave her more to fear.* "What did you do?"

For the first time, the old man's voice faltered. "I-I left it quarter of an hour. I hadn't heard her go out. I wondered what was up. The silence was funny, like. She was a noisy woman, always had been. I decided I ought to take a gander, just in case. Her door was ajar. She never had the faintest idea about security. I looked inside . . ."

"And you saw her hanging there," Nic finished. His stomach was churning.

"In the buff," the old man said. "Not a bloody stitch on. What a way to go, eh?"

"Jazz always put herself through hell," Misty Karl said. "As well as those of us who were fond of her. She fretted so much, it was tough to handle. Manic depression. Or bipolar disorder, should I say. You'd be amazed how many creative people have it. Most of the geniuses, actually. From the Hemingways to Tony Hancock, from Graham Greene to Edgar Allan Poe. The list is endless, Jazz used to say. Thinking that cheered her up at times. Years back, though, the bloody thing got the better of her. It was after an ex-boyfriend died. She shouldered all the blame. Poor Jazz, she always took everything so much to heart, sometimes she could be hard to take herself."

She and Nic were sitting on a bench in the Parks, casting an occasional glance at the punts passing by. Zack Flowers had said Misty was Jazz Delahayee's oldest friend; she was also Balliol College's senior research fellow in genre fiction studies. She was wearing a short white tennis skirt and sneakers. Nic's call to her cell phone number had caught her at the end of a tie-break. She'd been playing a friend from another college but had agreed to talk to him about Jazz. Her legs were sturdy and brown, and she'd done nothing to hide the crinkles around her eyes and mouth or first streaks of gray in her hair. She smelled faintly of patchouli.

"Did she keep a diary?"

"I don't think so."

He'd wondered if there might be something in her flat, something that would answer his questions. But of course it was too much to hope for. Even Dylan's laptop had finished up in a watery grave.

"Now, why are you so interested in Jazz? Is there any chance it wasn't suicide? Perhaps an accident—"

"It wasn't an accident," he interrupted.

Dylan had known that someone wanted Jazz dead, someone who had now got his way. Nic remembered her frightened voice on the telephone. She knew her life was in danger. She'd ended it herself, before that someone else did.

"I see." As if to suppress any display of emotion, Misty turned her gaze to the river, where a fat young man striving to impress a languid girlfriend was revealing his lack of mastery of punting technique. "Oh, it's a pole not a hockey stick, you silly oaf! Now, where were we? You were about to explain what it is about Jazz's death that has brought you here."

Nic hesitated, but he knew that soon he would have to confide in someone. "Jazz had an affair with a friend of mine. His name was Dylan Rees. Did she mention him at all?"

Misty shook her head. "I'd scarcely seen Jazz since last autumn. Partly my fault. I've been working on this book about Elizabeth Gaskell. Which argues, if you're interested, that the plot of *Mary Barton* marks her out as the first woman crime writer. Don't frown, Nic, it doesn't suit you. At least the synopsis earned me a decent advance. Trouble is, coming up to a deadline, I haven't had much chance to socialize. Anyway, Jazz wasn't around. The story goes she'd been pretty much wrapped up in herself. Then again, who am I to talk? I wish I'd made an effort to see her when I had the chance . . ."

Her voice broke, and again she fixed her gaze back on the sweating punter. He glanced in her direction, and she gave him an encouraging smile.

"Something was bothering her, according to Dylan," Nic said. "Several people had died suddenly and in strange circumstances."

"Is that why you're asking about her?"

"Yes." She wasn't someone to lie to.

"Sorry, I can't help you. Poor Jazz, she'd had to deal with sudden death before in her life. I'm not sure she ever quite got over what happened."

"Which was?"

Misty sighed. "She didn't mean to, but she killed her ex."

Nic clenched his fists. *Now for it.*

"How?"

"It was a pure accident. The police accepted that. So did everyone else. I was there. I saw her face when she realized what was going wrong. No one could have faked the look of horror on her face. I'll never forget it. Never."

"Tell me about it."

"A mutual friend of ours, a chap called Peter, was having a party. He'd sold a book about rugby football to Penguin, and he was celebrating. He asked Jazz and me to help out with refreshments at his little house in Jericho. There was only one fly in the ointment. Peter's best friend was Darrell Bergen, Jazz's ex. They'd split up a few weeks earlier. Darrell's decision. He was too easygoing to commit. At first, she was devastated. I wondered how she would feel about seeing him again. But she said she'd found someone else. She was going through one of her euphoric phases, so probably it was true, although I don't know. She didn't bring the new boyfriend to the party. I never met him, and I did wonder if she'd made him up."

"How did Darrell die?"

"It was horrible." The color drained from her face at the memory. "Jazz and Darrell said hello. She was putting on a brave face, and he wanted no hard feelings. She'd brought in a bowl of crisps, and he took one. Goodwill gesture, that's all there was to it. I went to have a word with Darrell. He was flushed, but I thought nothing of it. We were in the midst of a heat wave as fierce as this one. He was sweating, and he started to look anxious. I was chattering away, and when he began to cough, I asked if he was okay, but he couldn't answer. His face and lips swelled up; it was almost as if he had hives. I was frightened, and I called Peter to come and take a look. Darrell was scarcely breathing." Misty shivered, a faraway look in her eyes as she relived the past. "Peter went to phone for an ambulance. Poor Darrell began to throw up. Jazz was in hysterics, and the poor lad lost all control. He was having diarrhea—it was awful. I've never seen anything like it, not before or since. Thank God. By the time the ambulance arrived, Darrell was dead. There was nothing anyone could do. Not a bloody thing."

The punt finally drifted out of their sight. The young man was covered in sweat, his girlfriend dozing. Nic said, "And the cause of death?"

"It turned out that Darrell was allergic to peanuts. Of all the bloody stupid, totally innocent things to die of. The crisps he ate were plain. No problem there, but the bowl had had peanuts in it. Even touching a container that has held peanuts can cause a reaction if you have the allergy. Anaphylactic shock. He was a

fit man, played squash three or four times a week, but that
didn't save him. No, the medics said exercise exacerbates the
condition. Ironic, or what?"

The boy who died of shock. Nic said, "Did Jazz admit that the
bowl had contained peanuts?"

"That was the one thing that never stacked up. She sort of
went into denial. To listen to her, the bowl had never contained
peanuts, and she'd washed it thoroughly anyway before bringing it to the party. I must say, none of us believed that."

"What then?"

Misty's face hardened. "I'm sure it wasn't deliberate. There
was a bit of gossip at the time. One or two people suggested she
was trying to give Darrell a fright, to pay him back for being
unkind to her, without realizing she was going to kill him. That
was a wicked thing to say. She wasn't cruel. Okay, she knew
about Darrell's allergy, but it was obvious what had happened.
She'd simply forgotten that the bowl had held peanuts. Maybe
she hadn't washed it properly, either. When she realized the
truth, she couldn't cope with the guilt."

"Simple as that?"

"Simple as that." She considered him, not smiling. "Except
there's more to it than I realized, isn't there? Otherwise why
would you be asking me all these questions?"

An hour later, Nic was having tea and crumpets in Misty Karl's
aerie at the top of staircase sixteen, overlooking the Balliol
croquet lawn. Every now and then, through the open window,
they heard the thud of mallet against ball, cries of anguish and
glee. Inside, the furnishings were Spartan, the chairs hard, and
yet Nic felt as though he had arrived in the land of sybarites. If
you stayed here long enough, perhaps you might come to believe
that this was paradise, and the world outside a poor second
best.

"*Sex, Law, and Videotape*," Dr. Kennedy Brown said with a satyr's wink. "I owe the title to Jazz. I meant to dedicate the book to her, even before . . . this terrible, terrible thing happened."

When Nic had asked Misty if she knew anyone who might have seen Jazz lately, she'd immediately thought of the man she called JFK. He was on sabbatical from the Birmingham Law and Media Institute, and Jazz had commissioned him to write a book about film and the law. He was a thin, balding man who wore a white jacket and silk cravat and had an inexplicable liking for the sound of his own high-pitched voice. When he took Misty's call, he'd been at a champagne and strawberries party in the Master's Garden, and he freely admitted that he didn't have much of a head for bubbly. The main challenge was to keep him on the point. He'd already explained to Nic at length that he'd never forget where he was when the American president was assassinated in Dallas, since on that very day his mother had been giving birth to him in Warrington Hospital, and his parents had chosen to commemorate the event by naming him after the dead leader.

"Did you see much of Jazz?" Nic asked, buttering another crumpet.

"Oh, dear me, yes. I was always popping round to pester her, seek a second opinion. She was a marvelous editor, you know. She must have been, of course, to spot my talent!" Kennedy gave an arch smile. "She'd been having the blues quite a lot lately, poor thing. I was so sorry. This bloody bipolar disorder. She'd tried everything. Lithium, antidepressants, you name it. I'm no shrink, but to my mind the best remedy is a spot of tender loving care. I hoped that when she met Dylan, the headhunter, things would change."

"But they didn't?"

"Not much. He loved her and left her."

"They met at a conference, didn't they?"

"Oh yes, that was me playing Cupid! Quite unintentionally, I might add. My friend Alvin works for a hospitality company that organized a conference about careers in the law. This chap Dylan Rees was one of the speakers. There was a party on the Friday evening. Alvin invited me along, but he was going to be run off his feet, and so I asked Jazz if she'd like to come as my guest. She'd been pretty down, although she never wanted to talk about it. In the end she said yes."

"And she and Dylan hit it off?"

"I'll say so. I finished up as a gooseberry, and they finished up spending the night together. Talk about a pair of fast workers! I didn't mind. I was really happy for Jazz. A hard man is good to find, as Mae West used to say. They seemed to get on so well. Such a tragedy that it didn't last."

"And how did Jazz take that?"

"Perhaps not as badly as I might have expected. They kept in touch as friends, I believe. She said to me once that she'd found him easy to confide in, that before she realized what she was doing, she was sharing her innermost secrets with him. I thought that was going too far. I mean, nice guy and all that, but he was obviously only interested in one thing."

"Did she confide in you?"

"We were good pals," Kennedy Brown said. "Not every author can say that about his relationship with his editor. I used to worry about her. She seemed—oh, I don't know. Bothered. No, worse than that. Scared. But she didn't want to tell me what was wrong. That hurt a bit, I can tell you. She'd only known Dylan Rees five minutes, but we weren't bedmates. That was the difference."

After taking his leave, Nic found a quiet corner in the quad near the library. Leaning against the wall, he dialed the main switchboard at Creed. Soon he would be returning to Avalon Buildings. He had found the answers to most of his questions. Except for the most important one of all.

"Creed, good afternoon, this is Anji speaking, how may I help you?"

"I'd like to speak to Roxanne Wake."

CHAPTER TWENTY

"When are you coming to bed?"

Roxanne turned her head and saw Chloe standing in the hall, looking into the living room. White flesh luminous in the dark, but no provocation in her nakedness. Her shoulders were sloping, her eyes looked sore, and she was stifling a yawn.

"Just let me get to the end of this chapter."

"Do you know it's half past two?"

Roxanne glanced at the clock. "I got carried away."

She slipped a used train ticket into Nic Gabriel's book to keep her place. Once she'd started turning the pages, it proved impossible to stop. Crippen belonged to a different world, but Nic Gabriel had entered that world. He had woven music hall ditties, learned notes on the characteristics of scar tissue, and extracts from the doctor's private correspondence into a narrative web. The picture he'd conjured of Crippen's endless torments, his hapless efforts to cover up his wife's accidental death, his panic when the police came around: was it truth or illusion, fact or fiction? According to the critics, it scarcely mattered. If the whole thing was all made up, then at least Gabriel possessed the gift of seeing into the human heart. And if the little doctor had not gone through the hell that the book described, he should have done.

Chloe knelt beside Roxanne's chair. "Carried away, huh? You could have got carried away with me."

"Sorry." Roxanne ran her fingers along the long knobbly

spine, relished the sigh of contentment she evoked. "I've been selfish. I'll finish now."

Chloe took the book and peered at Nic Gabriel's face on the back cover. "He looks—restless. Like someone who will never be satisfied. Someone who can never bring himself to let go."

"Yes."

Chloe glanced at the biographical note. "So he used to be a lawyer himself. Might have guessed. What's your verdict, then?"

"Spooky, the way he reads Crippen's mind. Especially when it came to destroying the corpse with quicklime." Roxanne forced a smile. "I'm all goose bumps."

"Uh-huh." Chloe edged away and squatted on the rug in front of chair. Her skinny body had begun to shake.

Roxanne stiffened. "What's wrong?"

"I'm afraid for you," Chloe said. Her voice was muffled. "I don't want him ever to read your thoughts."

Ten minutes after they had arrived at Avalon Buildings, Chloe burst into Roxanne's room. "He hasn't turned up."

Of course Roxanne knew whom she meant. Only one man occupied their minds. They had spoken in monosyllables over breakfast, and conversation had been impossible on the train. Not that they wanted to talk any more about the Situation. The last twenty-four hours had drained both of them. Besides, what more was there to say?

"How do you know?" Roxanne was cautious, not wanting to let her hopes rise too soon.

"Joel told me. Well, to be honest, I asked. Don't worry. I was careful to sound casual."

"Uh-huh." Roxanne's heart sank. Chloe was no actress, and Joel no fool. The last thing she wanted was for other people in the firm to start wondering why Nic Gabriel meant so much to a personal assistant and a lowly paralegal.

"It's all right. Promise." Chloe saw the doubt in her eyes. "He didn't guess a thing. All he said was that Gabriel rang up first thing. He was meant to be here again this morning, but apparently he's been called away."

"So he's not coming back?"

Despite herself, Roxanne felt her spirits lifting. Perhaps he was not interested in her after all. He might have been struck by a prettyish face, and that was it. She had worried so much, and for no purpose.

"Oh yes, he is." Chloe spoke through gritted teeth. "He said he needed to do some urgent research, but he expected to be back soon."

"I see."

And suddenly, Roxanne thought she did. Nic Gabriel was an assiduous detective. *Crippen* was the proof of that. He could never have explored the doctor's mind so thoroughly if he had not first familiarized himself with every byway of the little quack's life. The clothes he wore, the music he liked, the food he ate. If he was toying with the possibility of writing about her, he would need to be even more meticulous in ripping the curtains aside. She wasn't like Crippen, cold in her grave and largely forgotten. He could not risk making a mistake in any point of detail. She would be allowed to have no shred of privacy, no space left in which to keep a secret. For all she knew, he was on his way up north at this very moment, traveling to interview Hilary Metcalf.

Roxanne had been seven when her grandmother died. Granny Lee had been pretty in her youth and didn't take kindly to old age. She compensated for it by making the most of every opportunity to be unpleasant. Roxanne didn't remember much about her except for the smell of peppermints which she refused to share around and a favorite phrase which she rolled out whenever she had to do anything. *No peace for the wicked,* she would say, with a malicious cackle. Roxanne only learned the truth of that after doing something wicked herself.

All she wanted for the present was to think about the Situation and what she could do to change it. She switched on the "engaged" light on her door, set the phone to "do not disturb," and spread bundles of documents across her desk, to give the appearance of intensely lucrative activity. None of it helped. The hands on the computer clock that recorded her chargeable time did not move, but she might as well have been working feverishly for all the good the break did her. It was true: there was no peace for the wicked.

Chloe popped in and said she had to catch up with her work over lunch. Roxanne bought herself a salad sandwich and an orange juice from a sandwich bar in the Strand, but when she tried to eat, she found she could not bear the taste. For the first time in years, she remembered an old superstition of hers: that if she kept her stomach empty, her thinking would sharpen up and her spirits would lift. Lately she'd been eating too much anyway. Chloe was inches taller, but her clothes had not been such a bad fit as she'd expected. For a little while, until the Situation was sorted out, she could afford to lose a few pounds. She hated feeling bloated, especially in this heat. It wasn't healthy. At a time when she must focus on trying to save herself, the last thing she needed was to waste time and effort gobbling down food.

Returning to the office, she bumped into Joel Anthony in reception. When he smiled at her, Roxanne nodded and hurried past. To her dismay, he followed her to the lift and started making pleasant conversation about the heat wave. Roxanne's stomach muscles clenched as she watched the lights showing the lift's descent. She wasn't in the mood for company, and she feared giving herself away. It would be the final irony if, after all her anguishing over Nic Gabriel, she let something slip which caused Joel to realize that Roxanne Wake did not exist and that the woman he and Ben had recruited was the freed killer, Cassandra Lee.

"Chloe seems bothered by something today," he remarked as the lift arrived at last, and they stood back to let the occupants out.

"Like you say, it's so hot. Even the air-conditioning isn't enough."

He gave a satisfied nod. "Strange, isn't it, how the heat takes us in different ways? Fast workers slow down, likeable people find their tempers starting to fray . . ."

She thought he was casting around for another example and, for a mad moment, was tempted to add: "And mild-mannered paralegals decide to kill their enemies."

Joel had that sort of effect. With a simple word or gesture, he helped you to articulate what had been swimming around in your head for a long, long time. Quite a talent. She contented herself with a nod of agreement, but it was as if a door had opened in her mind, a door she had believed was shut for ever.

Later, as she walked back into her room after a visit to the loo, the phone was ringing. She pressed the loudspeaker button and the receptionist said, "Nic Gabriel for you."

For a moment, Roxanne could not breathe. She felt dazed and light-headed. It was not simply hunger, but the suffocating awareness that he was closing in on her. She could not escape and, oddly, she was not even sure now that she wanted to escape. What would be, would be.

"Put him through."

Two long seconds passed before Nic Gabriel's voice filled the room. "Roxanne Wake?"

"Yes."

They had never spoken to each other before, yet it was as if she had known him all her life. When she was a girl, her grandmother had told her stories of the Bogeyman. Now he had tracked her down to her hiding place.

"Our paths crossed yesterday, although we weren't introduced. I—"

"I know who you are, Mr. Gabriel." She marveled at the steadiness of her voice. "As a matter of fact, I bought your book yesterday. Just to see if it lived up to its reputation."

A pause. Perhaps he had not expected her to sound so self-possessed, had hoped to take her by surprise, like the advocate who commences cross-examination with his most devastating question. A classic technique, but Roxanne thought it flawed. If the witness keeps her wits about her, the initiative is lost.

"I'm flattered," he said.

"Don't be." She was determined not to let him off the hook. He needed to understand that she wasn't a born victim. Crippen had been a soft target; she would be different. "I was curious, that's all."

"And?"

"Congratulations. You write well. I'm surprised you haven't published a second book. Or is a follow-up in the works?"

"I haven't even typed the first chapter heading."

"Oh dear. Writer's block?"

"No, it's just that since I laid poor old Crippen to rest, I haven't found another subject I wanted to write a book about."

"Nothing worthy of your talents?"

"It's simply," he said, "that I need a subject that takes over my life. Becomes an obsession."

"Well, good luck in your search," she said calmly. It struck her that, in his own way, he was nervous. He'd never spoken to Crippen. Now he was exchanging small talk with a woman who had murdered her lover. She didn't feel light-headed any more. She had the exhilarating sensation that he wasn't sure how to deal with her.

"I was wondering if we could talk. Not on the telephone. Face to face."

"You want to meet?"

"Please."

"I don't suppose I have any choice, do I?"

"Of course you have a choice," the disembodied voice said. "All the same, I would like to see you. Tomorrow? Not in the office, of course."

"No, not in the office."

"Perhaps I could offer you dinner?"

For God's sake, Roxanne thought. The man who is planning to shatter my life is inviting me out for a meal. It's like going out on a date with your appointed executioner. Like having sex with someone who is about to kill you.

"Thank you," she said. "I'd like that."

After Chloe rolled off her that night, they lay side by side, thighs touching. Roxanne's eyes were closed. Chloe liked to pull hair and rake with her fingernails as they made love. Tonight she had been fiercer than ever before. Roxanne wished she hadn't had anything to drink at the bar. She wished Chloe hadn't hurt her so much. Sex and starvation had left her melancholy.

Chloe always liked to talk afterward; Hilary had been the same. "Remember our first time, when I asked you to take control, remember what you said? You were right, it did take me a while to learn how to let go. But now that I have, I see what you meant. There's nothing like that sense of power. Having someone else under your thumb."

"Mmmmm," Roxanne said.

She breathed in her lover's perfume. She wondered how things would work out when they got through all this—if they did get through it all. Suppose she managed to get Nic Gabriel out of the way, so that he would never bother her again, what did the future hold at Creed? Would the two of them still be together in a month's time? A year's? She couldn't forget what Hilary had said to her at the time she'd moved out of the house they shared. Every relationship she'd ever had, she had wrecked.

"You're still awake, aren't you? There's something I want to say."

Roxanne shifted onto her side. "Hush now."

"No, this is important." Chloe propped herself up on her elbow so that they were facing each other. She peered at Roxanne, as if hoping to find the solution to a riddle. "You're not going to like it, though."

"What is it?"

"I love you."

Roxanne went cold inside. "I told you that first time, remember? I don't believe in declarations of undying passion. I've played that game before. In the end, no one wins. Trust me. It's dangerous. Let's just—"

"I know, I know, I know. I'm sorry. I'm sure you think I'm such a pain. But this is all new to me. New and strange and frightening. I can't help myself." Chloe traced round Roxanne's breast. "I'd do anything for you. Anything. Even . . ."

Her voice changed for a moment before it trailed away, became harsh and defiant. The bedroom window was wide open and had let in a chill. Roxanne said roughly, "Even what?"

Chloe enveloped her with her arms and squeezed tight. "If it meant I could save you, and be with you forever, I'd kill him."

Roxanne summoned up a few last ounces of strength and broke free of the grip, pushing her lover away from her and rising up above her. "You don't understand what you're saying."

Chloe looked up at her, breathing hard. "You may not believe me, but it's true."

Perhaps it was. Chloe saw everything in black and white, not shades of gray. Was she capable of murder in cold blood? Why not? Most people were. What they lacked was the final push to tip them over the edge, the prompt to translate fantasy into the real thing.

All I have to do, Roxanne thought, the blood rushing to her head, is to say one word. Let her know what I want from her—and she will do my bidding. I'm in control. I have the power of life and death. She's like a robot at my beck and call. If I want, she will murder Nic Gabriel. She is sure to be caught, but I will be innocent. I can walk away, and I will be free.

"If it wasn't for him," Chloe said dreamily, "everything would be so perfect."

"You think so?" Roxanne let out a little groan. She wasn't sure what she believed any more. Perhaps Chloe was right, and before Nic Gabriel had showed up, everything in the garden was lovely.

"It can be. He's the one obstacle in our way, I'm telling you. The only one."

Roxanne clenched her fists, summoning up her resolve. "Forget it, okay?"

"He's poison! Why don't you face up to it? You saw what he did to bloody Crippen, who's been pushing up daisies for the past ninety years." Chloe choked back a sob. "He acts like Prince Charming, but the truth is, he's cruel. He'll bleed you dry, if you let him. He'll do it so he can satisfy his curiosity, that's the ugliest part of it. If he makes another fortune, that's a bonus. After he's done, he'll move on, leaving you for dead. Is that what you want? Is it what you really want?"

"I suppose you're right."

"You can bank on it."

"Don't forget," Roxanne said, "I have a little experience of men who want to use me."

"Exactly! That's precisely why—"

Roxanne held up a hand as she interrupted. "Leave this to me."

Chloe stared at her. "So, you'll—"

"Let's not talk any more about it," Roxanne said. She realized now. This was her business. Chloe would never be able to deal with it. She meant well, but she mustn't be allowed to blunder in. In destroying Nic Gabriel, she would also destroy herself. Only one person was responsible for this mess, only one person could bring it to an end.

"The less we say, the better, huh? Listen, it's all down to me. I'll do what needs to be done, I promise." She felt her knees trembling as she saw the horror in Chloe's eyes. "I've saved myself before, remember."

CHAPTER TWENTY-ONE

"I'm a simple man," Mickey Aldwych said and took another puff at his cigar. Even for a twenty-first-century media tycoon, it was an outrageous lie. He was a frog-like fellow poured into a Bruce Oldfield suit, a prominent supporter of good causes who made a fortune from sadomasochistic porn, a caring father of five whose energetic flings with blond weather forecasters and game show presenters kept gossip columns in business. His opening gambit had been to offer to commission an article about Crippen's erotic inner life for a sum larger than most midlist authors received for a hundred-thousand-word novel. "I'm loyal, too. I liked Jazz Delahayee, and that's why I kept her on for so long. Despite everything. That it should end like this is an utter tragedy. A terrible accident."

"An accident?" Nic repeated softly.

Not accident, not even really suicide, but murder. Murder by someone who was desperate. Someone who would not give up. Someone who couldn't give up.

"Yes, yes, of course. A cry for attention gone wrong . . ." Mickey frowned. "I'm sure Jazz would never mean to harm herself."

"She worked for you for a long time, I gather."

"I realized when I first took her on that she was a good editor. A clever lady, and rather gorgeous, too." Mickey chuckled, as if reminiscing about a long-ago conquest. "In her early years with us, she never put a foot wrong. Her authors loved her, the—"

Nic waved at the photographs. "Authors like Will Janus?"

"Sure, sure. Before he became a household name, naturally. He made generous acknowledgment of Jazz's contribution. But she lost it. I gave her plenty of rope, but"—it occurred to him just in time that he'd chosen an unfortunate metaphor—"even I had to admit that she couldn't hack it any longer. She missed glaring errors in manuscripts, turned down book proposals which other people gobbled up and made a killing on. Our legal publishing division started losing money hand over fist. Frankly, that's quite an achievement. Any half-decent book about the law ought to make a return. What are law firms' library budgets for?"

"I gather she suffered from bipolar disorder."

"Of course, I made allowances. She had time off, but it didn't help. Our funds aren't limitless, Mr. Gabriel." Mickey contemplated his Rolex sorrowfully. "I had to do something."

"So you put her on a freelance contract?"

"Only way she could remain on the payroll. She'd become a luxury we could no longer afford. I thought things could only get better. So did Jazz."

"Did they?"

Mickey Aldwych's flabby jaw slackened in mock astonishment. "Surely, Mr. Gabriel, you've learned the eternal truth. When people say things can only get better, that's precisely the time they really take a turn for the worse."

"So what did you do about it?"

"For a long time, nothing. That's the trouble with me, Mr. Gabriel. I'm an old softie at heart." He brushed his eye with his thumb. He might have been wiping a tear or getting rid of a piece of grit. "Besides, I'd stemmed the drain on cash flow. I was paying Jazz less, and she wasn't complaining, so I let things ride. We lost our best legal writers, people like dear old Will Janus, but our business focus had changed. I was devoting my energies to erotic torture and fur fetishism. In an exclusively literary context, of course."

The boom of his laughter shook the oak paneling. Nic said, "So you were happy to keep her on, even though she still wasn't performing?"

Mickey sighed, a quick gust of regret. "Nothing is forever, Mr. Gabriel, you know that as well as I do. I won't rewrite history simply because the poor girl's dead. Even if I did, you would soon find out the truth anyway."

He chortled for a few moments at his own candor before continuing. "Fact of the matter is, the market has changed. Electronic publishing, virtual communication systems. One needs to focus nowadays. It must be true. Even the stupidest business analysts keep saying the same thing. So I decided that it made sense to dispose of our legal list. The main challenge was finding a buyer. Fortunately, Will and his people helped out. His firm has acted for me for years. They put me in touch with a prospective purchaser."

Nic stifled a groan. So easy now to see it coming. "Ali Khan?"

"My goodness me, you are well informed." Mickey frowned, but then a calculating light came into his small eyes. "Expect an announcement within twenty-four hours. It's not big news, admittedly. There's an obvious synergy between our businesses."

"So what was going to happen to Jazz?"

Mickey clicked his tongue. "There are always casualties when a firm moves on, Mr. Gabriel. Thrust has plenty of in-house resources at Tottenham Court Road. They didn't need an incompetent freelance to help them run a tiny legal list. I'd been consulting Creed about redundancy."

"Who was advising you?"

"Ben Yarrow, as it happens. Ugly little chap, but mustard as a lawyer. I asked Jazz to come in to see the two of us last week, said I'd briefed Ben that I wanted to be generous. He would be sorting out the details of the severance package. Making it tax-efficient, that sort of thing."

"How did she take it?"

"How do you expect?" Mickey pursed his lips. "She made a number of comments that were entirely unwarranted. Not to mention unwise. I'm a good friend, Mr. Gabriel. Personal loyalty is my Achilles heel—but I can be pushed too far."

His voice had dropped, and for a few seconds his chubby pink cheeks lost their color. "However, for Jazz, I was prepared to make allowances. We went back a long way together. For old times' sake, I wanted us to part as friends. I told her I'd ignore what she'd said. She was due to come back to Creed with her answer by noon yesterday. Of course, she never made it to the deadline."

"What did Jazz say?"

Mickey flapped a hand. "Oh, stuff about some conspiracy against her. Wild allegations about Creed. Nothing specific. It was all pretty hysterical. I told her to shut up before she embarrassed herself any more in front of poor Ben Yarrow. I must say, he took it well. He realized she was a sick woman, but as soon as he expressed his sympathy, she began to rant at him. All very sad."

"So you didn't pay any attention to what she had to say?"

"Of course not. It was nothing but tosh. I tell you, she didn't even expect me to take any notice. She said as much. I hate to say so, but it's even crossed my mind that what happened to poor Jazz was no bad thing. She didn't have much left to live for. Perhaps her death was a blessing in disguise."

Some disguise, Nic thought as he wandered among the gravestones at Highgate that afternoon. He leaned against a cherub-heavy tombstone. The cemetery was among his favorite places in the city, one of the few parts of London where he felt almost at home. He'd rather not dwell on what that said about him, but he liked wandering alone through the labyrinth of curving paths, pausing in peaceful corners in the shade, reading eulogies to the dear departed.

He hadn't believed in God since the day he'd seen his mother's broken body, but he understood why people needed something to cling to. Something stronger than logic and man-made laws. Like his own belief that his father was not a murderer. Every day it was there, at the back of his mind, the gnawing awareness that everyone else had thought the case cut and dried. People liked there to be a reason for things, to have them explained. To them, the myth of the Questing Beast would make no sense at all. With Dylan, as with the others, the story seemed so simple. Amy Vinton was a tragic avenger, exacting belated justice on the man responsible for the death of her sister. Sure, but the last few pages of the script were missing.

Advocacy. He was certain now, this was all about advocacy. People talked about the science of advocacy, the technique of persuasion, but that was in itself a kind of advocate's devilry. Teach-yourself books told tyros how to do it, but they came no closer to revealing the secrets than texts about necromancy or any other black art. Face it, Dylan was right. Litigation is like sex. The best advocates are as sensitive to mood and timing as infinitely skilled lovers. The closing speech pulls everything together, brings the case to a climax. At last the truth is laid bare. Or, at least, as much of the truth as the advocate wants the court to believe.

Too many people dead before their time. He realized that he'd started clenching and unclenching his fist. He was no longer calm. Too many people sacrificed. Dylan Rees and Amy Vinton. Matthew Creed and Bradley Hutton. Jazz Delahayee and even Darrell Bergen. Their deaths angered him, but they also made him shiver, even in the heat. He didn't want to join them and become, like his mother, one of the dead-too-soon.

Advocacy. All that talk about the advocate's art was misleading. It suggested a civilized, gentlemanly skill, reminiscent of all that nostalgic prewar crap about the advocate as a priest in the Temple of Justice. The temple was more like a mausoleum in this cemetery, where gargoyles leered at images of the saints, where reason, mercy, and discretion fought a losing battle against sentiment, prejudice, and fear. Persuasion so often took on a sinister guise. When you bent another person to your will, who could say where it might lead? Flattery, blackmail, even murder.

Shaving for the second time that day, he nicked his chin a couple of times. It shocked him to realize why his hands weren't steady. Within an hour, he would be seeing Roxanne Wake again. It gave him a buzz to think of looking at her, listening to her speak. This wouldn't be like the research he'd done for *Crippen*. Roxanne bore no resemblance to any other lawyer he'd ever known. He was sure that that she couldn't care less about driving a Porsche or taking skiing holidays in Aspen. She had killed, killed brutally, and yet seven years later, here she was, alive and well and working under a false name for Will Janus.

Why Creed, of all firms? Had the partners chosen her, or had she chosen them? Soon he would have all the answers he was seeking, but even that was not the reason his skin was pricking, why it took him longer than usual to button his shirt and straighten his tie. Something drew him to her, a fascination that was partly sexual—might as well admit it, even if only to himself: from the moment he'd seen her in Joel's room, she'd stirred something deep inside him—and partly the temptation of the dangerous unknown.

Not that she was dangerous any longer, he told himself as he slipped on his shoes. Lightning never struck twice. On the phone she had sounded calm, but that must be an act. He'd seen her fear when it dawned on her that she'd been recognized. He held all the cards. With one word, he could finish her career. She had so much to lose.

He dialed a cab. This evening, for once, he would not trudge along the London streets to his destination. Tonight was special, and yet he had no idea of how it might end. With the two of them in bed together? He imagined her bare arms around him, hugging him to her breasts. The picture he'd conjured up shocked him. He'd never gone in for one-night-stands. More often than not, like Phil, women sought him out rather than the other way around. None of the affairs lasted. This was different. He did not know her at all. Although he knew what she had done, he could not guess her thoughts. Yet none of that mattered. He could not wait to see her again. In the confessional of his mind, he must acknowledge it. He wanted her for himself.

At last the cab arrived. Traffic was bad, and they crawled along the streets leading to the center. The driver provided a running commentary on the iniquities of those in government who cared nothing for the poor downtrodden overtaxed motorist, allowing jams to build year after year while asleep in the back of their chauffeured limousines. Nic replied in monosyllables. To kill time, he was rehearsing in his head what he might say to Roxanne. None of it seemed right. There was sweat on his forehead, and his stomach had tied itself in knots.

He'd booked at an Italian restaurant near Trafalgar Square, a place where he sometimes met people he was interviewing for magazine stories. He'd decided that Roxanne would hate somewhere trendy and exotic, the sort of place where Grant used to take Cassandra. Because he had set off early, he arrived just on time, despite the gridlock. The street was packed with people sitting at the tables outside the bars and cafés, laughing and drinking. He shared a joke with the maitre d' and was led to his usual table at the back. It was near the kitchens, but he didn't mind. He liked the cooking smells and, besides, he and Roxanne would be out of the earshot of fellow diners.

Roxanne was nowhere to be seen. Ten minutes passed. Nic's spine felt thin and brittle as he kept shifting in his seat to glance over toward the door. He had been so sure she would turn up. He didn't see what else she could do. She couldn't take the risk of provoking him. She was at his mercy.

Suddenly he spotted her in the doorway, wearing a halter-neck minidress that showed plenty of flesh. She didn't have a tan like the other women dining, but now she was there, he could not imagine why anyone would give the others a second glance. To Nic she looked cool, elegant, formidable. A cross between a gazelle and a praying mantis.

Their eyes met at the same moment the maitre d' touched her arm and asked her to follow him. Nic could not read her expression. He stood up and smiled at her, and she made a slight dismissive movement with her shoulders. Something told him that neither of them would ever forget tonight. His heart beat faster. This was the first time he had ever dined with anyone who had taken the life of a fellow human being. To everyone else, she was a pretty young woman, out on a date. He noticed a group of city traders watching her progress as she shimmied between the close-packed tables. She turned heads, did Roxanne Wake.

They didn't shake hands. She was keeping her distance. He guessed her plan was let him make all the running. He didn't have a plan, except to keep talking and just see what happened. He felt a pang of remorse. He hated hurting people. Feared it. He couldn't take his eyes off her, despite what she had done. Or was it, he asked himself with a stab of self-loathing, *because* of what she had done?

Chapter Twenty-Two

Roxanne woke at five and couldn't get back to sleep. She should have been exhausted, but her head was buzzing. In fourteen hours she would be seeing Nic Gabriel. She could not face going in to work. Contracts and collective agreements, policies and procedures, none of them mattered any more. A world existed beyond the law, and she was about to step back into it.

Chloe's peaceful face was turned to her. Without makeup, her complexion was blotchy, but it didn't matter. Was Chloe serious about killing Nic Gabriel? She was a romantic with a reckless streak who would sacrifice anything for love. Herself included. But Roxanne could not let her do it. She owed it to both of them to deal with Nic herself.

The clock on the bedside table ticked loudly. As the minutes crawled by, Roxanne found images of Grant Dennis crowding together in her head. Grant laughing with her, Grant kissing her, Grant hurting her. The final scene crept back into mind, making her squirm. Grant on fire, Grant in agony, Grant staggering away to hurl himself to his death.

At last the alarm rang, and Chloe stirred. Roxanne shook her by the shoulder and, when she had come round, told her that she meant to take the day off work.

"Good idea," Chloe said, rubbing her eyes. "I'll call in sick as well."

"No need." Roxanne touched Chloe's side. "I know what must be done."

"Forget it. I'm not leaving you alone," Chloe said. "Not today of all days."

"It's sweet of you," Roxanne said. "I know you'd do anything, but—"

"I would, too." Chloe's jaw jutted out. "Believe me. Anything."

Roxanne squeezed her lover's hand. Chloe might think she understood murder, but she didn't. No one did; no one who had not committed the act. The emptiness when you'd ended someone's life, there was no imagining it. It resembled no hunger even she had ever felt.

People on the train and in the street were bad-tempered, quick to take offense. Everywhere they went, petty arguments kept breaking out. Chloe said it was the weather. The British couldn't cope with extreme heat. Neither of them cared. They were wearing summer dresses with nothing underneath. Chloe's idea. She said her last boyfriend had persuaded her to try going around minus underwear, and she'd found she loved it. It gave Roxanne a buzz, too, stealing a sidelong glance at her lover's curves underneath the thin cotton dress. She'd not been so turned on since the early days with Grant.

At Marble Arch, they paused at a bookstall, and Chloe flicked through the women's magazines. "Look at this," she called, pointing to Roxanne's horoscope. " 'Today's stars. Mars and Uranus make this an unforgettable day. You have to make an important decision. Trust your instincts and be brave.' Many a true word! Are you nervous?"

Roxanne shrugged. She didn't want to talk about tonight.

"Let's go to Harrods," Chloe said, putting a hand on Roxanne's rump, rubbing it gently through the thin dress. "I'll treat us to a smoked salmon lunch. How does that sound?"

Roxanne laughed and said it sounded fine, although a bottle

of mineral water was all she wanted. She picked at her food. The hunger pangs were constant, but she told herself it was a good thing. The gnawing in her stomach would help to keep her wits about her. If she were to make it through the evening, she would need to be alert. Right now, she didn't want to talk about it, but Chloe had other ideas.

"I ought to be jealous. What happens after you've had dinner? Suppose he takes advantage, asks you back home with him, what then? You *can't* just say no."

"Listen." Roxanne leaned across the table and took Chloe's hand. "The less you know, the better. Okay?"

Chloe tried another tack. "What are you going to wear? It needs to be great. A man like that, he'll be used to having the best-dressed girls on his arm."

Roxanne hadn't even given it a thought. She preferred to play things by ear. One more reason, maybe, why she would never make it in the law. Instinct was no substitute for a comprehensive skeleton argument.

"I'm not much of one for posh clothes," she said. "Cassandra Lee was different. She loved spending money on stuff she might only wear once in her life."

"Cassandra wasn't such a fool," Chloe said dreamily.

"She only ever thought about herself," Roxanne said. "You'd have hated her."

Chloe squeezed Roxanne's hand. "You're always too hard on yourself. Me, I feel sorry for Cassandra. She only did what a lot of other people would have done in that situation. She was a victim. There's no shame in that. It wasn't her fault."

Roxanne snatched her hand away. "I don't want to talk about Cassandra Lee."

"Sorry." Chloe was meek. "Clothes, then. Like I said, you need to wow him. Not just any old dress. I'm going to treat you."

It finished with an unexpected squabble. Chloe found a halter-neck minidress and persuaded her to try it on. Gucci, ultraglamorous, perfect in every way except for the price. Even Cassandra would have thought twice about asking Grant to fork out for it. But Chloe was in raptures and, on impulse, announced that she would buy it for her. At first, Roxanne assumed she was joking. But Chloe kept insisting.

"I can't let you do that," Roxanne said. "Honestly, it's sweet of you, but please forget it."

"I'm buying it, and that's that. Whatever you say. Even if you walk away from here, I'm paying for it. Trouble is, it's too small for me, so you'll have to take it. You can't stop me, so why not get used to it?"

Roxanne was aghast. "But the money. You can't possibly—"

"Listen to me." Chloe put her mouth to Roxanne's ear. "My ex, he wanted to part on good terms. He put some cash into my account, sort of a goodbye gift."

Hush money, Roxanne thought, but she kept her mouth shut. Had Ben been afraid she'd embarrass him, wreck his marriage, maybe even his career?

"I won't tell you how much he gave me, but it was enough to make your eyes water. More than I've ever had to my name in my life. I could have gone on a cruise, but I'm glad I waited til I met you. There's no one I'd rather spend his loot on. Even when I've put my plastic back in my purse, I'll have a few quid left over."

In the end, Chloe prevailed. Roxanne watched her signing the credit card slip with a flourish. She was beginning to realize how strong Chloe was. Her secret was simple: she never took no for an answer.

Outside, car and taxi horns hooted furiously at every minor infraction; sweating tourists jostled each other as they swarmed along the pavements. Roxanne felt her forehead burning. Her lips were dry and sore. They had a grapefruit juice in a café in Dean Street, just to cool down. Roxanne blinked at the tang in her throat. As long as she kept up her intake of fluid, lack of food wouldn't bother her. Tomorrow, she would begin to eat again.

Chloe sucked the last dregs noisily through her straw and said, "You're off home to get ready soon, then?"

She was solicitous, Roxanne thought, like a boxer's second. "Uh-huh."

"He'll aim to put you at your ease, soften you up." Chloe cast her eyes down and added, "Ready for the kill."

"I told you before," Roxanne said. "I'll make sure there's no need to worry. Depend on it."

"Well, if you're confident you can take care of yourself—and things . . ."

"Yes."

"It's a gorgeous dress." Chloe paused. "You'll knock him dead."

They said goodbye in Soho. Roxanne needed to get back to Leytonstone and said she was going to pick up the Tube. Chloe started to say something, but Roxanne stopped her.

"It will be okay."

"You'll give me a ring?"

"When I can."

Roxanne gave her a peck on the cheek and turned away. For a moment she wondered if she would ever see Chloe again, but she told herself not to play the drama queen. Before heading for the Underground station, she stopped off at a sex shop in Wardour Street, the first time she'd been through the doors of such a place since a visit to a seedy fetish shop where Grant Dennis had an account. She knew what she was looking for, and they had it in stock. A pair of bondage handcuffs in a gaudy package: *Guaranteed escape-proof or your money back!*

After taking the train home, she unpacked her new dress and laid it out on the bed. The handcuffs she put in the top drawer of her bedside cabinet. She had the key to the downstairs flat while Dee the happiness researcher was away. Her neighbor had once invited her around for coffee and proudly pointed out the storage area under the floor of the utility room. The butcher who'd kept shop here had used it as an additional storage space for keeping meat fresh. No one would guess it was there without being told, but close inspection revealed a small ring set into the stone tiles under the cupboards that ran along the wall. By pulling the ring, it was possible to lever up a cover four feet by five.

At first she wasn't able to move the cover at all. It was stiff from lack of use, and her first abortive effort left her sweating and swearing. She was frail from lack of food. After downing a Diet Coke, she tried again. Still nothing. She was panting hard and felt her heart thumping inside her chest walls. Wouldn't it be ironic if her heart failed while she was trying to lift up the floor? After sitting down for a couple of minutes to summon up her last reserves of strength, she took hold of the ring and heaved again. This time she felt it give. Slowly, she raised the cover, groaning aloud with the effort. The butcher must have been built like a circus strongman. Perhaps it was natural, after years spent cutting up joints.

The cavity under the floor was six feet deep. Its white tiles were dirty and cobwebbed. Twenty years might have passed since food had last been kept down there. But it didn't matter. She swung her legs over the side and jumped down into the hole. The air inside felt chill, but to her surprise it was not damp. Airtight, then. She was peeping over the edge, along the surface of the dusty stone tiles. For a few scary moments she wondered if she would be able to get out. The sides of the hole were sheer, lacking holds for either hands or feet. Standing on tiptoe and stretching, she managed to grasp the edge of the floor and haul herself up and out. Muscles hurting, she replaced the cover. The stone tiles fitted together perfectly. They hardly looked as though they had been disturbed.

She squatted on the floor for a few minutes, staring at the tiles and picturing the hole beneath them. Imagine being entombed down there. No way out. No oxygen to breathe. Impossible to conceive the horror of realizing that one would never escape, the dread certainty that one was going to die there through lack of air and that, chances were, one's body would never be found.

This wasn't like last time. Perhaps she would wake up and find that this had all been a bad dream. But, she reminded herself, there had been moments after the death of Grant Dennis when she had taken refuge in much the same fantasy. It hadn't come true.

Chloe was right. Nic Gabriel had nothing to lose by exposing her and plenty to gain. It was Nic or her. The choice was so simple.

Back upstairs in her own flat, she swigged from a second can while hunting around in the kitchen. She wiped the foam from her mouth and checked that the matchbox she was putting in the bedside cabinet was full, just like the bottle of Glenfiddich she had hidden next to the bed.

CHAPTER TWENTY-THREE

"I wasn't sure you would come," Nic said as the waiter folded napkins over their laps.

She meant to keep cool. Give nothing away. "How could I say no?"

"I suppose you've guessed why I wanted to meet you."

"I have no idea, Mr. Gabriel."

The meal passed in a blur. The sight of the food made her gorge rise, and she had to pretend to pick at her spaghetti, pushing it around on her plate, occasionally taking the smallest nibble, afraid to swallow in case she was sick. She'd intended to avoid wine, but found she couldn't say no. She needed an anesthetic.

He was nothing like Grant Dennis—and yet. When she was looking down at the food and pretending to eat, he would steal a glance which she caught out of the corner of her eye. The look in his eyes was almost proprietorial. He fancied her, she was sure of it. For an instant she was reminded of Grant.

I don't think I can do this.

She gulped in air.

I must. It's the only way.

He put down his glass and leaned over the table. "So tell me. How did the woman who killed Grant Dennis manage to end up in Creed's flagship department? A tribute to your ability to reinvent yourself, but—"

"I told them what they needed to know. They appointed me on merit."

"Sure, but would the partners at Creed take kindly to having the wool pulled over their eyes? What's the good of being liberal and caring if you don't get a photo opportunity out of it? A bit late now to hold a press conference to announce your arrival."

"They can say they didn't want to exploit me," she said. "That they wanted me to settle in without being bothered by the media."

Nic laughed. "Sure, but they won't mean it. If the story comes to light, they will hate it. And they will hate you, for having caught them out."

"You make me feel so good."

"I'm telling it as it is."

"Don't only the lousiest journalists say that?"

He poured again for both of them. She watched him drink the wine, then gave a so-what movement of the shoulders and had some herself.

"So what do you want?"

"To find out some more. About what you did and how you came to join Creed. And how you find the firm, now that you are a part of it."

"How does that song go?" She murmured: " 'Someday you're gonna write the story of my life'?"

"In case you're wondering, I don't have tape recorders up my sleeve. No hidden microphones strapped to my chest."

"How do I know that?"

He grinned and said, "If you want, I'll rip my shirt open for you."

"Don't make me swoon."

"The night's young."

"Should I be flattered?" She gritted her teeth. "Things could be worse, I suppose. At least I can expect the stuff you write

259

about me to be elegantly phrased."

"Who said I want to write about you? And if I did, would it be such a disaster? By the time a book came out, we'd all be two years down the line. You'd have carved a niche in the law for yourself by then. You'd survive."

"Oh yes," she said. "Survival is one thing I know about. Even if Creed sacked me, I should be able to find something else. That isn't the point."

"What is?"

She picked up her handbag and pulled out her copy of *The Innocence of Dr. Crippen*. "I've read this. You walked through Crippen's mind, trespassed on his thoughts. You imagined what he felt when he was fucking first Belle, then Ethel, and when he lied to Scotland Yard about what had happened to his wife. It's full of those telling little details which seem so authentic, even if we'll never really know how near to the truth you came. Or how far out your guesses were."

"You're not Crippen."

"And I don't want the same treatment. I don't want someone else to trample through my brain, rooting around for a nice form of words to convey my emotions when I killed the man I used to fuck. Crippen is dead, but I'm alive, that's the difference."

"You don't have anything to fear."

"Is that so? Even if you don't write a book, you can pay the rent for a few weeks by phoning up Murdoch's papers to tip off some hack. The tabloids will love it—I can see the headline." She put on an excited, breathy voice. " 'Murderer Goes into the Law, Makes Another Killing.' But the way I see it, there's more to it than that. It's the partners at Creed. You want to dish the dirt about them."

"I've found you."

"If you want me to give you a juicy inside story, forget it. I've enough skeletons in my cupboard without looking for any more at work. Sorry to disappoint."

"One thing you don't do," he said, "is disappoint."

She flashed a bleak smile. "The wine is starting to talk, I think. I'm right, though, aren't I? You've stumbled across me, but that wasn't what brought you to Creed. By crucifying me, you can have a go at Will and Fergus and Uncle Ben Yarrow and all."

Nic shook his head, as if in a vain effort to sober up. "What makes you think I want to crucify you?"

"Oh, I'm sure it's nothing personal. You'll regard it as a necessary evil. All the same, I'm puzzled. Paying off an old grudge, are you? Did you cross swords with Will Janus when you were in practice?"

"No grudges, Roxanne."

"So you just like knocking down people in the public eye. Is it a bit like the reason people climb mountains—because they are there?" She finished the wine. When she spoke again, the venom hit him like a slap across the cheek. "Will Janus and his partners are successful, so they are to be shat upon? The British disease. You couldn't hack it as a lawyer. It's been a few years since you wrote your book. It's easier to destroy than create."

The waiter arrived with their espressos. Nic took a sip of the scalding liquid, then leaned back in his chair and said, "You're the one who knows all about destroying, Roxanne."

She tapped her spoon against the saucer, as if it were an aid to thought. Finally she said in a subzero tone, "You've forgotten something. You're not talking to Cassandra Lee."

"Different person?"

She gave an elaborate yawn. "Let's not go on, shall we? You know everything and still—"

"Not everything, not by a long, long way."

"Everything you need to know," she said obstinately. "My

only question now is—what comes next?"

For perhaps half a minute they looked at each other without a word. Finally he said, "What comes next is, I call a cab to take you home."

"No alternative?" She lifted her head, face stripped of all expression. "Why don't you come home with me?"

The car was airless, like a tomb. She was in the back, not the trunk, but somehow it reminded her of the journey home on the night Grant Dennis had died. She and Nic sat in silence on opposite ends of the back seat, no parts of their bodies touching. It was dark now, and she stared out of the window as though mesmerized by the lights of the clubs and bars. She might have been a French aristocrat, destined for the guillotine. Their driver, a ringer for the late Richard Nixon, kept glancing in his mirror at the stranger in the skimpy dress.

"Is this it?" the driver asked as they arrived outside the old butcher's shop.

"Yes," Roxanne said, "this is it."

"What else?" she asked.

She was straddling him on the floor of the bedroom in her flat. They were both naked and panting. Hearts pumping. The carpet was thin and the floor hard. She had nibbled him all over before first pulling him on to her, meticulous in her attention to detail. Finally she had let go, biting and gouging, screaming her commands. His dignified dining companion had become a wild animal, knowing no restraint.

He opened his eyes again and considered her. Hair in a mess, lipstick gone. If she was exhausted, she gave no sign of it. She was surveying him, as a sea captain in colonial days might have looked over a small island, newly conquered. Since leaving the restaurant, she had scarcely uttered a word, except to urge him on.

He shook his head and gasped, "Nothing else. Not for now. Enough."

"It's not enough," she hissed. "Not for me. Not nearly enough."

He grinned, exhausted. "You've taken my breath away."

She rolled off him and padded away to the bathroom. He hauled himself up off the floor and collapsed on to the bed. He closed his eyes again. He hadn't meant this to happen—or had he? Better leave worrying about payback until the morning. The morning, when their bruises would begin to show.

She came back into the room and fiddled in a drawer of the cabinet by the bedside. "Sleepy?"

"Mmmmm."

She climbed back on top of him, breasts brushing against his chest. He groaned with boozy contentment. She took his right hand in hers, and he was aware that she was putting something on his wrist. It felt cold. He heard two clicks. He blinked. She had taken his left hand now and had slipped a handcuff on it. She snapped it shut and then linked him to the metal rail that held the headboard. He was manacled to the bed.

"Well, well," he murmured. His words were slightly slurred. "So that's your game."

"You like this?"

For the first time, she smiled at him. He grinned back dozily. "I'm at your mercy."

"True."

He opened his eyes wider. She was staring down at him. The smile had vanished.

"What's the matter?"

"You should have signed your name when you wrote to me," she said.

"What?"

"Oh, it doesn't matter. Water under the bridge."

"I don't understand." He flexed his wrists, experimentally. The cuffs cut into his skin. No chance of freeing himself. "What are you—?"

"Let's not talk," she whispered. "It's too late for words."

She climbed off the bed, keeping her eyes on him all the time. She picked up the bottle of Glenfiddich she had crammed between the bed and the floor, unscrewed the cap. With infinite care, she opened the drawer of the bedside cabinet, took out the little oblong box and dropped half a dozen matches, one by one, into her hand.

She tipped the bottle and let a little amber liquid trickle onto his belly. A tremor ran through him, and she saw his Adam's apple move. As if he were finding it difficult to swallow. Tension constricting the throat, she guessed.

"What are you going to do?"

"What do you think?"

He muttered, "Tell me."

She supposed it was a mistake to talk. But she had said so little for so long. If Cassandra was to come back to life, even for a little while, she ought to find her voice. She was entitled to be heard.

"Well," she said gently, "you know what happened to Grant Dennis."

"I'm not Grant Dennis."

You can change your name, but you can't change who you are.

"But to you, I am Cassandra Lee."

Her mouth was dry. He was not the only one who was afraid. There was a clawing in her stomach. Was she drunk, and if so, with wine or power? Her thoughts seemed to have become disconnected. One moment the man on the bed wore the furious face of Grant Dennis, the next he became Nic Gabriel again. If he felt anger, he was choking it back. Perhaps he was desperate not to provoke her. Grant had never scrupled about that. The two men were so different. Their bodies, for example. She could never forget how Grant had looked on that last night. Six-feet-three, with the beginnings of a beer belly. Nic's stomach was flat, his skin pale and covered in bite marks. Her doing.

"Penny for your thoughts," he said. He wasn't slurring now. Fear must have sobered him.

She poured a little more whiskey on to his chest. It dribbled down his body, dampening the bed. "Not worth it."

"Cassandra Lee didn't kill in cold blood."

"She killed to save herself."

"You don't need saving. Not from me." His chest rose as he sucked in air. "Cassandra lost control for a few short minutes. Shouldn't have done it, but anyone could understand. Anyone who had a glimpse into the life she'd been through."

She lifted the bottle over him and poured again. "I've got news for you. When I lit that match—I had a sense of power. Absolute power."

He exhaled. "So that's your guilty secret, is it? The rush you had, when you killed him? You hate yourself because of the triumph you felt? Doesn't make you a monster, Roxanne. Just a woman who once lost control."

She put down the bottle and picked up the box of matches. "That's enough, Nic."

"I got it wrong," he said.

"Yes, I think you did."

"My fault. I really believed I was in charge this evening. When all the time someone else was pulling the strings."

"Silly you."

"I'm simply wondering—just *who* is pulling the strings?" he said. "Have you figured it out?"

She took a single match out of the box. "You're shit scared, aren't you?"

"Someone's been talking to you, haven't they? Not encouraging you to murder me, nothing so crude. But dropping hints that add up to a message loud and clear. Making you understand that I'm the one who stands between you and your freedom."

"You think someone's manipulating me? Wrong, Nic. This is Cassandra Lee you're talking to."

"It's not true, and you know it. There's someone you trust, and they've eaten away at you. Talk about the worm in the bud. They want you to kill me."

"I've good cause to want you dead, haven't I? You shouldn't have stalked me, sent me that anonymous note. It wasn't kind."

"I didn't send any note. Whatever it said, I didn't write it."

Her palms were moist, and her hands were starting to shake. She struck the match. At the second attempt, it lit up.

"Who did you let into your secret?" Nic asked. "Who has been egging you on?"

"What makes you think someone egged me on?"

"You're not the first, Roxanne, I promise you. This has happened before. It's why so many people have died. Matt Creed, Bradley Hurst, others you haven't even heard of. Someone at Creed has found the Holy Grail. Absolute power coupled with a perfect alibi. How to commit murder for pleasure, and get away with it, time and again."

She stared at him, still holding the lighted match. "You're crazy."

"I'm not crazy, Roxanne. Neither are you. It isn't me you have to fear. It's someone else. Isn't it?"

She blew the match out, hurled the matchbox over her shoulder, and flung herself down, curling up on the carpet like a fetus. Wailing like a child, because even though there was little that she understood, she saw at least that she had been betrayed.

Much later, she picked herself up and stood over him. He

was still watching her every movement. She guessed he hadn't taken his eyes off her all the time she had been sobbing. She was small and thin and naked, and even though he was in handcuffs, he saw in her crushed expression that she felt utterly defenseless.

"Chloe," she said in a croaky voice. "It was Chloe."

CHAPTER TWENTY-FOUR

"Tell me the story," Nic said.

Standing there in silence, Roxanne collected her thoughts. Presently, she cleared her throat and said in a businesslike tone, "I'd better release you first."

She found a towel to dry him, watching the whiskey soak into the white cotton as she unfastened the handcuffs. It was as if, despite everything said and done that evening, she had suddenly become shy. Lovers shared intimacy, so did killer and victim. With the climax over, they were embarrassed strangers.

When he was free, they sat next to each other on the edge of the bed, legs not touching. Her gaze fixed on the knife which lay at her feet, she started talking. Engulfing him with her secrets.

Listening to her reminded Nic of a stormy January when he was a boy. His father had taken the family up the Yorkshire coast to join a crowd of onlookers at a little fishing port, watching from a safe distance to see whether the sea wall would collapse. While they waited, Bryn Gabriel told tales about King Pellinore and the Questing Beast; perhaps they were age-old legends, perhaps he'd made them up to kill the time. To a child, the stone barrier looked impregnable at first, but soon the waves forced a breach in the defenses.

She held nothing back, told him everything about Hilary and the death of Howard Haycraft. About the anonymous note and her growing closer to Chloe Beck. About the fear that haunted her.

You can change your name, but you can't change who you are.
Or what you did.

"How can I explain?" she said. "You must think I'm mad or bad, probably both. You're more of a lawyer than I'll ever be. I don't have a rational mind. It was stupid to kid myself I could ever make it in the law."

He shrugged. "So we have something in common."

"I needed to prove something to myself: that I wasn't born to kill. Ever since—ever since Grant died, that's the fear that's haunted me. I needed to have another chance, for the choice to be in my hands. I set everything up so that I could murder you and not be caught. I had the motive and the means. I could have dumped your body in the cold storage pit downstairs until I found somewhere to bury you permanently. I might have got away with it, even though questions would be asked when you disappeared. Your family would raise the alarm."

"I don't have a family." Days might pass before he was missed. Maybe weeks.

"Of course, it could never have worked. Who would believe me when I said you were fit and well when we parted? The police would have talked to the waiter and the taxi driver who brought us here. I'd have been caught, same as before. But I had to find out what I would decide to do."

"Chloe Beck encouraged you," he said. "Subtly, maybe, but she urged you on."

Roxanne considered. "She made a fuss of me, made me feel that I was all she cared about. She hinted she might kill you herself, to save my soul."

"Sure," he said. "Self-sacrifice. Altruism. Greater love hath no woman."

"That's what I thought then." She put her head in her hands.

"All of a sudden, I see it differently. Shaking the kaleidoscope, you know? I feel grubby. Used."

"You're not the first," he said. "That's the way it works."

"I don't understand this," she said, turning to face him. "Not any of it."

"It's a long story."

"I'm not going anywhere." She yawned, stretching out thin arms. "I'm exhausted and that wine hasn't helped. It's late, but I'll never sleep."

"I don't sleep anyway," he said. "Why not make some coffee? The stronger the better. It's been quite a night already, and there's a long way to go."

While she was in the kitchen, he marshaled his ideas about what had been happening. Even now there were gaps in his knowledge. He was guessing, filling in the last few blanks of the crossword by intuition. When she returned with two steaming mugs, he cleared his throat.

"I can't begin at the beginning. This started long ago. A friend phoned me one night. He'd heard part of the story, and it fascinated him. But the woman who told him had a history of mental breakdown. He couldn't take her word as gospel. To him, it was a game, a puzzle, a bizarre bit of fun. A chance to play detective. If only he'd taken it seriously before it was too late."

"He died?"

"Stabbed by the sister of an old girlfriend who killed herself because he'd deceived her. Years had passed, and I couldn't see why the sister had waited so long for revenge. I wondered what was the catalyst. She must have had the desire to murder him, but what broke her restraint? Suppose someone encouraged her, led her on?"

"Chloe said she wanted to protect me," Roxanne said. "Keep me safe."

"Ask yourself what effect she had on you." He rubbed his wrists where the handcuffs had chafed his flesh. "You danced to her tune, even if you didn't realize it. The more you're told not to contemplate killing, the more you toss the idea around in your mind. She might have been clumsy at times. She's scarcely a seasoned advocate. Even so, she's strong-willed. Persuasive. This all about trust. Blind trust. You let down your guard when you talked to her, because she was the one person you trusted."

"But why?"

"I'm a threat," he said, taking a sip from the mug. On its side was the legend *When God made man, she was only practicing.* "Just like my friend Dylan Rees and Jazz Delahayee, the woman who confided her suspicions in him. She hanged herself a couple of days ago. She'd been used, too. Years ago, a young man died from anaphylactic shock, an accident she'd caused. Someone talked her into giving him a nasty scare, to teach him a lesson for hurting her, but that someone made sure the allergic reaction was strong enough to kill. Later, that someone finished up at Creed, and the body count began to rise."

As he explained about the deaths, she kept her eyes fixed on him, and he saw the dread that perhaps he too was insane, that she had spared him only to find herself at the mercy of a madman with an obsession about extravagant homicides.

"You're a lawyer," he said, touching her hand. Her skin felt cold. "Remember there's a precedent for everything. So think of Iago. He would have made a marvelous litigator, don't you agree? The perfect trial advocate. Master of suggestion, always knowing when to tug on other people's strings. Othello never had a chance."

"It couldn't happen. It's impossible."

"The genius lies in the simplicity of it. This isn't a matter of suggesting the desire. The desire is a given. It's always there first. The skill lies in breaking down the resistance. Matt knows he's being an old fool, going to the sauna after having a few drinks, but—hey!—where's the harm? Easy to wound Bradley's drunken pride, so he wants to show he can drive even when he's drunk."

She shivered. "How can you be sure?"

"It's the art of advocacy, Roxanne. When Dylan Rees became a threat, the answer was Amy Vinton. She was bitter about her sister's suicide. It had ruined her life—but she'd never taken the law into her own hands. It was simply a matter of finding the right switch to throw, to turn her into a murderer. Same with Caron Isley, I suppose. Dylan would have kept the record of his investigations in his laptop. It was his life support, everyone knew it. No point in killing the man and leaving the laptop around to tell his story. So Caron was persuaded to punish the man who'd let her down by throwing the computer in the Thames. See how it's done? Shades of Iago, the untouchable. The crimes were never his, at least not directly. He never put a foot wrong, not until the end when Shakespeare had to make sure the baddie got his just deserts."

She shifted away from him slightly and said in a croaky voice, "The baddie doesn't always get his just deserts."

He remembered coming home to Ravenscar and finding his mother's corpse. "True."

"This isn't making sense to me," she said, shivering at the strangeness of it all. "Chloe isn't a murderer. I just can't believe that. Whatever she's done to me. And as for all these other people—it's all wrong. Wrong, wrong, wrong."

"Of course she wasn't responsible for their deaths," he said. "No more than she pushed Howard Haycraft into the path of a wagon in Chancery Lane."

"Well, then? What are you suggesting, that she hypnotized people?"

"No, no, no. Chloe was a dupe, don't you see? Acting out a

script written by someone else. Someone who craved power."
He was remembering his father's tale about chessmen guided
by an unseen hand. "Someone who wanted to control people's
fates, so that it was within his gift whether they lived or died."

"So someone put Chloe up to it?"

"I guess he was her lover, the man who paid for the flat in
Greenwich. As well as the gorgeous dress you wore tonight. But
the affair isn't over. He can twist her around his little finger.
She's become his slave."

Silence. He didn't need to say any more, was content to wait
while she cast her mind back, filled in the gaps. For the first
time, he had an inkling of how it might have been for his father,
telling a child fantastic stories of the Otherworld.

"Why would he want Howard Haycraft dead?"

"Maybe it suited Ali Khan. The man who must be kept sweet
at all costs. The crony who held the purse strings." Another idea
occurred as he spoke. "This someone, he wanted to be sure that
even you might do his bidding. Yes, maybe that was the purpose
of Haycraft's death. A trial run for murdering me."

"Bullshit," she said, flushing. "Haycraft's accident wasn't my
fault. It was nothing to do with me."

"There didn't have to be an accident, don't you see? Once
he'd talked to you, Haycraft realized he was finished. That was
what mattered. In his desperation, he might have done anything.
Taken an overdose, whatever. If he didn't, no problem. There's
always another day. But our man never gives up. He can't. He
has to keep refining the Iago technique, playing variations on a
theme. I ought to be flattered, for me he went to extraordinary
lengths. A *tour de force*. He wanted two women, not one, to do
his dirty work. This is someone who doesn't think of his dupes
as people. They are just his creatures. So he had Chloe incite
you to murder me."

"I just can't—"

"Remember how it was done," he murmured. "Think of the little things which point to one conclusion."

She glared at him, not wanting anyone else trying to read her mind. But he was right, of course. She said nothing.

"It was Ben Yarrow who handed you the Haycraft case, wasn't it? You guessed he'd had a fling with Chloe. The mysterious boyfriend, same scenario as Amy and Jazz. But it was more than a fling. I guess it's still continuing. Who knows what he's promised her?"

"You're saying Ben killed those people?"

"He could never be convicted in a court of law, could he? All he does is to influence. Easy for a control freak with a silver tongue. He had people in the palm of his hand. He was in the crowd drinking champagne with Bradley Hurst the night of the crash. Let's say he urged Bradley not to drive, warned that he was over the limit and would never get away with it. Other people were saying the same thing, but Ben managed to get under Bradley's skin. I can picture him determined to prove Ben wrong, intent on showing how well he could hold his booze. Exactly what Ben wanted."

"The others?"

"He knew Matthew Creed's weaknesses, went out drinking with him and encouraged him to go to Paradise. This is all about control, isn't it? I suppose he thought that when Matt died, he would take over as senior partner. Even though that didn't work out the way he planned, it didn't stop him. Ambition wasn't his main motive, I'm sure of that. He always wanted to pull other people's strings, get them to do his dirty work." He remembered Amy Vinton, making her way unsteadily toward Dylan Rees. No wonder she'd reminded him of a marionette. "With Amy, even Caron, the seed of hatred was already planted. All it needed was a little help with germination. Ben sought them out, contrived an acquaintance, wormed his way into their confidence."

"You could never find proof, never convince a court of it."

"No, but persuading people is what advocates do, Roxanne. Like lovers." He paused, recalling Dylan's speech to the young lawyers. The man had forecast the means of his own murder. "Think of it as the technique of seduction."

"It's so risky. Leaving so much to chance."

"Maybe that's part of the fun. Trial and error. Never quite knowing what's going to work, and when. Who's to say that he hasn't had a hundred failures? Like in the end, he failed with you."

Cheeks white, she said, "Ben recruited me to Creed. Perhaps he knew all about Cassandra Lee. All that stuff about my great ability as an advocate was bullshit."

"And perhaps he saw a woman with that kind of secret as ideal for his purposes. He plans ahead, this man. When he discovered I was taking up where Dylan left off, he had an ideal candidate for you to kill. But he was tempted to experiment. He didn't encourage you to murder me himself. Instead he reached you through Chloe."

"Oh, God." She blinked away tears. "All the time I thought I was making a fresh start, someone was playing me like a fish on a line."

He said nothing, watched her thinking it out, struggling to understand.

"And in the end, I'd be convicted of murder again. No appeal this time round."

"No," he said, putting his arm around her. "That's where he got it wrong. Ben thought he'd discovered the perfect murder weapon. Someone who had killed a man before. Someone who could be tipped over the edge again by his go-between. Yet you couldn't do it. You chose of your own free will not to do it. You're not a murderer."

He could feel her trembling. "I killed Grant Dennis."

"Anyone might kill," he said, "given the circumstances. That's what Ben trades on. Dennis hurt you, and for a few moments in your life, you lost control. Manslaughter, yes. Murder, no. You shouldn't have been sentenced to life, never would have been if you'd run the best defense at your trial." He hugged her skinny body to him, mustered a grin. "Trust me. I'm a criminologist."

"You only have my word for it. How can you be sure I didn't mean to set fire to you, the way I did with Grant?"

"Sometimes," he said quietly, "you have to take innocence on trust. Even if your trust has been betrayed before. That's where law and logic let you down. Sometimes you need faith. You're not a murderer, Roxanne. Neither was Cassandra Lee."

"Okay, you win." Suddenly she laughed, and he realized he'd never heard her laugh before. "Had you worried, though, didn't I?"

A humid morning, the sun masked by cloud. Thunder forecast, and the atmosphere so close that Nic found himself fighting for breath as he walked along the Strand. The pavements were crowded; even on foot, getting anywhere in the city center was a nightmare. All the main routes from Whitehall to St. Paul's Cathedral were closed to traffic. Thousands of people were demonstrating. The media was full of rumors that terrorists were going to highjack the protest and turn it into a riot, maybe even a bloodbath. Here and there, cops on motorcycles muttered into walkie-talkies. Makeshift barriers had been set up along the pavement. As Nic approached Avalon Buildings, an ambulance screamed past, blue lights flashing, heading east toward the danger zone.

Roxanne had pleaded with him not to confront Ben, but he'd said he must. Nobody had done it before. What was the alternative? No one else would believe him. If he talked to anyone, he'd be warned of the cost of defending an action for slander and encouraged to invest in a lengthy course of therapy. He was a blocked writer who had sought to rekindle his career by making up a calumnious story about a distinguished representative of all that was finest in the legal profession.

"Easier to believe in abduction by aliens or Elvis shopping for groceries in Canning Town." Nic shook his head. "I have to confront him face to face. It's the only way to make him understand that he can't go on. It's over."

"If you're wrong," she said, "you're committing professional suicide. If you're right, it's just plain suicide."

"What's he going to do? He's like a stage illusionist. His magic only works when people don't keep an eye on what he's up to."

"What about Jazz Delahayee and Dylan Rees? Their knowledge didn't save them."

He didn't say so—didn't want to tempt fate—but the truth was, he felt invincible. For a while last night he'd thought he was about to die. In the end, he had not only survived, but also learned how Ben had used Chloe Beck to seduce Roxanne. Where Jazz and Dylan had failed, he would succeed. Ben's luck had run out.

The Stepford Wives told him Ben was in a meeting with Joel but would be free shortly. Would he like to go up to the boardroom and wait there? As he pressed for the lift, Nic wondered if he should have worked out a script. All good advocates did their preparation in good time. But he'd never claimed to be a star advocate.

On the penthouse floor he turned into the corridor that led to the boardroom. The door to Will Janus's office was ajar, and Nic could hear him talking.

"Can you hear the shouting?" Will sounded panicky. "They're getting nearer. Fergus, these people say they believe in civil rights, but it isn't true. They're just wreckers."

"I told security to let me know at the first sign of trouble." Fergus McHugh, calm as ever. "Everything's under control."

Nic strode into the boardroom, making for the roof garden. The window doors had been pulled back; he could hear the protesters' cries and the beating of a drum. The air was smoky, made his eyes water. Not far down the Embankment, a van had been set on fire. Alarms shrilled, sirens had begun to wail.

As he stepped outside, he realized he was not alone. Joel Anthony was sitting on the low parapet, his eyes fixed on the big wheel. A shaft of sunlight glinted on the stud in his ear. Nic stared at him. For a few moments he felt robbed of the power of speech. He couldn't move; it was if he had been paralyzed. One thought screamed across his mind. He voiced it.

"I got it wrong."

Joel turned and gave an elegant smile. "You certainly did, Nic. I won't ask how things went last night. Obviously not quite the way I'd hoped. Never mind. If at first you don't succeed, eh?"

Nic whispered, "You're losing it, Joel. It happens with addicts, even murder addicts. And you've been addicted ever since Bergen died."

"Oh, Darrell wasn't the first. There was a boy at school. We were friends, but he didn't want us to become as close as I'd hoped. We used to play the 'fainting game.' It's popular in boarding schools, a fun way for teenagers to pass the time. All about getting kicks from making yourself lose consciousness." Joel smiled reminiscently. "I discovered I was able to persuade him to go a little too far. Mainly by urging him to be careful, you see. His heart stopped; it was a tragic accident. Everyone said so. It's quite something for a young person, you know, learning that one possesses such a gift. As time passed, I decided it would be a crime to waste a talent so rare. I chose the law for my career. As a kid I always fancied being a kind of Perry Mason. Seducing the jury, you know."

"Dylan talked about advocates as experts in seduction, the night he died."

"I owe him a debt of gratitude. We used to talk a lot. Headhunters are incurable gossips, as you know. If he hadn't opened his mouth once too often, I might never have worked out that Jazz was agonizing over whether I was up to my old tricks."

"You were her boyfriend, weren't you?"

Joel nodded. His calm struck Nic as extraordinary. "We met at a party. She decided to initiate me, wouldn't take no for an answer. I thought maybe I'd be better off with an older woman. With girls my own age, things never seemed to work out. Trouble was, when I didn't enjoy myself, she decided to make me jealous by talking about Bergen. Telling me all the time what a hotshot lover he was. Poor psychology, when you think about it. Served them both right when he died."

"She blamed herself. Years passed before the truth began to dawn on her."

"She put two and two together when she heard about the deaths of Matthew and Bradley. Funny thing is, she might have been off her head, but she had more lives than a cat. I just couldn't finish her off. Yet with Dylan, as soon as I ran across Amy Vinton, I was sure she'd kill him. She hated the guy. She only needed the gentlest nudge." He giggled. "It's a power thing, of course. Nothing to touch it, the knowledge that you can decide who lives, who dies. I don't believe in God, Nic. But I do like impersonating him."

"Jazz is dead. Your doing."

"Suicide ran in her family, poor thing," Joel said, his gaze on Nic. "Both her parents offed themselves. I mentioned that when we spoke on the phone. Naturally, I begged her not to do anything rash."

"And Roxanne?"

"I suppose I was guilty of overelaboration there. But it was so much fun to plant seeds in her mind. I told her that Haycraft was in deep, deep trouble and hey presto! She did the necessary. It was so satisfying, Nic. One needs to stretch one's talents, don't you agree? Roxanne truly was the perfect dupe. Ben doing battle with her in the tribunal was a lucky break. So was Hilary Metcalf shooting off her mouth to anyone who would listen. I persuaded Ben that we should offer her the job. Such a luxury, to have an experienced murderer in the team. Ready to fire, like a loaded gun."

"You read her wrong," Nic said. "She has a mind of her own. Not what you wanted at all. So—what do you do about me? You never killed anyone by yourself before."

Joel smiled. "You've a sharp brain, Nic. You'd have made your fortune in the law. Pity you didn't stick to it. Now why don't we talk? Come and sit here on the wall with me. Be good, and I'll tell you something you don't know about your mother's death."

His tone was coaxing, his manner eminently reasonable. It seemed impertinent not to go along with what he wanted. Nic perched on the low wall, keeping his feet on the ground.

Quietly, Nic said, "What about my mother's death?"

"Oh, I know all about your interesting family background. Surely you've identified the secret of my success by now? I'm a terrific lawyer, Nic. I understand how people think and behave— and I always do my research. It makes all the difference between success and failure. We have something in common, you and me." Joel smirked. "I've committed murder. So did your father."

"He was a storyteller, that's all," Nic said. In the humid atmosphere, he was finding it hard to breathe. "He never killed anyone."

"Come on, Nic. It's a blind spot with you, but you ought to face facts. Your mother found out he was having an affair, they quarreled, he tipped her over the side of the cliff. Then he weighted himself down and jumped after her."

Far below, someone was blowing a whistle. A police officer with a bullhorn was making a muffled plea for calm. People were chanting.

Burn it, burn it, burn it.

"You made up that story," Nic said. "That's what you do."

"I told you before, I'm a good lawyer. The truth is what I want it to be. But seriously, Nic, he did kill himself, you must know that in your heart of hearts. He saw there was nothing left in life for him. You weren't enough. So he ended it all."

"You're not in control anymore," Nic murmured. "You see, I don't believe you."

Joel's eyes widened. "You truly believe your father was innocent?"

"Yes."

Joel shook his head. He smoothed down his hair with an ostentatiously casual sweep of the hand. "It's the one thing that has kept you sane, all your life long, isn't it? This ludicrous credo, that your old man didn't kill your mother."

"You don't know anything about either of them," Nic whispered.

"I know about you," Joel said. His voice was gentle, soothing. "Like I say, I've done my homework. Do you dare to look over the wall? It's a long, long way down, but the fall won't take more than an instant and then there's peace forever. You're going to do what he did, that's what I think. It's the best way out, no matter what either of us say. We both understand that. *Think the unthinkable.* You're going to jump. I know it."

Nic closed his eyes for a moment. When he opened them

again, he looked over the wall. The rioters seemed so small, so far away.

He looked back at Joel. "You're lying about my father and my mother. Someone else killed them, God knows who or why. I'm not Jazz. Suicide doesn't run in my family. So no, I'm not going to jump."

Joel gave his broadest grin. "Hey, that's not playing the game."

"Game over."

"Come on, Nic. You know it makes sense."

"Uh-uh."

Another grin, rueful this time. Nic was reminded of the way Joel had appealed to him on first meeting. The man was so easy to like. "You realize, if you don't take the plunge, I'll have to? I like to think of myself as a fighter, not a quitter, but I really don't fancy facing the music. Besides, the truth is rather like that wretched crap we get piped in here, twenty-four hours a day. Uneasy listening."

"Go on, then, why don't you just fucking well jump?" a woman's voice asked.

Nic spun round. Chloe Beck had opened the French windows and was looking at them from the boardroom. Her hair was a mess, and tears had caused her makeup to run. Behind her, in the shadows, he could make out a white face. Roxanne.

"Pissed off with me, darling?" Joel asked. His tone was jokey. "I did make such an effort. Especially since I find shagging women such a bore. Even when I'm not regretting the cost of your implant surgery."

"You shit," Roxanne said.

"Ah, Roxanne. Only one thing I need to remind you of. Like I've said before, you can change your name, but you can't change who you are. Don't forget that, will you? Ah well, ladies and gentleman, the dogs bark and the caravan moves on. The thought of cheating justice has always turned me on. I really am a true lawyer, you see. So I won't detain you any further."

Joel gave them all a little bow, then swung his legs over the parapet and slipped off the wall into nothingness.

CHAPTER TWENTY-FIVE

"Yes, I am afraid," Will Janus said. "Afraid we'll never know the truth of what really happened on that dreadful day."

His voice was hushed, his head bowed. He might have been saying a prayer, invoking the Almighty to explain the death of his junior partner. A few seconds passed in silence. For Will, as for his interviewer, the television studio was a sacred place.

The interviewer cleared his throat. "Your firm has relocated into temporary accommodation while salvage crews sift through what is left of Avalon Buildings?"

"That's right, Amin." Will looked up. His makeup for the camera, applied with a light touch, did not obscure the dark patches under his eyes. No one seeing him could doubt that he had been severely wounded by the shocking turn of events. "We've been touched by the support we've received at this difficult time. Everyone has rallied round."

The interviewer leaned forward. "People are suggesting—"

"I can't comment on ill-informed speculation," Will snapped. "It's all froth. Froth and bubble."

"I was going to say," the interviewer persisted, "people are suggesting that Joel Anthony must have been watching the riots, the arson attack on your offices, when the accident happened."

Relief spread over Will's face like a stain. "Who knows, Amin? I mean, who really knows?"

"Clearly, there must have been an incident of some kind. Perhaps—"

"It was a cruel twist of fate," Will interrupted. "A tragedy."

He took a breath, straightened his shoulders, looked into the camera. "And yet, you know, we can't let the firm be destroyed by the disgraceful antics of a handful of mindless thugs bent on wrecking everything we hold dear. The work goes on. We must stand shoulder to shoulder, we must keep fighting for justice. That's what Joel would want, actually."

Roxanne flicked the remote. Will's close-up froze on the screen in a rictus of sincerity, then vanished. "Excuse me while I go and puke."

From downstairs came a muffled "Aaaah," an answering squeal of pleasure. Dee and the new boyfriend she'd brought back from holiday. Happiness research in the old butcher's shop had taken a practical turn and reached a new pitch of intensity.

Roxanne jabbed him in the ribs. "Are we going to let the bastard get away with it?"

"This is all about getting away with murder."

"He's lying to save his face."

"You don't understand. Every word he utters is true, to him. That's the secret. His special gift."

"It takes my breath away." She shook her head. "You should have told the whole story when you talked to the police."

"Like you did?" Nic asked gently.

She hung her head. "I was scared. I was the wise monkey—see no evil, hear no evil. Okay, I was wrong, I ought to have explained about Joel. What he said to me, I suppose it scared me. 'You can change your name, but . . .' "

"You're Roxanne Wake," he said. "Cassandra's gone forever."

"Even so. We both ought to have said something when we had the chance."

"Who would have believed us? Where's the evidence, now that Chloe's fled?"

"She won't go far. The way she spent, the money Joel gave her won't last long."

"He didn't tell her anything that mattered about the other deaths. When it came to seducing you into doing what he wanted, she was under his spell. She was crazy about him. She would have killed to please him."

"So where does that leave us? Anyone with half a brain is putting two and two together and making Christ knows what."

"It only adds up to a nine-day wonder. Any moment now the media will find a fresh tale to tell."

"Will is giving an exclusive interview. Why not follow his example? You know people with influence."

"Haven't you and I had enough of people with influence? Besides, most of them have taken Ali Khan's shilling, and Ali's standing by his man. He's invested a lot of money in Creed. If the firm goes belly-up, he writes off a small fortune. On top of which he has to waste time scouting round for another law practice looking to sell its soul."

"Are you kidding? He'd get trampled in the rush."

He laughed. "I suppose."

She seized his wrist, hurting him. "So it's all about money and power, then?"

"Isn't it always?"

"We still ought to do something."

"Like what? Remember Conan Doyle's line about the story for which the world isn't yet prepared? Even if I wrote it up and sold it to the highest bidder, what would that achieve? Think about it." He paused, choosing his words. "You've had your life crawled over once before."

She flinched. He guessed she could see in her mind that bleak press photograph taken when she was under arrest, could almost hear her calculating how many times it would find its way back into print.

"So we say nothing?"

"Who else needs to know?"

"What next, then?"

"Who for?"

"Your own mystery." She took his hand in hers, squeezed it hard. "It still bugs you, doesn't it, what Joel said about your parents? Forget it. He was playing mind games right to the end. He made it up, he didn't know a thing. How could he?"

He stared at the floor. "Of course you're right."

"But?"

He shrugged. "Christ, Roxanne, there's always a but, isn't there?"

Back in the green room, Will said, "I think that went pretty well, actually."

Fergus McHugh grunted. "Uh-huh?"

Will poured from a carafe of water. "Look, you know me. You can read me like a book."

"Yes," Fergus said, "that's right."

"I'm a pretty straight sort of guy and frankly, I don't like all these ugly rumors."

"Relax, relax. You're still the most popular lawyer in town. No one has better name-awareness, and now people want to smother you with sympathy. Don't fret about malicious gossip, innuendo from a few troublemakers. Don't bother about the likes of Nic Gabriel. Ali Khan is still on board. He wants what we want, so that's all fine and dandy. You can leave the worrying to me."

"I want you to know," Will said, draining his glass, "that I'm so grateful for everything you do for me. You've earned your stake in the firm, actually."

"It's my pleasure," Fergus said, almost to himself. He straightened his shoulders. "Hey, this is only a setback. I'm planning already for the future. You think that Creed has influence now, but you ain't seen nothing yet. There is so much more for us to do."

Will inclined his head. "I still can't come to terms with what's happened. The tragedy of Joel's death."

"He could so easily have turned into an embarrassment."

A sigh. "I suppose you're right."

"At least he kept his sense of timing, right to the end. There couldn't have been a better day to bury bad news." Fergus rubbed his chin. "You realize he envied you?"

"You think so?" A smile started to tiptoe across Will's face.

"I know so. He saw you had everything. He wanted to be like you. Maybe even *become* you."

"Really?"

"Oh yes. He wanted to be in control, the way you are. But even if he had your style, he didn't have your substance. I told him, never mind the sound bites. The hand of history really *is* on Will's shoulder."

Will savored the thought. "You know, sometimes I think you're the one who's really in control."

"Oh no." Fergus shook his head in modest disclaimer. "I'm just a messenger."

Will cocked his head to one side, contemplating a truth revealed. "So you think Joel became jealous—of everything I've achieved?"

Fergus's features twisted. For an odd, foolish moment Will wondered if he trusted his old friend more than was wise. Unworthy thought—he banished it. He was in charge. Fergus was just the hidden persuader. Of course Fergus was on his side. They both believed in the same things. Surely.

"Joel and I talked a lot, as you know," Fergus murmured. "He worked on special projects with me, all for the good of the firm. But he had psychological flaws. He became, let's say, curiously detached. Frankly, I think he was beginning to outlive his usefulness. The poor misguided creature."

"Really?"

Fergus smiled. His gaze settled lovingly upon Will. "Yes," he said. "Poor misguided creature."

ABOUT THE AUTHOR

Martin Edwards is an award-winning crime writer whose fourth and most recent Lake District mystery, featuring DCI Hannah Scarlett and Daniel Kind, is *The Serpent Pool,* published in February 2010. Earlier books in the series are *The Coffin Trail* (short-listed for the Theakston's prize for best British crime novel of 2006), *The Cipher Garden,* and *The Arsenic Labyrinth* (short-listed for the Lakeland Book of the Year award in 2008). He has written eight novels about lawyer Harry Devlin, the first of which, *All the Lonely People,* was short-listed for the CWA John Creasey Memorial Dagger for the best first crime novel of the year. In addition he has written a much-acclaimed novel featuring Dr. Crippen, *Dancing for the Hangman.*